Unknown love . . .

Ursula stammered, "I hardly know you, so how can I possibly guess what kind of man you are?" And she thought, *I only know that when I look into your eyes, I feel more alive than ever before. . . .*

Conan smiled. "Well, I know as little about you, Miss Elcester."

"Sir Conan, I rather think you know much more about me than I do about you. You had a chance to speak to Mr. Glendower concerning me, whereas until last night I did not even know you existed."

They gazed at each other, both trying to conceal their feelings. Then, for the second time since meeting her, he stretched down a hand to help her to her feet. And, for the second time, the physical contact engulfed them in a tidal wave of erotic sensations that quickened their hearts and dragged at their guilt with an undertow of unconsummated desire . . . .

Breaking the Rules

Sandra Heath

A SIGNET BOOK

SIGNET
Published by New American Library, a division of
Penguin Putnam Inc., 375 Hudson Street,
New York, New York 10014, U.S.A.
Penguin Books Ltd, 27 Wrights Lane,
London W8 5TZ, England
Penguin Books Australia Ltd, Ringwood,
Victoria, Australia
Penguin Books Canada Ltd, 10 Alcorn Avenue,
Toronto, Ontario, Canada M4V 3B2
Penguin Books (N.Z.) Ltd, 182–190 Wairau Road,
Auckland 10, New Zealand

Penguin Books Ltd, Registered Offices:
Harmondsworth, Middlesex, England

First published by Signet, an imprint of New American Library,
a division of Penguin Putnam Inc.

First Printing, March 2001
10 9 8 7 6 5 4 3 2 1

*To my friend Joan King,
who helped me so much with
the title.*

In and out the dusky bluebells,
In and out the dusky bluebells,
In and out the dusky bluebells,
I am your master.

Tipper-ipper-apper—on your shoulder,
Tipper-ipper-apper—on your shoulder,
Tipper-ipper-apper—on your shoulder,
I am your master.

"In and out the dusky bluebells"
is a pre-Christian singing ring game played
all over England and Wales. Said to be magical,
its words can be construed as rather sinister.
Its origins lie in Druid customs. . . .

With apologies to Macsen Wledig for the
liberties I have taken with his dream.

1

"I fear poor, dear Reverend Arrowsmith will never recover from the shock," declared his high-strung wife as she languished wanly upon a mound of pillows.

Mrs. Arrowsmith had recently been brought to bed of twin boys, who had been promptly banished to the nursery at the other side of the rambling vicarage in order to spare their mother's delicate nerves. Except that nerves had very little to do with it, for she was always more concerned about herself than anything else. She had made an inordinate fuss from the moment her babies were expected; indeed, she had raised the trials of prospective motherhood to an art, wallowing in the anxious attentions of her sorely tried husband. Even now her bedroom curtains were almost fully drawn to prevent the late-April sunshine from spoiling her treasured pallor, and a log fire roared and crackled in the hearth, rendering the room almost suffocatingly hot for anyone else except herself, for *she* was always cold, no matter what. It was as if there was something missing from her life, an omission that rendered her dissatisfied and self-absorbed. Ursula's father declared her to be a woman in search of something she would never find. Perhaps he was right.

"Whatever shall I do?" the wilting invalid declared. "How can I possibly offer him comfort when he has suffered such a calamity?" Her lips quivered expertly, and she dabbed a handkerchief to eyes that were devoid of real tear.

Ursula Elcester, her rather unwilling visitor, was a young lady who was occasionally unable to help deliberately misunderstanding, especially with such an impossible woman. "Calamity? Oh, surely he does not see the babies in that light?"

"Babies?" Mrs. Arrowsmith looked blankly at her for a moment. "Miss El-sester, I wasn't referring to my darling cherubs."

Ursula gritted her teeth at the mispronunciation of her surname. Why did the awful creature still insist on saying "El-sester," even though she and her husband had been in Elcester village for four years now? It was time she accepted that no matter how the name was *spelt,* it was *pronounced* Elster! Ursula was the only child of Mr. Thomas Elcester, the renowned clothier and antiquarian, who owned the village and a large portion of the surrounding area, as well as several mills along the River Frome in the nearby Stroud valleys, and she was very proud indeed of her ancient name.

Mrs. Arrowsmith continued. "I was referring to the theft of the chalice from the church."

"Ah, yes, the chalice." Ursula's face was the very picture of righteous sympathy, although to be sure she was hard put not to smile, for the lidded goblet in question wasn't what most people thought it to be—an Anglo-Saxon communion cup—but a very unholy thing indeed. A minute examination of its elaborate frieze revealed pagan goings-on that had nothing whatsoever to do with Christian martyrdom! How on earth it ever came to be in the church was a mystery. The staid Bishop of Gloucester would not approve at all, and Mrs. Arrowsmith herself would no doubt have a fit of the vapors to end all fits of the vapors.

That lady dabbed her eyes again. "This is 1816, and I cannot believe there is anyone so base as to steal from an altar. Why, I said to dear Lord Carmartin before he left for London that the world is now a wicked, wicked place."

Ursula could just imagine his lordship's response, for he was not a man to suffer fools gladly, and Mrs. Arrowsmith was definitely a fool. Lord Carmartin's country seat, Carmartin Park, stood on an outlier of the Cotswold escarpment in the wide vale of the River Severn, five miles away from the village, which was high on the escarpment itself. He was not an easy man, nor even a pleasant one, and he was certainly not a man about whom Ursula wished to think. Not now, not ever really.

Mrs. Arrowsmith was still speaking. "And as if the theft of the chalice was not bad enough, this morning I have learned that the yew tree has had *another* piece of bark removed."

"Another?" Ursula knew the two-thousand-year-old tree had been tampered with at least twice already, once prior to her father's recent financial difficulty and then again just before Jem Cartwright suddenly sold up the village inn and departed, no one knew where. Each time a six-inch square of bark had been carefully cut away.

"Oh, yes. There are now three rectangles spoiling the trunk." Mrs. Arrowsmith gestured toward the window. "See for yourself, Miss El-sester."

Ursula went to hold the curtain aside and look through the fresh young leaves of the walnut tree that grew against the sunny vicarage wall. She wore a riding habit that was the same shade of lilac as her eyes; indeed, lilac was her favorite color, and on her head there was a little black beaver hat with a net veil that was at present turned up to reveal her face. She was pale and slender, with a mane of silver-blond curls that required the control of numerous pins. At the moment it was gathered into a black net at the nape of her neck, to which she had pinned a bow of wide lilac ribbon that was prettily embroidered with white dots. She did not often succumb to fripperies of any kind, but had not been able to resist purchasing several yards of the ribbon when she had last been in Cheltenham.

The vicarage drive curved away between lawns to wrought-iron gates set in a Cotswold stone wall. Immediately to the left of the grounds stood the ancient church with its squat tower and crowded country churchyard, and overhanging the lych-gate was the venerable yew tree. The three square scars on the trunk were clearly visible. Who on earth would do such a thing? And why? she mused.

Mrs. Arrowsmith echoed her thoughts. "It makes one wonder what manner of being is walking about in the village. I mean, what possible reason could anyone have for carving three pieces of bark from a tree? And not even at the same time, but on three separate occasions?"

Ursula was about to turn back into the room when a movement in the walnut tree caught her eye. It was a copper-colored squirrel, pert, quick, and daring enough to come quite close to the glass, flicking its long bushy tail and gazing at her with bright, intelligent eyes. Ursula was surprised at its temerity, for squirrels were usually timid creatures that fled at the merest approach of a human.

Mrs. Arrowsmith was complaining again. "Oh, I declare that all this will prove the very end of me. How am I supposed to worry about chalices and yew trees when I am so fragile?"

Ursula returned to the bedside. "I'm sure you will benefit from the asparagus I have brought from the manor stovehouse. It is a capital remedy for ragged nerves." The asparagus had been received with gushing superlatives that still rang in her ears. There was *never* such asparagus in all the world, so tender, so straight, so green, so perfect, so beautifully cut, so cleverly bundled, so immaculately matched, so everything-under-the-sun! To be sure, Ursula thought wryly, the Almighty had only created asparagus to please the vicar of Elcester's wife.

Mrs. Arrowsmith's face brightened. "A capital remedy? Is it really?"

"Indeed so," Ursula replied untruthfully, for she had no idea whether it was or not, but Mrs. Arrowsmith was the sort of person one reassured by saying such things.

"Then I daresay I will eat it this very day," the vicar's wife declared.

The clock on the mantel chimed midday, and almost immediately the nearby church bell boomed out as well. Ursula was relieved. "I must go now, Mrs. Arrowsmith, but I will come again soon."

"You do not mean to come to my churching tomorrow?" The question was put in a reproachful tone.

"Tomorrow? Why, yes, of course. I had not realized . . ."

"I do hope dear Mr. El-sester will come too?"

"I'm sure he will."

Mrs. Arrowsmith's face was wreathed in smiles again. "That would be *most* agreeable, Miss El-sester. Thank you again for the wonderful, wonderful asparagus."

Ursula forced another smile, then made her exit. She had hoped to be able to "forget" the churching, but that wouldn't do now.

Pausing beneath the vicarage porch to lower the veil of her riding hat, she turned to glance up at the walnut tree, but the squirrel had gone. She took a deep breath of the sweet spring air, and closed her eyes for a moment. Most people regarded her as quite a beauty, which together with her expectations should have long since seen her suitably married off, but she had always been far too contented with her quiet country life to want to come out in London; indeed, she stubbornly refused to consider the Season. Cheltenham was the only fashionable place she had ever cared to visit, for even Bath she considered to be too much of a market.

But apart from this resistance on her part, the plain fact was that she was also an incurably overeducated bookworm. Reading was her greatest delight, and she could speak French and German, as well as the fluent Welsh she had learned from her dear late mother. Her great passion was Celtic myths, which she had begun to painstakingly translate into English from ancient manuscripts that had come to her from her mother's family. It was her dearest hope that one day the resulting volume might be published. Such a studious turn of character made her virtually unmarriageable, except under the peculiar circumstances that now prevailed, for the dread prospect of *having* to marry had begun to loom in the form of an arranged match that she loathed to even think about.

Ursula sighed and began to walk down the drive toward the gates, for she had left her new white mare tethered by the churchyard wall. If she could make time stand still right now, she most certainly would! Why dwell on horrid things like marriage contracts when she was about to enjoy a delightful ride home through the woods? It was Saturday, April 27th, 1816, and for the moment at least all was well with her world. The weather was glorious, the hedgerows were white with hawthorn, the orchards pink with blossom, and gardens were filled with lilac, forget-me-nots, wallflowers, and jonquils. Skylarks sang ecstatically against the bright blue Gloucestershire sky, and the sound of lambs drifted from the stone-walled fields surrounding the village that took its name from her family.

Elcester was a picturesque community of gabled stone houses and cottages that from medieval times had owed its existence to wool and weaving. It nestled around its church in a dip just behind the western edge of the Cotswold escarpment, at a spot where four roads of varying importance met, and where there was shelter from the southwest gales that roared up the Bristol Channel. It wasn't a large village, possessing one general shop, an inn, a smithy, the church, and a tiny school set up with funds provided by Ursula's widowed father. A mile away to the northwest, on the far side of a hidden valley through which no road passed, stood Elcester Manor, her beloved home.

As she emerged through the vicarage gates, Ursula found Daniel Pedlar, the village blacksmith, soothing her mare, which had been in a very odd mood coming through the woods earlier. There had been Pedlars in Elcester for as long as anyone could remember, and they seemed to have always been the village smiths. Daniel's forge was opposite the lych-gate, and he had seen how nervous and unsettled the horse was when Ursula arrived by the lych-gate. He was a widower, a burly man with a shock of gray hair, and leathery skin that was darkened by years of sweat and heat. His low-crowned hat was seldom set aside, no matter how hot he became, and his old leather apron was shiny and worn. His shirtsleeves were permanently rolled up to show his muscular arms, but his touch upon the mare was feather-light, for he was not only a strong man but a gentle, artistic one too. Smithying was his trade, but delicate wrought-ironwork was his hobby, and many a fine garden chair, armorial gate, and elaborate weathercock had come from his forge.

"Is Miss Muffet all right now, Mr. Pedlar?" Ursula asked anxiously, hoping the mare wasn't still as nervous as before.

" 'Er'll need a tight rein, Miss Hursula," he warned as he helped her up onto the sidesaddle. "You and your hinsistence on white 'osses. This time I reckon as 'ow you've come unstuck. 'Er's a skittish one, and no mistake."

"She's been quite all right until now. Besides, I adore white horses, and would not be happy with any other color."

"Each to their own, but white 'osses is fairy 'osses."

"That's nonsense."

"Mayhap so, but whatever the shade, you'm to promise to take special care."

"You have my word." Ursula tucked a stray curl of her silvery hair back beneath her hat.

"See that you do." He gripped the bridle and looked earnestly up at her. "And go around by the top road, don't go tekkin' the way through the valley."

"Why ever not? It's a beautiful day, and—"

"And those woods ent a good place to be no more," he interrupted. "There's sommat bad down there, Miss Hursula. Sommat awful bad."

2

Ursula stared at the blacksmith in astonishment. "Bad? Whatever do you mean? I came that way and everything was perfectly all right. Well, except for Miss Muffet playing up, of course."

"I don't rightly know what I mean, Miss Hursula, and mayhap this 'ere mare knows more'n you think. There's whispers about the woods. Rufus Almore saw sommat there last full moon, and 'e've been in a state ever since. 'E won't say what 'appened, just that it weren't no place to go no more."

"But Rufus is the most inveterate poacher Elcester ever produced. He's almost an institution, and my father's keepers have given up trying to catch him. I can't imagine him *ever* being afraid in the woods at night."

Daniel nodded. "Which just goes to show 'ow bad 'e've tekken this whatever-it-were. He's turned no better'n sommat stupid stuck on a stick, and won't go near the woods now, Miss Hursula, so you'm to promise me as you'll go back to the manor by the top road."

"But that's the long way," she protested.

"I know, but nevertheless—"

"Oh, very well, you have my word."

"Good. I don't know what the world is comin' to, Miss Hursula. What with that there chalice goin' missing, and the spoilin' of that beautiful old yew." He nodded toward the tree, which overhung the lych-gate and the street, casting a dark shadow over his forge. His words were such an echo of Mrs. Arrowsmith's that Ursula almost smiled, until he added, "And now there's a plague of darned squirrels too!"

"A what?" She thought of the walnut tree.

"Squirrels! Ent you seen 'em, Miss Hursula? Why, they'm overrunnin' the place good an' proper."

"Oh, surely not."

"Well, 'appen I'm exaggeratin' a mite, but there's too many on 'em, all the same. And on top of all that there's sommat queer down in the woods." He shook his head sadly.

"I'm sure it isn't quite Armageddon, Daniel," Ursula said with a smile.

"Mayhap not, 'ceptin' at the vicarage, where 'tis *always* Armageddon." He grinned wryly, for the entire village found Mrs. Arrowsmith a trial. "Not that it meks a great deal of difference to me what goes on there," he continued, "on account of I'm not a churchgoer anyway."

"The Pedlars never have been, as I recall," Ursula observed.

"That's right, and a few other families in the neighborhood as well. The old ways suit us best, so the seasons and the land are what we look to, not what the fancy Bishop of Gloucester might decide. We marry by the yew, not the altar."

"What do you mean?" Ursula asked curiously.

"Mm?" He pulled himself up. "Oh, don't mind me, Miss Hursula, I'm inclined to chunter now and then."

Chunter was one thing Daniel Pedlar did not do, Ursula thought. "Marry by the yew" was a very strange phrase, and conjured vivid scenes in her mind. She could imagine that Robin Hood would have married Maid Marian by the yew, and not in the confines of a church. Silence hung for a moment, and then she changed the subject. "I've been wanting to ask you, Daniel. How is Vera these days?" His daughter Vera—actually, Severa, but no one called her that—was the cause of a great deal of scandalous chatter at the moment, and Ursula only felt able to inquire because the blacksmith knew he could count upon her discretion.

His face changed. "I believe 'er's well enough, Miss Hursula."

"So she hasn't come home yet?"

"Nope, 'er've just upped and thrown 'er good character out of the window by goin' to live with that devil Taynton. The world knows as 'e only wants 'er on account of 'er's the finest cook 'twixt 'ere and Land's End. 'Er's a foolish little trot as can't see 'e've no intention of mekkin an honest woman of 'er! What 'er poor dear mother would have said, I 'ardly dare think. 'Twere bad enough that she married beneath 'erself with me, then 'ad to go to all that trouble to mek sure our Vera spoke as proper as she 'erself did, but to 'ave seen the foolish little trot throw it all away on sommat as low as Taynton . . ." Further words failed the blacksmith.

Bellamy Taynton was the new landlord of the Fleece Inn, which was now called the Green Man. He was an unusually young man to own an inn, handsome, genial, and generally well liked. Vera had always been a quiet girl, obedient, dutiful, gentle, but no sooner had Taynton arrived than she left home to go to him. It had been the talk of Elcester for weeks now.

Taynton brought about a great deal of change in Elcester. He had moved into the old Fleece the very day the previous landlord left, and had quickly proved that he could run a far better establishment. Elcester's situation on a crossroad meant that its inn could hope to gain much passing custom, but the old innkeeper, Jem Cartwright, hadn't bothered much. The newly named Green Man had swiftly become a prosperous posting house, with excellent stables that were filled with fine horses for the various stagecoaches and by-mails that now used the inn. Carriages, chariots, coach and saddle horses could be hired there, and numerous grooms and ostlers were always to be seen going about their work.

The Green Man had the best ale, sparkling dry mead, and the most potent Severn Vale perry, or sparkling pear juice, for miles around, and—thanks to Vera Pedlar's renowned culinary skills—its table was simply superb. So all in all Taynton had proved a welcome new resident, and was forgiven his insistence upon the inn's peculiar new name. Most people—except Mr. Pedlar, of course—had also forgiven him for Vera.

Neither Ursula nor her father had yet met the new landlord, but for Vera's father's sake she was predisposed to dislike him. Mr. Pedlar was right. Why didn't the man marry Vera? Why make certain of ruining her reputation by taking her as his mistress?

The blacksmith lowered his eyes. "I tell you, Miss Hursula, that if I ever meets Taynton on a dark night, I won't be responsible for my actions. 'E's so full of 'imself, so 'ail fellow-well-met all the time, but I can see through 'im. Villainy's 'is middle name, you mark my words."

"Well, perhaps all will be well yet," Ursula said sympathetically. Oh, how she hoped so, for she had always liked the Pedlars.

"Nothing will be right while Taynton's in Elcester," he said quietly. Then he cleared his throat and summoned another smile. "Enough of that, Miss Hursula, for I've been 'earing a whisper or two about you as well."

"Oh?" She could guess what was coming.

"That you might be about to tek your marriage vows. Oh, don't fear that the world and 'is wife knows, Miss Hursula, for I can keep my trap shut well enough. I only know it from your father 'imself. He and I shares a companionable jug of perry from time to time."

Ursula looked away. Oh, how she shrank from this proposed match! It wasn't that she loathed her prospective bridegroom—she hadn't even met him—it was just that she wanted to stay exactly as she was. A sliver of guilt passed through her, for her opposition was entirely selfish. Her dearly loved father, hitherto always so doting and indulgent where she was concerned, had suffered a grave financial setback six months before—on November 1st, 1815, to be precise. On that day a certain Mr. Samuel Haine had baited a very skillful hook, to wit a South American emerald mine that only needed a little financial investment to become wildly successful, and Thomas Elcester had bitten like an obliging fish from Hazel Pool. Now if Elcester, its manor, and weaving industry were to remain secure, she was faced with a marriage contract she simply could not decline. This was because, quite out of the blue, Lord Carmartin had offered a very handsome financial settlement if she would marry his recently discovered nephew and heir, the Honorable Theodore Maximilian Glendower. The settlement would secure Elcester, manor and village in her father's possession until he died, when it would become her husband's property. A stay of execution maybe, but far better than the immediate alternative. Lord Carmartin's well-known ambition was to own a swathe of Gloucestershire from Cheltenham in the north of the Duke of Beaufort's land at Badminton in the south. He was a ruthless man, and his family and the Elcesters had been foes for two centuries, so if he found out about the parlous state of the manor coffers, there was no doubt the handsome financial settlement at present on offer would be substantially reduced.

The blacksmith watched the expressions flitting over her face. "I knows you don't want a 'usband, Miss Hursula, but 'twill be a good thing for the village if that darned feud atween the Elcesters and Carmartins is finished with. And all over fishin' rights in 'Azel Pool. 'Ang me if the bream and tench from there can ever 'ave been up to much."

"Maybe because the likes of Rufus Almore poach them before they have a chance to grow," Ursula pointed out with some accuracy. "Anyway, the quarrel was clearly serious back in sixteen-hundred-and-whatever." The calling of a truce would indeed be a good thing, but as far as she was concerned the price was very high indeed. The Honorable Theodore Maximilian Glendower was the son of Lord Carmartin's disinherited sister, who had scandalized her family by running off with a young Welsh gentleman of very modest means. His parents were now both dead, and he had spent most of his life abroad in various places, latterly Naples, where he learned by chance of his noble connection and had come to England to see his uncle. Ursula did not doubt he was as resentful of the match as she was, and that he would strongly disapprove of her bluestocking ways. A man who had a bride thrust upon him would wish her to be meek and malleable, not with a mind of her own!

Daniel gazed sympathetically at her as he patted Miss Muffet's flawless white neck. "Well, arranged matches 'ave always been the way of it where fancy folks are concerned, Miss Hursula," he said gently.

"Maybe, but right now I 'd like to hie me to a nunnery," she replied with feeling.

He chuckled as he glanced at her silvery hair, lilac eyes, and lissom figure. "I can't see you as a nun, Miss Hursula. No, by Jove, I can't!"

She smiled. "Let's change the subject to something more agreeable. How is the weathercock coming along?"

'Oh, it's doin' nicely, Miss Hursula. I reckon 'twill be one of the finest I've done. Mind, I could 'ave done with a sensible drawing to work from."

"I know, but it was the best I could do."

"Well, I didn't reckon as 'ow a Roman eagle would 'ave bandy legs and a crooked beak, so I've smartened 'im up a bit. 'Twill look proper 'andsome on the manor roof."

"I sincerely hope so." She had ordered the weathercock for her father's birthday in a week's time. He was deeply interested in all things Roman, so she had sifted through his vast collection of books and papers for an illustration of one of the eagle standards carried by the legions. She had found only a second-rate engraving, then copied it to the best of her ability—which wasn't much when it came to drawing.

Daniel patted the mare's neck. "Will you and Mr. Elcester be attendin' the May Day junket on the village green, Miss Hursula?"

"Oh, I expect so. I hear the fair is to be especially lavish this year, and there's the morris dancing, of course," Ursula added, knowing that Daniel was one of the Elcester morris men. He dressed in a black hooded robe and pranced around with a long staff that was decorated with posies of flowers, fluttering ribbons, and little bells. Other morris men had hobbyhorses or St. George; Elcester had a black monk. At least, in the absence of another identification it was presumed that the figure was a black monk.

To her surprise, mentioning the morris dancing did not bring a smile. "Well, I don't know as 'ow I'll be donnin' my robe this year, Miss Hursula, on account of there bein' a plan to sup at the Green Man before *and* after the dancin'. And on account of one or two of the others 'ave become a mite too pally with Taynton for my likin'."

"Oh, I am sorry, Daniel."

"So am I, Miss Hursula, so am I. Well, I suppose I'd better get back to work. You 'ave my word that the weathercock will be ready in time. Good day to you, Miss Hursula." He touched his hat and stepped back.

"Good day to you, Daniel," she replied, and rode away along the village street toward the crossroad.

The blacksmith gazed sadly after her. It was a shame she had to marry into the Carmartins, he thought. Lord Carmartin was a bitter man who had let life's adversities rule him. He had closed his heart to his sister when she fell in love with a man of whom her family could only disapprove, and for years he had been sunk in anger and disappointment. Then he had become the guardian of a little girl, Eleanor Rhodes, who had brought him to life again. He had no children of his own, so he doted upon her, vowing to leave her everything he had. At the beginning of August one year, when she was still a child, she vanished. Not a trace of her was ever discovered, and her disappearance still remained a mystery. Lord Carmartin was at first distraught, then he hardened against the world again, and that was how he remained to this day.

3

Ursula was greeted warmly by everyone as she rode through the village, for there wasn't a soul in the neighborhood who did not like her. They didn't *understand* her, but they liked her immensely. As far as they were concerned, she could read every book in the realm!

Elcester had remained a small village because of its isolated position, but its roads were often very busy. Wagons, carts, flocks of sheep, stagecoaches, private drags, everything came this way, sometimes just making the dust fly, but now often stopping at the Green Man. There were many towns in the surrounding area—Stroud, Dursley, Tetbury, Nailsworth, Wotton-under-Edge, Thornbury, Berkeley, Gloucester, and Cheltenham, even Bristol— and Elcester was where the ways crossed. There was a little village green, where in four days' time there would be a maypole and the May Day fair with all the traditional distractions of which the Arrowsmiths had made known their righteous disapproval. All was peaceful now, with packhorses drinking from a stone trough while their owner sat on the grass, enjoying bread and cider from his leather satchel. Near the village store there was a pony and cart laden with yarn from Mr. Elcester's mills in the Stroud valleys, where the rivers and streams ran with blue dye. A shepherd and his dogs were going out to the fields, and women were gossiping on doorsteps. A number of cottage windows were open, and Ursula could hear the clack of looms and the voices of the two-person weaving teams as they produced the superfine blue woolen broadcloth for which the area was justly famous.

It all seemed so timeless, yet this way of life was endangered. Increasingly the weaving was being done at the mills, as well as the fulling and spinning, putting people like the villagers out of work. Her father was one of the few clothiers who had adhered to the old ways, but how long he would be able to continue and still stay in business had been very much in question even before the advent of tricky Mr. Samuel Haine.

Ursula urged Miss Muffet on, taking the Stroud road, which led northwest out of the village. The last building it passed on the right-hand side was the Green Man, which now possessed a rather fearsome new inn sign depicting the face of a horned man peering out of thick green leaves. The inn itself, which like all the other buildings in the village was built of Cotswold stone, was not unlike the vicarage, with three stories, gables, a stone-tiled roof, and ivy on the walls. It faced directly onto the road, with an archway that led through into the cobbled yard at the rear. Just beyond it was the gate into the field, where a well-trodden path led down into the hidden valley, and the woods through which Ursula usually rode to and from the village. But Daniel Pedlar's warning was ringing in her ears, and she knew she would heed his words. She would tell her father about it, however, for if there was something or someone in the woods, he, as the landowner, should be kept informed.

She would have ridden past the inn, except that a glance through the arch revealed her father's chestnut hunter, Lysander, tethered to the rail by the back doorway. Her father had been to the town of Dursley on business, and she guessed he was making his overdue courtesy call upon the new landlord. Perhaps it would be as good a time as any for her to do the same, she thought, and headed Miss Muffet into the yard as well.

A stagecoach had not long departed, and the next was not expected for another ten minutes, so there wasn't any bustle at all as she maneuvered the mare next to Lysander. Almost immediately she heard her father's clear tones emanating from the open window of the tap-room. "So you mean to stay on now, eh, Taynton?"

"That I do, sir."

"Excellent. From all accounts you've already turned the old place to profit."

"Almost, sir. Come May Day it will be accomplished." The landlord was oddly well spoken, Ursula noted in surprise. Certainly he sounded like an educated man. She dismounted, keeping out of sight of the window, for she meant to eavesdrop awhile to see if she could gain the measure of the man who had lured Vera Pedlar from the straight and narrow.

Her father was replying, "May Day, eh? That's only a few days away. Well, it's a time of celebration anyway, but for an innkeeper it is doubly so. Am I not right?"

"Indeed it is, sir. It's the most important day of our year."

"How do you mean to celebrate?"

"Well, there will not be any stagecoach races actually starting or ending here in Elcester, but several will pass through, which is always an exciting spectacle. The Green Man will have decorations, music, dancing, and the prettiest serving girls I can find to serve free drinks and food. I shall commence from the very stroke of twelve the previous night."

"Ah, Walpurgis Night."

"Indeed, so, sir, and some call it the onset of Beltane, but to me it's just the start of the best time of all."

Mr. Elcester laughed. "What with the Green Man's considerable contribution, the annual fair, the maypole, and all the usual local festivities, I vow this will be a May Day to remember."

"It will indeed, sir, it will indeed," murmured the innkeeper.

"How long have you been here in Elcester now?"

"Since Imbolc, sir."

Ursula was taken aback, for the innkeeper had now mentioned two ancient Celtic festivals. Mr. Elcester was startled as well. "Imbolc?" he repeated.

"February the first, sir."

"Ah, yes."

"I'm, er, told you are interested in the Roman period, Mr. Elcester," the innkeeper said then.

"Er, yes, I am very interested indeed. Why do you mention it?"

"My father was an antiquarian with a similar interest, which I have inherited. And if you think me impertinent for saying so, sir," Taynton continued, "I feel that you and my father would have formed a friendship, for he too was of gentle birth, although without fortune, I fear."

"Ah." Mr. Elcester's sympathy was almost tangible, then he cleared his throat. "As a fellow antiquarian he'd certainly have appreciated this part of the country, which is so rich in sites of archeological interest."

"And treasures like the stolen chalice."

"Eh?"

"The chalice, sir. I was able to examine it before it was taken, and I could see that it was much older than the Reverend Arrowsmith said."

Mr. Elcester chuckled. "Much older, and much less holy than he believes as well!"

The innkeeper laughed. "That's what I concluded too. Still, what the good reverend does not know cannot harm him."

"Very true. Actually, I wasn't referring to things like the chalice, but ancient landmarks in the neighborhood. There's Uley Bury, an Iron Age promontory hill fort on the way to Dursley, and the chambered long barrow just off the Stroud road. Actually, when I rode past the latter this morning, I checked to see that all was well, and would you know? Some brainless scoundrels have ransacked it recently for no good reason. Oh, it grieves me greatly to think of it. What with that, the yew tree, and the stolen goblet, I fear Elcester has become a lawless place."

Ursula pursed her lips, for her father was the third person she had heard say as much in the last hour.

The landlord gave a sigh. "It is the times we live in, sir."

"You are right, sir, you are right. However, to return to matters antiquarian. This area must have been of considerable strategic importance, and I have always contended that the Roman occupation hereabouts commenced with a stronghold on Carmartin Hill. Then when times were more settled, those of high rank built fine villas here in the nearby hills."

"I'm sure you are correct, sir," Taynton murmured.

Ursula was intrigued, for it was almost as if the innkeeper *knew* her father was right.

Mr. Elcester went on. "My theory would be given some weight if only I could discover some villa remains. I am certain there would have been one in our valley behind the inn. There is an ample spring line there, and the scenery is beautiful—two very good reasons for a noble Roman to choose the spot. Maybe even the *Dux Britanniarum* himself, who knows?"

Ursula smiled, for her father dearly wished the most important Roman villa in Britain could be found on his land.

"I mean to start the search again soon. Perhaps you would care to join me?"

"I would like that very much, sir," the landlord replied.

"I'll be sure to send you word. My, it will be most agreeable to have a fellow soul with me." Mr. Elcester paused, then returned to a previous topic. "I can't help thinking about what you said about being in handsome profit by May Day. Knowing what I do of old Cartwright's business here, your success seems little short of miraculous to me."

"Well, sir, Cartwright only had to seek the trade as I have done. Turnover is excellent. I expect the Cheltenham *Flying Machine* stagecoach in a few minutes—it passes through both ways several times daily, as do the *Age* and the *Meteor*. The by-mails now frequent the inn as well, to say nothing of all the locals and market traffic. It all provides a more than comfortable income, especially if a man knows how to part people from their money."

Mr. Elcester gave a bark of wry laughter. "Oh, I know all about being parted from money!"

By now Ursula had decided that Daniel Pedlar was right about Bellamy Taynton, who seemed to have an answer for everything, and was too smooth by far. It was time to meet him face-to-face. She turned to the inn entrance, which was like that of a church porch, and entered the low passageway beyond.

4

For a moment Ursula found it hard to see after the brilliant sunshine outside, but then her eyes grew accustomed to the shadows of the long, wainscotted hall. The floor of uneven stone flags was scattered with sawdust, and the dark oak walls were lined with coat hooks and smoke-stained sporting prints. An old long-case clock ticked slowly beside a narrow table, on which stood bowls of water, soap, and clean towels for the passengers of the Cheltenham *Flying Machine* stagecoach, which would arrive shortly. There was a mixture of smells, ale and strong coffee, the dried herbs suspended from a beam, and the roast beef that was ready and waiting in the kitchens.

The door to the main dining room, which was empty at present, opened to the left, and that of the taproom to the right. At the end of the hall was the staircase to the upper floors and cellars, and beside it the narrower passage leading to the kitchens, private accommodation, and other offices. The voices of her father and the innkeeper were suddenly much more clear now she was inside. They still did not realize she was there, so she went softly to the door, and peeped inside. The two men were out of sight, but she could see much of the room.

It was used as much as the dining room for serving meals, so there were a number of round, white-clothed tables set in readiness. A huge dresser laden with pewter and blue-and-white crockery stood against the wall next to the chintz-curtained window through which she had eavesdropped, and in a mirror she could see the cavernous, soot-darkened inglenook where a fire flickered.

Gleaming copper pots and pans reflected the leaping flames, and a large kettle sang softly on a trivet. There were settles and Windsor chairs, as well as benches and stools, and a long trestle on which stood bread, cold meats, jars of pickles, a pat of butter, and a Double Gloucester cheese. Behind the trestle was a row of tapped barrels containing the expected selection of beer, ale, perry, and cider.

Vera Pedlar was laying out cutlery on one of the tables. She was as buxom and pretty as ever, her rounded figure neat in a beige linen dress and starched white apron. Her brown hair was pinned up beneath a neat mobcap, and her cheeks had that country bloom that always looked so healthy. Her soft brown eyes were downcast as she went about her work, and she did not seem any different, although Ursula somehow expected her to have changed.

Then another movement caught Ursula's attention, and to her dismay she saw a squirrel in a metal cage; not an ordinary red squirrel, but an almost white one that gazed directly at her as it clung forlornly to the side of the cage. Only its head was the usual russet red, and even its eyes were unusual—they were a vivid green, almost like emeralds. She hated to see such a beautiful wild creature caged in such a way. Where had it come from? she wondered. Was it one of the "plague of squirrels"? If Daniel Pedlar saw it, no doubt he would say it was a fairy squirrel, for he was convinced all white animals belonged to the little people.

Her father suddenly realized she was there. "Why, Ursula, m'dear, what a pleasant surprise to see you here. Why on earth are you lurking at the door? Come on in."

Feeling a little embarrassed to have been perceived before she was quite ready to make her presence known, Ursula went in. "Hello, Father," she said, but her gaze was upon his companion. Bellamy Taynton was in his early thirties, tall and well made, with patrician features that might have seemed more appropriate at Almack's than at a country inn. His eyes were a very pale blue, his flaxen hair was combed back from his face, and he wore a faded indigo coat, fawn breeches, and top boots. Such attire was plain enough, but in his neckcloth there was a gold pin such as any London lord would be pleased to wear, and on his lapel was pinned a handsome nosegay of woodland flowers, bluebells, wood anemones, and violets. There was a half smile upon his lips, and his eyes bore a bland expression that made him a closed book. Everything about him made her want to shiver.

Mr. Elcester came to kiss his daughter's cheek. He was unlike Taynton in most respects, shorter and broader, with hair that was now little more than a gray monastic tonsure. His pine green riding jacket had flat brass buttons and a velvet collar, and his cream corduroy breeches were of very fine quality. He wore a mustard-colored waistcoat, and his neckcloth also sported a gold pin, but it was more discreet than the innkeeper's. His bushy-browed face was amiable, but his tired hazel eyes showed the strain of the past few months. "How is Mrs. Arrowsmith?" he inquired.

"Very well, and the babies are the bonniest I have ever seen."

"With such saintly parents, they are most likely cherubs." Mr. Elcester chuckled.

"Mrs. Arrowsmith thinks so."

"No doubt."

Ursula smiled across the room at Vera. "Hello, Vera."

The young woman bobbed a quick curtsy. "Miss Ursula." Her voice was low and clear, and far more well spoken than her father's. That was because her mother had been an apothecary's daughter from Stroud, and had been brought up in an educated background. Vera's maternal family never had anything to do with her, having frowned upon the marriage to a mere blacksmith.

Mr. Elcester hastened to do the honors between his daughter and the innkeeper. "M'dear, allow me to present Mr. Bellamy Taynton. Taynton, this is my daughter, Ursula."

The innkeeper bowed courteously. "Miss Elcester."

"Sir," she replied bluntly, fixing him with a glare that was disapproving because of both Vera and the squirrel.

Her father glanced at her in surprise. "Is something wrong, m'dear?"

"I couldn't help noticing the squirrel." She could hardly mention her displeasure over Vera as well.

"Squirrel?" Her father hadn't seen.

"Over there by the barrels."

Mr. Elcester turned. "Good God, an albino!" he cried.

Ursula shook her head. "Not quite, for its head is red and eyes are green," she pointed out.

"So they are." Her father turned to Taynton. "Where did you get it?"

"Oh, I've had it for quite some time." The innkeeper turned to Ursula, and for a moment she saw a glint of annoyance in his pale eyes, but then it had gone. "The creature comes to no harm, I assure you, Miss Elcester. Indeed, it is much loved, so you do not need to fear for its comfort."

Ursula was unimpressed, as the brief glint in *her* eyes bore full witness. Much-loved creature or not, one only had to look at the squirrel to know it was wretched! Battle lines were drawn in those few seconds, and she could tell that Taynton wasn't accustomed to defiance, least of all from a woman. She disliked him more with each second, and found it impossible to believe that someone as sweet as Vera could possibly find him worth the sacrifice of her good name.

The innkeeper changed the subject rather pointedly. "I understand you are soon to be married, Miss Elcester."

She was startled. How did he know? Her father was unlikely to have mentioned it to him, and Daniel Pedlar certainly wouldn't. And the blacksmith wouldn't have told Vera because she had left for the Green Man before the marriage was suggested.

Mr. Elcester frowned. "How did you come by that information?" he demanded.

"Someone mentioned it. I don't recall who." Taynton looked a little uncomfortable, and clearly wished he'd held his tongue.

"As it happens, marriage may indeed be in the offing,"

Mr. Elcester said then, much to Ursula's annoyance. Why confirm anything? Taynton had no need to know.

"May I ask who the fortunate groom will be?" asked the innkeeper.

"Lord Carmartin's nephew and heir, the Honorable Theodore Glendower."

The squirrel became suddenly excited, making strange little noises and twitching its bushy tail, at which Taynton's breath caught slightly. A new wariness entered his eyes as he looked at her, as if something had suddenly become clear to him. Was Mr. Glendower known to him? A direct question was necessary. "Mr. Taynton, are you acquainted with Mr. Glendower?" she asked.

"Why no, Miss Elcester. Why do you ask?"

"It's just that his name seemed to convey something to you."

"No, miss." But his eyes were veiled.

Mr. Elcester cleared his throat. "Well, I must ask you not to speak of this to anyone, Taynton. There is nothing final yet, so it wouldn't do for there to be talk."

"You have my word, Mr. Elcester."

"And that goes for you too, Vera," Mr. Elcester added, looking across at the blacksmith's daughter.

Vera bobbed another curtsy. "Not a word will pass my lips, Mr. Elcester," she promised.

Ursula noticed how often Taynton's eyes rested upon Vera, but his expression wasn't loving, more reluctant, almost as if he found her attractive and wished he didn't.

Mr. Elcester was ready to leave. "Good. Well now, Ursula, shall we ride back together?"

"I'd like that," she replied.

"Through the woods?"

"Of course."

At that Taynton spoke up quickly. "I would not advise that, sir."

"Eh? Why ever not?"

"I'm given to understand there is a villain of some sort lurking there, an escaped prisoner, it's said. I know nothing for certain, you understand, but it seems some of the local men have had unpleasant experiences, and have decided to give the woods a wide berth."

"This is the first I've heard of it," Mr. Elcester declared, clearly astonished.

"It may be a fuss over nothing at all, sir, I merely thought I should mention it."

Ursula did not like being advised by the innkeeper. "Mr. Taynton, I rode through the woods earlier on, and it was perfectly safe."

Their eyes met, and she knew that somehow he was aware of the difficulty she'd had with Miss Muffet. "That's as may be, Miss Elcester, but people have been badly frightened by something there, and I have had reports of several horses almost bolting."

He *did* know about Miss Muffet! But how? The only other person to know what happened was Daniel Pedlar, who was the very last man on earth to confide in Bellamy Taynton.

The innkeeper addressed her father again. "Mr. Elcester, I know I may be out of turn, but I have taken it all very seriously. I rode to Stroud yesterday to report matters to the authorities. I am assured that a watch will be kept, but in the meantime it is advisable to stay away from the woods. Just to be safe."

Ursula's father was in full agreement. "Oh, indeed so. Well, if the authorities have been notified, there is no need for me to act."

"No need at all, sir."

"Excellent."

The sound of a stagecoach key-bugle playing *"Oh, dear, what can the matter be?"* carried from the distance, announcing the approach of the Cheltenham *Flying Machine*. Taynton turned sharply to Vera. "Make sure they're ready in the kitchens!" he called out with an imperiousness that bordered on the theatrical.

"Yes, sir," Vera replied meekly, but as she began to quickly lay the rest of the cutlery she still held, Taynton became irritated.

"Remember, wench, I am your master!"

Now he *was* being theatrical, Ursula thought, not

knowing whether to laugh because he was so ridiculously pompous, or frown because he was so insufferably overbearing.

Vera's eyes widened, and as she hastened out, her starched apron rustling, "*Oh, dear, what can the matter be?*" was heard again.

The innkeeper turned back to his guests with a facile smile. "I trust you will both excuse me, for I will have guests directly, and this particular coach company allows only twenty minutes for the halt."

"Of course, of course." Mr. Elcester offered Ursula his arm, and they left the inn to emerge into the sunshine again. Ursula felt in more ways than one that she had come out into fresh air!

5

The key-bugle sounded imperative as the approaching stagecoach rattled into the village, past the churchyard and across the green, so that Ursula and her father had to step aside as it swept beneath the archway into the inn yard. There was dust, noise, and clatter as Taynton's men hurried out to attend to the passengers and horses, and Ursula was relieved to mount Miss Muffet and ride out to the road; relieved too to get away from Bellamy Taynton, who made her positively shudder.

Hawthorn hedgerows filled the air with scent as the village slipped away behind, and a light breeze trembled through the cowslips that flourished at the wayside. The road to Stroud led along the ridge between the hidden valley to the right and the great vista of the Severn's wide vale to the left. The valley was called hidden because only paths wound through it, and from spring to autumn it was concealed beneath a thick cloak of trees. Many a stranger traveling along the ridge had gazed down into it and wondered what secrets it held. At the moment the canopy of leaves was still not entirely unfurled, so that there was an occasional glimpse of a dell of bluebells, and of Hazel Pool, the contents of which had caused so much trouble in the past between Elcester and Carmartin.

Elcester Manor glowed in the sun on the far slope of the valley. It was a Tudor mansion of great beauty, with lichen on the roof, mullioned windows, and curls of smoke rising from the tall chimneys. Behind it climbed an open park, splendid with specimen trees, a herd of deer, and a drive that led toward the lodge over the horizon. To the front were three terraced gardens, then another area of park that gave way to the cloak of the woods filling of the valley floor.

The horses' hooves clopped slowly on the road, and Ursula and her father rode in companionable silence for a while, but then she couldn't hold her tongue a moment longer. "Why did you tell Taynton about the match?" she asked reproachfully. "I mean, there is nothing firm about anything, and it may not happen, so confirming it to anyone is—"

"I know," Mr. Elcester broke in guiltily. "I was so taken aback that he'd heard anything that I just didn't think."

"How do you think he found out?"

"Well, I did talk to Pedlar about it," her father confessed.

"He told me, but he'd rather flatten Mine Host on an anvil than exchange tidbits of gossip with him."

"True."

They rode on for a moment, and then Ursula looked at her father again. "Did you notice how Vera and Taynton addressed each other? She called him sir, and he reminded her he was her master. Very affectionate."

"Each to their own, m'dear."

"Maybe, but I think it very peculiar, and he is so melodramatic. What can Vera be thinking of?"

Mr. Elcester chuckled. "My dear daughter, I don't think the man exists who would meet with your approval. Be sensible now. Taynton is young, handsome, well-to-do, and clearly possesses charm when he chooses. If he is imperious when it comes to the running of the inn, well, that cannot be entirely bad. For someone like Vera Pedlar, he is what is vulgarly termed a catch."

"Catch or not, good innkeeper or not, I didn't detect much charm," Ursula replied caustically.

"You weren't exactly overflowing with civility yourself," her father pointed out.

"How can I be civil to a man who keeps a squirrel in a cage and pretends it is the happiest creature on earth? And who lures an innocent young woman from her home, then makes her the talk of the neighborhood by declining to marry her? I'm sorry, but Bellamy Taynton is *not* the sort of person to whom I can warm."

"That much is clear. Still, he has been good for the Fleece . . . er, I mean the Green Man."

Ursula pulled a face. "Hmm. It's a truly dreadful name, to say nothing of the atrocious sign he has erected. I'll warrant it terrifies the village children."

"It takes a great deal more than that to frighten country children. Besides, it's only a depiction of the old spirit of summer."

"The only summery thing about it is the leaves—the face is positively demonic."

Mr. Elcester raised an eyebrow. "I can see you are determined to find fault with everything."

"Mr. Bellamy Taynton has provided me with a great deal of ammunition." She lowered her eyes for a moment. "Father, isn't there anything we can do about the squirrel?"

"Do? No, m'dear, I'm afraid not. Keeping a squirrel isn't illegal, and the animal certainly doesn't look starved."

"Nor does it look happy," Ursula retorted.

"Well, the Green Man is freehold, so Taynton can almost do as he chooses."

"More's the pity." Ursula fell silent for a moment. "Father, have you heard anything about a so-called plague of squirrels in the area?"

"Not a plague exactly, although my keepers have commented that in recent weeks there seem to be many more than usual in the woods." Mr. Elcester sighed. "Squirrels in abundance, but not a shred of Roman evidence. Well, almost not a shred."

"What do you mean?"

"I took a stroll by Hazel Pool last week and found a coin that must have been dislodged from the bank during the winter. Anyway, I've examined it closely now, and it appears to be a late fourth-century gold solidus of Emperor Magnus Maximus."

Ursula reined in with interest. "Really? That's odd.

How many emperors were there with the name Maximus?"

Her father halted Lysander as well. "Why do you ask?"

"Well, it's just that the next myth I intend to translate from Mother's manuscripts is *The Dream of Macsen Wledig*. Macsen Wledig means Lord or Prince Maximus, and he was supposedly an emperor of Rome."

"Not supposedly, m'dear, he was. That is, if Magnus Maximus and Macsen Wledig are the same man. Magnus Maximus was sent here as *Dux Britanniarum,* but he rebelled against Rome, and was declared emperor by his troops."

Ursula gave a surprised laugh. "So the myth might be about a real figure?"

"It's possible." Her father chuckled. "How very agreeable it would be to think he might have lived right here in Elcester, but I must not place too much faith in the discovery of a single coin. I might be barking up entirely the wrong tree where that villa is concerned."

"If you are, then Taynton is too," Ursula replied, recalling the innkeeper's suppressed reaction to that particular subject.

Mr. Elcester gave her a wry look. "I think we've vilified him enough, don't you? Tell me, what exactly is this Macsen Wledig supposed to have dreamed?"

"He was out hunting one day and fell asleep. He dreamed about a beautiful maiden in a castle in a faroff land, and when he awoke he was determined to find and marry her. That's all I can remember. I was very small when Mother used to read the manuscripts to me. I'm looking forward to reading it again."

As they rode slowly on, the curve of the escarpment began to take the road to the rear of Elcester Manor, so that the village and hidden valley slipped out of sight behind them. The lodge at the manor gates was on the right about a quarter of a mile ahead, but on the left before that, on a level area dotted with bushes and soaring Scots pines, was the chambered long barrow called Hatty Pedlar's Tump, so called because one of Daniel Pedlar's forebears had once grazed her goats upon it.

Beyond the barrow was an almost precipitous drop to the vale of the Severn far below.

Ursula remembered what her father had said at the inn. "I'm afraid I eavesdropped a little at the Green Man, and heard you mention the tump. How has it been damaged?"

"I'll show you." Mr. Elcester turned Lysander off the road and rode across the springy flower-dotted grass, where the bushes rustled and the pines sighed in the breeze that played over the lip of the escarpment. They dismounted by the barrow and tethered the horses to a convenient spindle bush.

Hatty Pedlar's Tump was a mound about ten feet high, one hundred and forty feet long, and ninety feet wide, with a stone-slabbed entrance that gave into a deep passage and five burial chambers. The rough door that had protected the access was now hanging by a single hinge because someone had used a crowbar to force it open.

"Such unnecessary vandalism," Mr. Elcester said angrily as he tried to straighten the door.

"Like the yew."

"Yes, just like the yew."

Ursula climbed on top of the barrow, which at this time of the year was carpeted with primroses. "Let's sit awhile," she said, making herself comfortable at the western end, where the view over the vale was quite breathtaking. The River Severn, some seven miles distant and dotted with sails, wound its silver way southwest toward the Bristol, and over twenty-five miles to the north, beyond the grandeur of Gloucester cathedral, rose the unmistakable humps of the Malvern Hills.

Directly opposite where they were sitting, only half a mile away, was the outlier upon which stood Carmartin Park, but Ursula looked anywhere and everywhere except at Lord Carmartin's magnificent seventeenth-century house and park; and anyway, her thoughts had again harked back to the conversation with Taynton. "Do you really think there is someone hiding in our woods?" she asked as her father joined her.

"Taynton seems convinced so, and until the matter is settled I want you to promise faithfully not to go there."

She shaded her eyes to look up as a skein of seagulls flew noisily inland from the estuary. "Mr. Pedlar extracted a similar promise from me as I was leaving the vicarage." She hesitated. "Actually, he told me something that probably confirms what Taynton said." She related what the blacksmith had said about Rufus Almore.

Mr. Elcester was astonished. "*Almore* is afraid to go back to the woods? I never thought I'd live to see the day."

"Nor did I, but something frightened Miss Muffet near Hazel Pool this morning, so what with that and poor old Rufus, I have to wonder . . ."

Her father nodded. "Well, if there's a felon hiding there, the authorities will flush him out, make no mistake. They'll probably find the chalice at the same time, and the defacer of the yew and this barrow."

Ursula plucked a primrose and twirled it thoughtfully. "I'm sure Taynton knew I'd had trouble with Miss Muffet," she murmured.

"What makes you say that?"

"Just a feeling."

"So he's now clairvoyant as well, hmm?" Her father raised an eyebrow.

"Either that or he's the one frightening everyone."

"Now that *is* silly. What possible reason could he have?"

"I don't know, any more than I know why anyone should want to cut pieces of bark or wreck the door of a long barrow." She smiled then. "Daniel Pedlar thinks Miss Muffet misbehaved because she's a fairy 'oss."

Mr. Elcester laughed. "He's so steeped in country superstition he thinks all white animals are supernatural. Lord alone knows what he'd make of a squirrel with a red head and white body."

Ursula looked away. "Don't talk about the squirrel. I feel so angry about it that I could slip back right now and set it free."

"Don't you dare."

She pressed her lips stubbornly together and didn't reply. There was a long silence, and then Mr. Elcester spoke again, awkwardly.

"Ursula, m'dear, now seems as good a time as any to make a confession."

"Confession?"

He sighed unhappily. "It concerns this Carmartin marriage business. I'm afraid it's much more definite than I've given you to understand; in fact, it . . . er, has virtually been settled."

"Settled?" She leapt to her feet.

"Lord Carmartin is away in London at the moment, but he has sent word that his nephew is coming down to Carmartin Park tomorrow. You and he are to get to know each other, and then an announcement will be made in due course."

She was appalled. "Tomorrow? Oh, Father, how *could* you let things get to this stage without telling me?"

"Because I kept hoping against hope that I would find a way out. But thanks to swindling Mr. Samuel Haine, I have no choice but to take Carmartin's offer seriously. At least this way, we can be assured of keeping the estate in our control, and with it the welfare of the village. Please say you understand, and forgive me."

Ursula had to turn her back to him so that he wouldn't see her tears, but at last she was mistress of herself again. "You know I forgive you, Father. How could I not when it is for the sake of the manor and the village? I know you would not do this unless it was absolutely necessary, so I will be amenable to Mr. Glendower."

Relief lightened her father's brow. "Thank you, my dear. Anyway, look on the bright side, for perhaps you and he will get on famously."

Ursula doubted it very much. She was about to resume her seat when her hair felt a little odd. She put her hand to the nape of her neck to see what was wrong, and realized that the ribbon bow had gone. Where on earth had she lost it? She glanced back toward the road, but suddenly, instead of the flat grass, bushes, and Scots pines, she quite clearly saw a gracious and exclusive town square—London, she thought, although she didn't know—with a railed central pool containing an equestrian statue. A fine carriage was drawing up outside a house in the far corner, and she saw a gentleman glance out, a handsome fair-haired gentleman with arresting gray eyes. . . . A thrill of excitement trembled through her, a stirring of something, she knew not what. The gentleman's eyes were so direct, as if he would see into her very heart, and an irresistible longing washed her veins.

"What is it, m'dear?" asked her father curiously, for she had been standing quite motionless, apparently gazing at nothing.

The square and the gentleman vanished. "Mm? Oh, nothing. I just seem to have lost my ribbon." Her voice shook a little, for she couldn't quite believe what had happened in the last few seconds.

"It was there a moment ago. It must be lying here somewhere." He got up to glance around, but there was no sign at all of the white-spotted lilac ribbon.

Ursula was still unsettled by what she'd seen. "It . . . doesn't matter. I have more of it at home," she murmured. She had just seen a face that was her fate; she knew as surely as she knew her own name. Kismet, wasn't that the word the Ottomans had for it. . . ?

Mr. Elcester mistook her cast, and took her hand suddenly. "M'dear, I cannot begin to tell you how much I regret having to foist an unwanted marriage upon you. If I'd attended that damned meeting with Haine in London instead of sending my fool of a lawyer . . ."

"Your lawyer is anything but a fool, Father, so if he was gulled by Mr. Haine, then so would you have been." Ursula pulled herself together. She'd imagined the square, the carriage, *and* the gentleman! It would be ridiculous to think it had been anything more than that.

"Damn it all, Ursula, I have never even clapped eyes on Samuel Haine, yet because I was greedy for profit, he managed to dip his sticky fingers well and truly into my purse. I really believed that emerald mine to be a sound proposition. Emeralds? Pah! I now loathe the sight of them, even the ones in your dear mother's jewelry."

"I hope you do not mean to forbid me to wear them?" Ursula asked, thinking of a rather lovely necklace of which she was particularly fond.

"No, of course not, my dear, but oh, if I had Haine here now, I vow I would hang, draw, and quarter the villain."

"Then it's as well he left the country in such a hurry."

"With his ill-gotten gains."

The notes of the key-bugle sounded again as the Cheltenham *Flying Machine's* brief halt at the Green Man came to an end. Soon it swept into view out of the dip, and Mr. Elcester went to soothe the two horses as the stagecoach dashed past with its full complement of outside passengers holding on to their hats.

6

A few minutes earlier in London, where the weather
was very cold and windy, the fine town carriage
Ursula had "seen" was driving smartly along King Street,
past Almack's exclusive assembly rooms toward St.
James's Square. There were three occupants: Sir Conan
Merrydown, whose carriage it was, his new friend the
Honorable Theodore Glendower, and Theo's boisterous
white wolfhound, Bran—full name Bran the Blessed, Son
of Llyr—who was proving quite a handful in the confines
of the carriage. The two men had met only a couple of
weeks earlier at a Tattersall's sale and immediately
forged the sort of strong friendship that both knew would
stand the test of time. Now Theo was lodging with Conan
at the latter's house in Bruton Street.

Theo was twenty-two, and definitely not the fair-
haired, gray-eyed gentleman Ursula had glimpsed, for he
had inherited dark hair and dark eyes from his father's
Spanish grandmother. His wardrobe was what one would
expect of a newly arrived young gentleman of *ton*; or
rather, it was what one would expect of a newly arrived
young gentleman of *ton* who was finding it difficult to
make ends meet in the costly world of London's high
society, for it was all secondhand. He wore green cossack
trousers, a baggy style made fashionable by Czar Alexan-
der, and a wide-collared apricot coat that had a great
many gathers at the top of the sleeves. Thanks to Bran's
exuberance, his top hat had been knocked sideways,
there were muddy paw prints all over the greatcoat that
lay on the seat beside him, and his neckcloth had been
crushed beyond redemption because the wolfhound had

spotted a smug marmalade cat seated in a doorway! All this when Theo needed to look his best for an important meeting with his uncle, a fact he had been bewailing for several minutes now.

Conan, who *was* the fair-haired, gray-eyed gentleman, had listened enough. "If your appearance is so damned important, why on earth did you bring that great fool of a hound with you? You *know* how clumsy and overenthusiastic he is!"

"After what he did on your carpet this morning, I thought it best that he not stay in the house."

Conan gave him a look, for a rather costly Aubusson had suffered greatly on account of Bran the Blessed; Bran the Pest was more appropriate. There were times when he wondered if perhaps the new friendship with Theo would *not* stand the test of time after all! He leaned his head back against the carriage seat. At twenty-eight he was handsome to a fault, and as secure and privileged as Theo had it within his grasp to become. His thick fair hair had a habit of falling forward over his forehead, requiring constant pushing back, and the eyes that had so impressed Ursula were a deep clear gray. He had a quick smile, a ready sense of humor, and impeccable taste in clothes, as was clear from his superb charcoal coat, tight-fitting cream trousers, and immaculate Hessian boots. A single diamond glittered in the small folds of his neckcloth, and his top hat rested at a casual angle that many a gentleman spent hours trying to achieve; to Conan it came naturally.

The Merrydowns were an illustrious family from the Welsh marches, with considerable estates along the border between Shropshire and Montgomeryshire, and he was more often in the country than in London, so it was a stroke of good luck that had led to his meeting with Theo. No doubt the unfortunate Aubusson would consider it a stroke of very ill luck indeed!

Theo was contrite about the carpet. "I'm truly sorry, and when I'm in a position to do so, I will replace it."

"Yes, you will."

Theo smiled sheepishly, but then his face darkened

once more. "But first I'll have to marry an awful clothier's daughter!"

"Would that be the daughter of an awful clothier? Or
the awful daughter of a clothier?" Conan replied lightly.

"This isn't funny!"

"All right, so let us be serious. Theo, my old dear, I'm
very much afraid that Ursula Elcester is to be your bride,
and that is the end of it."

Theo managed to haul Bran from the window, then
straightened his hat and composed himself a little before
answering. "Why should I have to marry a woman I find
abhorrent?" he demanded.

"Why? Because your uncle says you must if you wish
to be his heir. It's all quite simple."

"Which is easy for you to say—you don't have to
marry her!"

Conan looked at him, perplexed. "Why on earth are
you so set against her as a bride? And how on earth can
you call her abhorrent? You haven't even met her, let
alone been able to form an opinion. She might prove to
be your perfect woman."

"Perfect woman? I think not. My uncle informs me
she is a bluestocking with yellow hair. Can you imagine
anything more vile? I simply cannot understand women
like that. They aren't natural." Theo scowled out at the
windswept street, where gentlemen's hats were in peril,
and ladies' skirts threatened to reveal far more of the
female anatomy than was wise, even in these days of
perilously thin muslins.

Conan smiled. "I prefer to reserve judgment about
Miss Elcester, who I am sure is as natural as anyone else.
I'm afraid I do not go along with the view that the female
of the species should not exercise her mind and talents
as much as the male."

"Then we agree to disagree. Women were put on this
earth to be empty-headed, sweet, and clinging."

"Such a creature would bore me to tears within a day."

Theo pulled a face and fell silent. Things had seemed
so bright when he'd come to London at the beginning
of February and made himself known to his uncle. Lord

Carmartin had accepted his identity and announced an intention to make him his heir. All well and good, but the price was this damned marriage. "Why, oh, why, couldn't the Elcester creature be an adorably dizzy redhead whose notion of intelligent reading is the latest edition of *La Belle Assemblée*?" he moaned. "From what I gather of dear Ursula, she delights in translating ancient Celtic myths! She probably spins her own yarn as well, and likes to design complicated patterns to weave into her own cloth! Oh, Lord, I feel positively suicidal."

"You shouldn't have drunk so much Diabolino last night. You were maudlin then, and you still are now," Conan replied unsympathetically.

Theo glowered at him. "I needed Dutch courage for today."

"Which ploy was singularly unsuccessful, because all you have to show for it now are the disagreeable aftereffects and precious little courage."

"Thank you for being so understanding!"

Conan grinned. "Anyway, to return to the matter of Miss Elcester's interest in Celtic mythology. What's so wrong with that? You've chosen to call your damned hound after a Celtic hero, a giant actually, which seemed rather appropriate, given that Brian is an extremely large hound."

"I didn't choose his name—he came with it." Theo gripped Bran's collar hastily as the wolfhound, which was tall enough to look out of the carriage window even when seated on the floor, suddenly saw a pug dog being carried from a house by a liveried footman.

Conan observed something suspiciously tiny and black jumping on the wolfhound's coat, and edged away in alarm. "Did you know he has fleas?"

"Oh, yes, but he'll soon be rid of them because I've immersed him in the usual infusion of wormwood, pennyroyal, and fennel."

"Is *that* what the stink is?" Conan muttered, pressing as far into the opposite corner as he could.

"It's a fine herbal fragrance, I'll have you know."

"Fine herbal fragrance? It's disgusting."

Theo persuaded the wolfhound to sit down again, then looked imploringly at Conan. "Can you think of a way I can dissuade my uncle from this damned Elcester match?"

"No, because there isn't a way, unless she obligingly marries someone else. Look, Theo, you can't have your cake and eat it. If you want to be your uncle's heir, you have to take Ursula Elcester, Celtic myths and all."

"I know, damn it, I know." Theo gave a long sigh. "This is 1816, not the Middle Ages. A man shouldn't *have* to marry because a tyrannical old curmudgeon of an uncle says he must!"

"He does when the tyrannical old curmudgeon holds the purse strings." Conan paused. "Carmartin is the way he is because of that business with his ward."

Theo looked at him in surprise. "Ward? I didn't know he had one."

"Oh, yes. A little girl, Eleanor Rhodes. She was the apple of his eye, but then she vanished one day, oh, years ago now. Your uncle cut up very rough about it, and quite frankly he hasn't been very agreeable ever since."

"How do you know so much about it?"

"Chance really. I heard my parents discussing it when I was a child. It seems that a branch of my family is called Rhodes, and it was wondered if Eleanor was actually my cousin. The possibility must have come to nothing, however, for it wasn't pursued, and she remained your uncle's ward."

The carriage entered St. James's Square, its team of white horses stepping high. Lord Carmartin's town residence was in the far corner, a three-story redbrick property with pedimented, shuttered windows on the two lower floors, and an imposing porch that jutted out to the iron railings that guarded the drop between the pavement and the basement. The square was a handsome area, with a railed octagonal pool where a flock of seagulls fluttered excitedly around the central equestrian statue of King William III. In the summer there was boating on the one-hundred-and-fifty-feet-wide pool, but there were no boats there at this time of year. The wind rippled the chilly water, and overhead small white clouds raced across the blue sky.

Conan watched the seagulls, and then realized what was attracting them, for a squirrel was perched on King William's head, for all the world like a red fur hat. How on earth had it crossed the water to get there? And why was it in St. James's Square anyway? There wasn't a tree in sight! The gulls fluttered and swooped, and when he saw the statue again there was no sign of the squirrel, although he was sure the gulls hadn't snatched it. The gulls flew off as the carriage drew closer, and Conan decided he'd imagined the squirrel.

Theo suddenly looked sharply at him. "Mm? What was that you said?"

"What was what? I didn't say anything."

"Oh. I-I thought . . . it doesn't matter."

The carriage continued around the square, then Theo sat forward with a start. "Come on now, Conan, you've just said it again!"

"I tell you I haven't said anything," Conan repeated a little testily. What was the matter with the fellow?

Theo stared at him. "You didn't say 'Eleanor'?"

"No. Well, not since mentioning your uncle's ward. Why?"

"Oh, I . . . ." Theo looked away a little awkwardly.

Conan smoothed the moment over. "It was probably a street call—this wind distorts everything."

"Yes, I suppose so." Theo let the matter drop, but a crease remained in his brow.

The coachman maneuvered the horses to a halt at the cub. Conan grinned at Theo. "Well, we're here, so you might as well get on with it."

"Will you look after Bran for me?"

"If I must," Conan replied without enthusiasm, for the likelihood was that his spotless attire would soon look as disreputable as Theo's.

"I fancy I'll need a good deal more Diabolino when this is over," Theo muttered as he flung open the door of the carriage and climbed down. The wind blustered coldly in for a moment before he slammed the door and approached the house.

As he disappeared inside, Bran whined suddenly, and Conan saw that the wolfhound was gazing alertly toward the central pool. A young woman was standing there beside her white horse, yet he hadn't heard her ride up. She wore a lilac riding habit and a veiled hat that cast her face and hair into shadow as she tied a length of ribbon to the railing that surrounded the pool. Bran whined again and pawed at the carriage door, distracting Conan. In that second both the young woman and her mount disappeared, just as the squirrel had a few minutes earlier, except for several more lengths of lilac ribbon that fluttered away on the breeze. Had he imagined her too? No, for the ribbon was there, fluttering in the wind.

Puzzled, he opened the door and climbed down. Bran scrambled out too, his long legs slithering and claws scraping, then he set off across the square, baying at the top of his lungs. He dashed around and around the square, searching for the young woman, but although he halted hopefully at each exit, tail wagging nineteen to the dozen, there was no sign of her. Conan reached the railing and removed the ribbon, which still bore the creases where it had been tied around her hair. The scent of flowers— primroses, he thought—seemed to cling to it, fresh, sweet, and so haunting that he closed his eyes. Bran returned and stretched up to snuffle the ribbon, then whined.

Conan slipped the ribbon into his pocket, then took Bran by the collar to lead him back to the carriage.

7

At that moment in the second-floor drawing room of Carmartin House, poor Theo was being torn off a considerable strip by his uncle, who was definitely *not* pleased to meet with any resistance to the proposed union.

"Now listen to me, you ungrateful whippersnapper, you are marrying Ursula Elcester, and that is the end of it!" Lord Carmartin slammed his glass down so hard that his pre-luncheon cognac splashed on the highly polished mahogany table beside his comfortable crimson velvet chair. "Unless of course, you no longer desire to remain my heir?" he added testily, his cold eyes peering over the thick-lensed spectacles wedged upon the end of his large nose.

Theo rose unhappily from his chair and placed a hand on the marble mantelshelf to gaze down into the gently swaying flames. Then he glanced back at his angry uncle. "Of course I wish to remain your heir, sir, but I simply cannot like Ursula Elcester."

"What has *like* to do with the scheme of things? We're talking about a marriage of convenience."

"I know, but it would help if I at least *understood* a woman who enjoys translating ancient Welsh myths!"

"Understood her? Damn it all, boy, you're going to *bed* her, not delve into the mysteries of her mind! Any man who is fool enough to make a study of female intelligence is doomed!" Lord Carmartin moderated his tone. "Look, m'boy, it ain't as if you're expected to live in domestic bliss with her. All that's needed is an heir or two, and then you can both go your separate ways."

"Yes, but the getting of heirs requires a certain, er, intimacy, sir."

"By the saints, if you can't manage *that,* you're no nephew of mine!" roared Lord Carmartin, losing patience again. His watery hazel eyes were bright, and spots of high color marked his lean cheeks. Jasper Octavius Carmartin was of a generation that had little time for such things as love matches. A man got married, and then, provided he was fortunate, affection followed. That was how it had always been, how it *should* be! He had married twice, so he should know! All this modern namby-pamby romantic nonsense had no place in the serious matter of increasing estates and fortunes. This match was a certain way of joining the Elcester lands to his own, and to that end he cared as little for the bride's wishes as he did his nephew's.

Theo returned his attention to the fire, and suddenly it seemed to him that he saw the image of a young woman shimmering among the flames. She had wonderful green eyes and a sweet, heart-shaped face framed with silky red hair. He had seen her before in his dreams, on the first of February, when he had arrived in London from Naples.

Hardly had she appeared in the flames, when the whisper he'd heard in the carriage was repeated. *"Eleanor . . ."* Dear God, he must have had even more Diabolino last night than he'd realized! But then the fire shifted, and the image was destroyed in a thousand glittering sparks that fled toward the icy sky above London. Startled, he stepped swiftly back from the hearth.

"What is it? What's wrong?" his uncle demanded.

"Nothing, sir, nothing at all." Theo glanced at the fire again. Could the image be of his uncle's lost ward, Eleanor Rhodes? Although why he should think that he really didn't know, for Eleanor was not an uncommon name. He turned to face the older man. "May I ask you something, sir?"

"Within reason."

"I'm told you once had a ward—"

"That is definitely *not* within reason!" interrupted the older man, his eyes suddenly alight with bright emotion.

Theo drew prudently back from the brink. "Forgive me, I did not mean to upset you. Er, about this match. I suppose you really are set upon it?"

"Most certainly. Thomas Elcester and I have decided that it will take place soon. Damn it all, as a widower I'd marry Ursula myself if I thought it would achieve anything, but two childless marriages do not bode well for a fruitful third. I'm nothing if not pragmatic about such things."

"Well, I may not be any more successful than you," Theo pointed out, for large numbers of offspring did not appear to be a feature of the Carmartins.

"Damn it, boy, *all* marriages are a lottery where such things are concerned. Both you and Ursula are healthy, and therefore the chances are good. That is my last word on the subject. I want you to go down to Gloucestershire tomorrow in order to dance suitable attendance upon the lady. It's a formality, because she won't have any choice in the matter either, but we must go through the motions."

We don't have to do anything, *I* do, Theo thought resentfully. It wasn't damned well fair, but an inheritance was an inheritance, and he'd be the fool to end all fools if he threw it away because of something like this. He could only hope his uncle was right, and he and the dreaded Ursula would soon be able to go their separate ways.

Lord Carmartin surveyed him. 'Well? What's it to be?"

"I'll do as you wish, sir," Theo replied.

Satisfaction lightened the other's face. "Excellent. I've already sent word to Carmartin Park, so you're expected late tomorrow evening. I've also informed Thomas Elcester, so no doubt there'll soon be a dinner invitation waiting for you when you arrive."

"How pleasant," Theo murmured under his breath, and then glanced once more at the fire. Why couldn't Ursula Elcester look like the divinity he had seen among the flames? He cordially desired the Elcesters, *père et fille,* to go to perdition and stay there.

Lord Carmartin's voice penetrated again. "It will be best bib and tucker time while you're there, m'boy, so there isn't to be any foppishness." His withering glance encompassed his nephew's cossack trousers.

"I'm *not* a fop," Theo replied, taking offense.

"Anyone who wears those damned ridiculous trousers is a fop as far as I'm concerned, and that's what Thomas Elcester will think as well, so temper it a little. Dress more like your friend, er, what's his name? Berrytown?"

"Merrydown. Sir Conan Merrydown."

"That's the chap. He always looks manly."

Theo managed to hold his tongue. Oh, how he hated these one-sided exchanges, his lordship loading the ammunition, his nephewship in the firing line.

"How is Merrydown?" Lord Carmartin inquired.

"Very well. Actually, I'd like to take him down to Gloucestershire with me. From your own account Carmartin Park in February isn't exactly cozy, and I'd be glad of the company."

Lord Carmartin cleared his throat. "Oh, I suppose it's all right, but just make sure you both behave faultlessly where the Elcesters are concerned. If the feud is resumed because of something you've done, you'll be out of my will as quick as a blink."

"I stand duly warned."

"Good." Lord Carmartin rose from his chair and went to pour some more cognac for them both. Then he came to press a glass into his nephew's hand. "This will be a wise connection, m'boy, for it means you will one day be master of a hefty slice of the county. You mark my words, this match will see the founding of a new dynasty. Here's to success between the sheets, eh?" He clinked Theo's glass.

Theo murmured something unintelligible, but drank the toast. Then his glance moved back to the fire, where the shimmering face lingered in his memory. A beautiful, vulnerable green-eyed redhead called Eleanor. Oh, if only . . .

8

Ursula was awakened before dawn the following morning. She didn't know what had disturbed her, and for a few moments she was too drowsy with sleep to stir properly. The oak-paneled room was in shadow, with only a faint glow of ember light in the hearth of the heraldic stone fireplace, and the faint silver of moonlight visible through the pale green curtains. It was a beautiful old room, with an intricately decorated Tudor plasterwork ceiling, and an uneven wooden floor that was scattered with green rugs. Her four-posted bed was hung with heavy lemon-white-striped silk, gold tasseled and fringed, and the fireside chairs were upholstered in the same material. There were two doors, one to the passage, the other to the adjoining anteroom, which served as a dressing room, with a washstand, dressing table, and wardrobes.

Ursula lay with the tendrils of sleep still curling all around. The air was cool, and she shivered a little, drawing the bedclothes up around the shoulders of her lace-trimmed nightgown. Then the window curtains moved a little in a draft. She looked drowsily toward them. Had she left the window open last night? Oh, it didn't matter now, for she wanted to sleep again. Her eyes began to close, but suddenly there came a soft scampering sound. The scampering became a scuffling, and she sat up in alarm, pushing her tangled hair back from her face.

A squirrel was sitting on the floor, looking at her. For a split second Ursula thought it was a rat, and gave a gasp of horror, at which the little creature darted away toward the window, then disappeared out into the night.

She heard the ivy rustling against the wall as the squirrel made its escape. Flinging back the bedclothes, Ursula got up to hurry to the window, where there was an upholstered window seat upon which she always knelt to look out. The predawn air was cold in the embrasure, and the mullioned window was indeed ajar, although she was certain she hadn't opened it on retiring.

Her room faced south over the hidden valley toward the Green Man and Elcester village. A spring mist enveloped the woods at the bottom of the valley, so that only the tallest trees were visible, but the sky far above was clear, and the moon, more than three-quarters full, cast a cold clear light over the countryside. To the west rose the ridge along which the Stroud road passed; to the east the valley descended gradually and secretly toward the hamlet of Inchmead, some two miles away, and two miles beyond that the small mill town of Nailsworth.

Below the window, the manor's terraced gardens descended into the mist. The fountain played in the topiary garden, where the paths were laid in a symmetrical pattern that had been set down in the sixteenth century. Ursula's attention was drawn to two squirrels playing around the base of the fountain; then she saw more running along the low urn-topped wall between the topiary garden and the rose garden on the hazy lower level. In fact, there were squirrels everywhere. Daniel Pedlar was right, there *was* a plague of them!

Then something else caught her eye, an incongruous bobbing light on the far side of the valley. Someone was carrying a lantern down through the field behind the Green Man. Who would be out at this hour? she wondered. Not Rufus Almore, that much was certain. As she watched, the lantern disappeared into the mist as whoever it was entered the woods close to Hazel Pool. Down in the gardens, the squirrels had melted away into the mist.

A dog began to bark in the grooms' quarters over the manor stables, and she heard the horses shifting nervously in their stalls. Voices drifted up to her as the men were aroused from their beds and went to see what was wrong. Ursula wanted to know as well, so she hastily donned shoes and a sensible aquamarine merino gown and dragged a brush through her hair before tying it back with a white ribbon. Grabbing her gray cloak, she hurried from her room.

Her father had been disturbed as well, and was down in the stables in his nightshirt, purple dressing robe, and tasseled hat. The dog was no longer barking, and the horses were quieter. No one knew what had upset the animals, for a search had revealed no sign of an intruder. The head groom shook his head in mystification, and then muttered something about it being "that whatever-it-was down in the woods." Ursula felt a chill finger pass down her spine as she remembered the lantern.

Mr. Elcester decided to make another search of the stables himself, and would not hear of Ursula staying outside. "No, m'dear, you go back to your bed."

"But—"

"Do as I ask, m'dear."

"Very well." She kissed his cheek, then began to return to the house, but as she passed the steps down to the first garden terrace, she paused to look in the direction of the woods and Hazel Pool. The first gray light of dawn now marked the eastern sky, and a vixen screamed somewhere, an eerie sound that always made her heart quicken a little. Then she thought she heard something else. Voices? She wasn't sure. A strange feeling of excitement and curiosity began to course through her. If something was going on in the woods—her father's woods—then she ought to find out what it was. Her father wouldn't know what she was up to, because he would think she was safe in bed. Valor nudged common sense aside, and she gathered her skirts to hurry down the steps.

She descended through the terraces, and on reaching the misty rose garden at the bottom, she opened the door in the tall boundary wall. Beyond it lay the lower park sloping away toward the woods. Rufus Almore crossed her mind briefly, but then she was outside and hurrying along the path through the dew-soaked grass. The mist swirled around her, sometimes cloaking everything, sometimes thinning so that she could see almost clearly.

The edge of the woods loomed before her, fringed with the creamy white of hawthorn blossom, which filled the dawn with perfume. She entered slowly, for the well-remembered trees seemed menacing, and she thought she heard odd little sounds; the squirrels maybe, for she sensed them nearby, and once or twice she glanced up to see one leaping from branch to branch overhead. There was no birdsong, she noticed, for usually the dawn chorus would be getting under way at this hour.

Voices sounded again. They were singing. No, chanting or reciting something. She felt she should know what they were saying, for there was something familiar about the rhythm. The woods folded over her, and the scent of hawthorn gave way to the more subtle fragrance of the bluebells that lay in drift upon moon-silvered drift all around. Wreaths of mist curled and uncurled, but always the path remained visible, leading her on toward Hazel Pool.

The gentle babble of water told of the little stream that overflowed from the tree-edged pool and made its way down toward Inchmead and Nailsworth. Its water was clear up here near the head of the valley, but the mill on the edge of the town would stain it with blue dye. Flowers bloomed close to the water—violets, golden kingcups, and forget-me-nots, which in daylight would be bright splashes of color, but in the mist and moonlight were as silver as the bluebells.

A squirrel bounded across her path, and Ursula began to wonder if she should turn back. She hesitated, but all was quiet now, no rustlings, no birds, no voices, just the burble of the brook. The scent of the bluebells was almost heady, as if the dew had freed it tenfold, and suddenly she realized what the voices had been chanting—an ancient ring game. *In and out the dusky bluebells, In and out the dusky bluebells, In and out the dusky bluebells, I am your master. Tipper-ipper-apper—on your shoulder, Tipper-ipper-apper—on your shoulder, Tipper-ipper-apper—on your shoulder, I am your Master . . .* She had watched the village children play it with laughter, but the words seemed threatening now.

A twig snapped somewhere ahead, and she halted with a sharp intake of breath. Something moved. A man was walking along the path toward her—a gentleman by his fashionable silhouette. She shrank back in alarm, for he must be able to see her as clearly as she could see him, at least . . . She could see *through* him. He wasn't really there at all. He held his hand out to her. There was something in it—a ribbon. Her ribbon! For a split second she saw his face in the moonlight; it was the fair-haired man she had seen in the London carriage! Who was he? What was he doing here? As she stared, he vanished as suddenly as he'd appeared, leaving just the path through the bluebell glades.

Ursula's heart lurched sickeningly. She was seeing things! Was she ill? Was she losing her mind? Rufus Almore's face flashed before her, and then Taynton's words to Vera echoed through her head. *"Remember, wench, I am your master!"* But even as the thought struck her, a hand suddenly clamped forcefully upon her shoulder. She screamed in utter terror.

'Don't be afraid, Miss Elcester, it's only me," said Taynton's soft voice.

She wrenched herself free and whirled about, not knowing whether to be relieved or still be frightened. "How *dare* you creep up on me like that!" she cried, taking refuge in attack.

He gave an apologetic smile. "I didn't creep, Miss Elcester. Indeed I spoke to you several times, but you didn't seem to hear me."

Spoke? He hadn't said a word! "Why are you here in the woods?" she demanded.

"I might ask the same of you," he replied.

The retort angered her. "The woods happen to belong to Elcester Manor," she reminded him.

"I know, Miss Elcester, but I thought you had more sense than to come here when it's so dangerous. It's as well I saw you, for who knows what might have happened."

"There was a lantern . . ." she began, then glanced back along the path where she had seen the gentleman.

"You saw it too? I wondered if someone in the village was helping the escaped prisoner. I came down to investigate, and then saw you. You really shouldn't be here, miss, a young lady alone . . ."

She didn't believe him; in fact she was sure *he* had been the person with the lantern. She couldn't prove it, of course, but his use of the phrase "I am your Master" was surely too great a coincidence. Nor could he be alone, for there had been a number of voices chanting. She wanted to challenge him, to confront him with her suspicions, but that would hardly be wise. No one at the manor knew she was anywhere but in her bed, and as he had pointed out, she was a young woman alone.

He gave her another of his facile smiles. "I will escort you safely home, Miss Elcester."

"I am quite capable of finding my own way back."

"I do not doubt it, but I feel it is my duty as a man of honor to see that you return unharmed."

"Mr. Taynton—"

"I insist, Miss Elcester," he broke in, quietly but firmly.

She did not argue further, and without a word began to retrace her steps toward the manor. She hurried, obliging him to quicken his gait to keep up with her, and she was very glad indeed when they emerged from the woods. The eastern sky was lightening by the minute now, and the mist was beginning to lift. All the birds began to sing, and then a cockerel crowed at the Green Man; normal enough sounds, but this morning they unsettled her more than ever. Taynton's close proximity made it worse. How Vera could have gone to live with him Ursula still could not imagine. Young, handsome, and eligible he might be, but he was also very strange, and not a little frightening.

They reached the door in the rose garden wall, and she hoped he would leave her there, but to her dismay he insisted on accompanying her right up to the house, where her disappearance had somehow been discovered.

Her father was in a great alarm, and a search party was being formed to look for her, so her sudden return with the innkeeper was greeted with much relief all around.

Mr. Elcester wasn't at all pleased with his disobedient daughter, whom he banished to her room without further ado. He didn't care how many lanterns she had seen; she should have informed him, not gone to the woods on her own, especially when she had been expressly forbidden to do so. Taynton, on the other hand, was a grand fellow who received warm thanks for finding her and bringing her home. As Ursula left to go upstairs, the invitation to assist in the locating of the lost villa was reiterated.

She paused to look back, a dark expression in her eyes. Bellamy Taynton was up to no good, and after this she regarded it as her bounden duty to find out what it was. *And* she was going to seize the first opportunity to release his squirrel from its cage!

At the same time that Ursula had first entered the woods at Elcester, Conan was asleep in his Palladian-fronted town house. His blue-and-white bedroom was furnished in classical style, and the curtains were tightly drawn against the lamps of Bruton Street. The bells of London struck the hour, but he didn't hear them. He was dreaming of being lost in a strange misty wood, his senses stirred by the scent of flowers. He was holding the ribbon in his hand while he searched for the young woman who had left it on the St. James's Square railing. He could see her on the path ahead. She was looking at him, and was unaware that someone was creeping up behind her! He tried to shout a warning, but his voice would not obey him. The person behind her was reaching out to put his hand on her shoulder. . . !

Conan awoke with a cry as a hand shook him urgently. He stared up to see Theo grinning down at him by the light of a candle.

"Are you all right, Conan? I fancy you were having a nightmare."

"A-a nightmare?"

"Yes, judging by the racket you were making. I could hear you from my room."

Conan hauled himself up in the bed. The fragrance of the woods was still with him, and he knew now what the flowers were—bluebells. A large white moth was fluttering around Theo's candle, its wings beating audibly.

"Better now?" Theo inquired, brushing the moth away.

"Yes, I think so." Conan turned the bedclothes back and got up. He felt very unsettled, rattled almost.

Theo went to the door. "Well, I'm getting some more beauty sleep. I want to be as fresh as a daisy for the journey."

"Journey? Oh, yes. Gloucestershire." Conan ran his fingers through his hair.

Theo gave him a curious look, then left. Conan pulled on his mustard paisley dressing gown, then lit a thin Spanish cigar from the dying embers of the fire and went to draw the curtains back. Mayfair was quieter than usual because it was Sunday, but there was a street call from a milkmaid with two brimming pails on her yoke. The first rays of morning were fingering the eastern sky, and an early carriage drove past on its way out somewhere. Or perhaps it was a late carriage coming home.

Conan couldn't shake off the dream, and turned to a small mahogany table beside the window where he had left the lilac ribbon, neatly rolled. Picking it up, he put it to his nose. The scent was no longer of primroses, but of bluebells. His fingers closed slowly over the fine silk, and he looked out of the window again. Something very odd was happening, and he couldn't imagine what it was, except that he had no desire to avoid it.

Fate beckoned, and he was eager to follow.

9

It was midmorning at Elcester Manor, and Ursula and her father were taking a very late breakfast in the sunlit dining room. They had been to Mrs. Arrowsmith's churching, throughout which the twins had screamed themselves blue in the face. Nothing daunted, the proud papa had thundered a sermon that should have concerned the joys of parenthood, but instead was all about the profanity of stealing from the church. If the missing chalice was mentioned once, it was mentioned a thousand times, and on each occasion a quivering finger swung toward the glaringly empty spot on the altar where the treasured item used to stand. Ursula and her father had exchanged more than one wry glance at the spectacle of such holy indignation about such a decidedly unholy cup.

It was the custom for the whole village to turn out for a churching, so the congregation was larger than usual. The only missing faces were those of Taynton and a number of his men from the Green Man, and of course, the usual absent faces. Those who married by the yew, Ursula found herself thinking. Rufus Almore had always numbered among these, but today he had broken the habit of a lifetime by attending service. He did not look at all well, and kept glancing nervously around as if he feared something. He was pale and had lost weight, so that he now resembled a beanpole more than ever. His red hair was combed neatly back from his foxy face, and he clutched his prayer book in white-knuckled hands. Ursula and her father resolved to speak to him afterward, to find out what had happened in the woods, but he dashed from the church before they had even left their pew, and when they knocked at his cottage door on their way home, he refused to answer.

After the fright of her encounter with Taynton in the woods, Ursula was now much more prepared to accept what Daniel Pedlar had said. *"There's sommat bad down there, Miss Hursula. Sommat awful bad."* She therefore made no fuss when her father rode back to the manor along the Stroud road. Not a word had been said about her misconduct, for which she was thankful. In the cold light of day she couldn't believe she'd been so utterly foolish, and she resolved not to repeat the exercise. But thinking about those strange minutes inevitably brought memories of the gentleman coming along the path toward her. Or rather, the gentleman who *wasn't* coming along the path, but whom she'd seen anyway. Oh, it was all quite ridiculous, she thought, as her common sense knew only too well; but common sense wasn't receiving much attention at the moment. She wondered who he was, because she was somehow sure he was a real person, not the product of her fertile imagination. He was constantly in her mind, and the intrusion was a little too pleasing for comfort. How novel and satisfactory if he turned out to be the Honorable Theodore Maximilian Glendower, for then the impending match would be far from disagreeable. But such a wish belonged in the land of cuckoos, she thought dryly as she applied raspberry preserve to her toast.

Dainty little white ribbons adorned the lace-edged day bonnet she resorted to when, as this morning, her hair was being difficult, and she wore an emerald-and-white checkered seersucker morning gown, high-waisted and long-sleeved, with a scooped neckline in which she had tucked a gauze scarf. A light cashmere shawl rested around her shoulders, and she looked very fresh considering her dawn excursion.

Sunlight poured in through the windows, for the room faced due south over the first terrace, where the gardeners had today placed the potted bay trees that always overwintered under glass. The room itself was oak-paneled like the rest of the house, with heavily carved Elizabe than furniture that must have been made actually within the four walls, because it was all far too big to pass through either the doors or the windows. A fine display of silverware shone on the great sideboard, and a fire danced in the hearth, making the room so warm that Ursula resolved to stop the lighting of fires until the onset of autumn.

Mr. Elcester's mood was one of disgruntlement, for he had come to breakfast hoping to find yesterday's *The Times* newspaper, which had failed to be delivered the previous day. Once again it was nowhere to be seen, and his annoyance was considerable. "Great Heavens above, with all those stagecoaches calling at the Green Man, you'd think the delivery of a single newspaper was not beyond their capabilities! It's not satisfactory, not satisfactory at all. I cannot abide breakfasting without my newspaper!"

"Shall I bring Friday's edition? I'm sure you haven't read it all."

"I have read every inch," he replied testily, drumming his fingers upon the table. Then he looked at her. "I have to ride to Stroud afterward," he said suddenly.

"Stroud? But it's Sunday."

"I know, but a message arrived while we were at church. It seems the cellar walls of Fromewell Mill are giving cause for concern again."

"Again? I didn't know anything was wrong with them."

"Yes, I'm afraid there has been a little subsidence, which in turn has weakened the foundations. If there's rain and the river rises, the cellars will flood and a great deal of other damage might result. I'd best take a look. Who knows, maybe I will find a copy of *The Times* in the town."

"I'm sure yours will be delivered soon," Ursula said patiently.

"I like my news to be reasonably current, not ancient history," he replied as he spooned some more kedgeree onto his plate. "Will you come to Stroud with me?" he asked then.

"I thought I'd make a start of *Macsen Wledig*."

"Hmm." He plunged his fork into a portion of hard-boiled egg in the kedgeree.

She knew the tone of voice. "Is something wrong? I-I mean, if you really wish me to accompany you, then of course I will."

"It's not that I wish you to come, m'dear, rather that I do not know if I can trust you not to go to the woods again."

"You have my word."

"I thought I had that before."

She colored a little. "This time I really will obey."

He looked at her for a long moment, then nodded. "Very well, you may stay here with your translating."

She nibbled her toast, thinking about the woods again. "Father, I am very suspicious about Taynton's so-called escaped felon. There were a number of people in the woods at dawn. I heard them."

"Heard them?"

"Yes, they were chanting."

He lowered his fork. "Oh, come now—"

"It's true." She told him about the dusky bluebell ring game.

Mr. Elcester gave a guffaw of laughter. "Ursula, m'dear, I think you are imagining things. I fancy you returned to your bed and dreamed."

"It wasn't a dream."

"Dusky bluebells, indeed. It's a *children's* game, not something adults would indulge in."

"I know, but—"

"But nothing, m'dear. You dreamed it, and that is that. Besides, I hardly think Rufus Almore would have been terrified witless by the sight of grown men cavorting around in the bluebells, do you?"

Put like that, it did indeed seem silly, but she knew what she had heard. And she knew that Taynton was mixed up in it. She decided to change the subject. "What about dinner tonight? Will you be back from Stroud, or will you put up at the Golden Cross again?"

"I'll come back. My business at the mill shouldn't take all that long." He paused, as if there was something he needed to say.

"Yes?" she prompted.

"Ursula, I'm afraid I still haven't been quite honest with you about things."

"What things?" she asked suspiciously.

"Er . . . about Mr. Glendower's arrival at Carmartin Park tonight. You see, I've sent him an invitation to dine here with us tomorrow night."

"You've what?" she said faintly.

"I rather think you heard."

"Yes, I rather think I did too. Oh, Father, the cook needs more warning when an important dinner is to be prepared, even if there *are* only three at the table!"

"Well, I'm sure the larder will have something suitable. I'm very partial to a nice bit of boiled mutton."

"Boiled mutton? Father, I refuse absolutely to serve *mutton,* boiled or otherwise!" Flustered, she thought, what was at its best right now? Was there time to send to Gloucester for some Severn salmon?

"I also rather like guinea-fowl," Mr. Elcester went on.

"Guinea-fowl? Oh, yes, I suppose that will do. Daniel Pedlar is sure to let us have a couple of his."

Her father beamed. "There, it's settled then."

"Is there anything else you mean to spring on me? Lord Carmartin and the Bishop of Gloucester aren't coming too, by any chance?"

"No, just Mr. Glendower. Nor is there anything else I should have told you."

"I'm relieved to hear it."

"But it *is* all for the manor and village," he added.

"A fact that right now I am having to force myself to bear in mind," she replied crossly. Just let him say one more word about her disobedience at dawn, just one word, and she would have a few things of her own to say!

A respectful tap came at the door, and a maid entered with the overdue edition of *The Times.* "Begging your pardon, sir, but Mr. Taynton at the Green Man says he's very sorry, but he inadvertently sent it on to Gloucester on the stagecoach. The mistake was only discovered this morning, and the innkeeper of the New Inn sent it back with the first stage."

Mr. Elcester was a little placated. "Oh, very well. By the way, tell the cook that I like a little more curry in my kedgeree. That was a little bland."

"Yes, sir." The maid curtsied and hurried out.

Ursula eyed her father's empty plate. "I notice you managed two helpings of it, bland or not," she observed.

"That's as may be, but I *do* like a little more spice." Mr. Elcester poured himself a cup of strong black coffee and settled to read awhile. Silence descended, except for the rustle of the paper, but then he gave an exclamation as a certain name leapt out at him from the close-packed columns. "Well, I'll be damned!"

"What is it?"

"That fellow Samuel Haine hasn't left the country after all! A false trail has been uncovered, but his actual whereabouts remain unknown. All that can be said with any conviction is that he is still somewhere in England. No doubt he is rooking some other poor gull. By God, if I had him here, I'd break his vile neck!"

Ursula forbore to reply. She couldn't think of a fate horrible enough for Samuel Haine, whose devious activities had brought about the untimely demise of her cherished spinsterhood!

It was noon, and her father had departed for Stroud when Ursula went to sit on the steps of the topiary garden with her notebooks, her mother's old manuscripts, and a freshly sharpened pencil. She still wore her checkered seersucker gown, and the ribbons on her day bonnet lifted gently in the slight breeze. Some gardeners were at work planting the tubers that in summer would produce the new white double dahlias her father had gone to so much trouble to acquire, and a boy was brushing the flagstones around the fountain, where the squirrels had played at dawn. Squirrels were in the offing now, she noticed almost casually. One was sitting atop the wall, and another was digging busily in a far corner, as if searching for nuts it had buried and mislaid.

Soon she was lost in the world of *Macsen Wledig*. The manuscripts had been in her mother's family for generations, and whoever had written them had a spidery hand that was sometimes difficult to decipher, but she felt she was translating accurately.

> "*The Dream of Macsen Wledig—being the story of how the Emperor Macsen, who was as handsome a man as ever came out of Hispania, found his bride, and how she gained her name, Elen of the Ways. One evening at the beginning of February a long, long time ago, after a day's hunting near Rome with his favorite white wolfhound—Macsen, the emperor, dreamed of a Welsh princess called Elen, who lived beyond the north wind. It was Maytime, and he saw her castle at C———, on an island rising out of a spring mist.*
>
> "*Inside, the castle hall was bright with jewels and gold, and he found two young noblemen, Kynan and his younger brother, Cadfan, playing a board game that reminded Macsen of chess, except that the ivory and blue glass "men" were animals—horses, dogs, and squirrels. The brothers' betrothed wives sat by a window nearby, embroidering fine gloves for their future husbands, and the young men's august uncle, Eudaf, High-King of Britain, was seated on a golden throne, carving new pieces for his nephews, while his beautiful daughter, the Princess Elen, sat at his feet. She wore a white gown embroidered all over with golden squirrels, her hair as red as the sunset, and her eyes as green as the woods in summer.*
>
> "*When Elen saw Macsen, she rose gladly to her feet and went to him. 'Oh, my dear lord,' she said, 'I have waited so long for you to come. If you will but love and marry me, all my father's lands and treasures will be yours. What you see around you now is but a fraction of his wealth, most of which is kept fast in his summer house nearby.'*"
>
> "*The High-King nodded, and said that his land needed an emperor's hand to rule it. At this Kynan, the elder of his nephews bowed his head, knowing that if Macsen ac-*

*cepted he himself would be passed over. Kynan was a wise
young man, but untested, and he knew his uncle was right.
The younger nephew, however, was hotheaded and bitter.
Kynan could stand meekly aside if he chose, but Cadfan
would not do the same. In a fury he overturned the game
board, scattering the precious pieces in all directions, and
as they fell they became living creatures, and went to Elen
of the Ways, whom they revered and loved. The High-
King stretched out a soothing hand to Cadfan, but he
would have none of it. Cadfan ran from the hall, shouting
that he would never accept a Roman usurper.*

*"Macsen was too enchanted by the maiden to pay heed
to Cadfan's anger. He gazed into her magical eyes, and
reached out to touch her, but his hand passed right
through her. At that point the emperor awakened, and
vowed to find her."*

Ursula had been working for nearly two hours when
she reached this point, so she set everything aside and
stretched. She wished she could decipher the name of
the castle, but that fragment of the manuscript was too
worn to make out, beyond beginning with a C. She could
only imagine that if Macsen himself was real, then the
castle might also be. A number of Welsh castles began
with C—Caernarvon, Carmarthen, Conwy, and Caerleon,
for instance—but none of them stood on an island, unless
one accepted that the British mainland was an island
in itself.

She drew her knees up and rested her chin on her
hands. The squirrel by the fountain came to the foot of
the steps and looked cheekily up at her. It curled its long
fluffy tail up in the air and flicked it occasionally, then
turned and bounded away again. Ursula watched it almost resignedly. Would it be too foolish to see a coincidence in all these squirrels and the mention of the same
creature in the myth? she mused. A green-eyed maiden
with red hair and a white gown. A green-eyed squirrel
with a red head and white body . . .

She got up, feeling cross. Yes, it would indeed be too
foolish! Just because for some reason Taynton was trying

to frighten people out of the woods, *she* was letting her imagination run away with her. She looked across the valley at the Green Man. She disliked Mr. Bellamy Taynton more each time she thought of him, and she had not forgotten her resolve to release the caged squirrel. But how and when to do it without being caught in the act? The best time would probably be when the inn was very busy, preferably when a stagecoach had just arrived and Taynton and the others were distracted. She knew the interior of the Green Man like the back of her hand, having often gone there as a child because Jem Cartwright's wife made particularly fine sticky gingerbread, and could be guaranteed to press a slice upon her. A back way led past Taynton's private quarters to the rear of the taproom. A convenient curtain screened the end of the passage from eyes in the taproom, and all it would require would be a few quick tiptoed steps to the cage, the turning of the little door handle, and that would be it. The squirrel would do the rest!

Ursula warmed to the idea. The Tetbury *Arrow* had recently begun to halt at the Green Man every evening at eight. It was always crowded with passengers eager for one of Vera's fine dinners, so the taproom would be a hive of activity. Shadows would be lengthening then too. She smiled. She would do it tonight!

10

Conan and Theo were destined to be at the Green Man at that time too, although they had no idea of this as their traveling carriage neared Elcester. Darkness was in the offing, and the journey from London had been wearisome. First they had been held up by a wagon overturn that blocked the turnpike. Then one of the horses had cast a shoe in the middle of nowhere, and now they were both tired and hungry and there were still at least six miles to go, with a hazardous descent from the escarpment, and then a long toil up Carmartin Hill.

Both men had endured more than enough of the open road for one day, and now wished they were at journey's end. They slumped in opposite corners, Theo with Bran sprawled on the seat beside him. Neither of them had spoken of their seemingly supernatural experiences in London, but both were thinking about them. Conan had brought the ribbon with him in his greatcoat pocket, although he didn't really know why. He still felt he was in the hands of fate; a novel feeling, but a stimulating one. Currents he didn't understand were swirling in the shadows all around him, and he meant to let them take him where they would.

Suddenly, the horses were frightened by something, and both men jolted forward as the coachman shouted and tried to bring the startled animals under control. Bran scrambled to his feet and began to bark. The carriage slewed across the road and lurched to a standstill, and Conan, fearing highwaymen, reached under the seat for the pistol he always kept there. He gestured to Theo to keep Bran quiet, and after a few moments the wolfhound was prevailed upon. Then they listened, but there were no strange voices, no demands, just the coachman doing his utmost to soothe the rattled team.

Conan opened the door and jumped down. The carriage had come close to an overturn in a wayside ditch, but was safe enough. Apart from the uneasy horses, their white coats ghostly in the fading light, all seemed quiet. There wasn't even another vehicle in the road. Nothing. He looked inquiringly at the coachman. "What happened?"

"I don't rightly know, sir." The man's face was pale and uneasy in the half-light of the April dusk.

Conan knew he wasn't being truthful. "Come on, Gardner, spit it out."

"Well, sir, I-I thought I saw a man standing in the middle of the road. The horses saw him too, and that's what set them off."

"What sort of man?" Conan asked, glancing around, pistol at the ready.

The coachman swallowed. "A tall man in white robes, with antlers on his head."

Conan stared at him. "With *what* on his head?"

"Antlers, sir, and I-I could see right through him. Like he was made of glass!"

"Have you been at the contraband brandy again?"

"No, sir! I swear it! Upon my mother's grave, there was just such a man in the road!"

Theo had heard by now, and alighted from the carriage with Bran. The wolfhound growled and stared straight ahead, where the lights of Elcester were beginning to glimmer. The church bell sounded the half hour, and some sheep called in a nearby field. There was a wooded valley to the right, and on the far side of it some illuminated windows of what seemed to be a big house. A key-bugle sounded, and Conan looked across the field to the north of the village and saw a stagecoach pulling out of a well-lit inn and driving off in the direction he knew Stroud to be. He had had more than enough now. If the inn had room, he intended to stay overnight and continue in the morning, when sanity should again prevail. Antlers indeed! he thought.

"Come on," he said to Theo. "We'll walk the damned team the rest of the way."

"What, six miles?" gasped Theo, appalled.

"No, just as far as that inn."

"Oh. Very well." Theo was a little mollified.

Bran was obliged to resume his place in the carriage, much to his vociferous disgust, but Conan wasn't about to have an enormous wolfhound charging all over the road and adjacent fields. The wretched dog was too enthusiastic by far, and certainly didn't count obedience among his attributes.

Gardner clambered down from his seat, and Conan, and Theo coaxed the horses to walk on. It was a quarter to eight when they reached the crossroad in the middle of Elcester, then turned north toward the Green Man. Neither Conan nor Theo much liked the leering face on the inn sign, but the general atmosphere of the inn seemed to bode well for good food and a comfortable bed. Another key-bugle could be heard faintly in the distance as they led the horses into the rear yard, where grooms hastened to attend them. Conan glanced around. It was a tightly run establishment, he decided with approval, and counted his blessings, for it could so easily have been little more than a lowly village tavern. The stables were all very well stocked, the yard itself was regularly cleaned, and there were various vehicles drawn up, including another stagecoach. Through the lighted windows of the inn itself he could see a number of people seated at tables covered with snowy white cloths.

A small gate next to the coach house opened into the field at the back, which sloped down toward the treed valley he had seen from the other road. The lights of the big house glimmered in the virtual darkness, and he was about to ask a groom what house it was when Theo chose to open the carriage door and release Bran.

The wolfhound leapt out joyously and immediately stood on his hind legs, his front paws on his master's shoulders. His tail wagged so much it caused a draft, and if a dog could grin, it was clear that Bran the Blessed, Son of Llyr, was doing just that. The wolfhound minded his manners for once, and observed the rule that there should not be any barking in a yard where there were strange horses, so it certainly wasn't his bad behavior that brought the head groom running in dismay.

"Oh, you can't bring that hound here, sir!" he cried.

"Why not?" Theo demanded.

"The landlord, Mr. Taynton, would not wish it, sir." The man's eyes moved to the team of white horses, and he became more agitated. "Perhaps it would be best if you drove on, sir."

Conan interceded. "Drove on? Certainly not."

"Why can't I bring Bran here?" Theo demanded again.

The man hesitated. "Because he's white, sir."

"What sort of answer is *that*?" replied Theo, astonished.

"Please, sir—"

"Bran stays." Theo dug his heels in, daring the man to make a further issue of it.

The man exchanged uneasy glances with some of his underlings, then shrugged. "No doubt you will take it up with Mr. Taynton," he muttered.

"Oh, I will indeed," Theo replied firmly. Damn it, he thought, Bran was being a veritable angel, so if this lout thought he was about to travel on because the landlord had some foible or other, he was very much mistaken! And so was Mine Host! He turned to speak to Conan in a low voice. "What in God's own name has white got to do with it?"

"Superstition, most likely."

"This is Gloucestershire, not darkest Africa!"

Conan grinned. "If that fearsome inn sign is anything to go by, it might as well be Africa."

The approaching key-bugle sounded again, very loudly now. The stagecoach was virtually at the inn. Conan's coachman was urgently requested to move the carriage farther in, to make room, and in seconds there was an uproar as the *Arrow* clattered beneath the archway.

Conan perceived the remaining tables would soon be snapped up, so he caught Theo's arm. "Come on, let's confront this Taynton fellow."

"With Bran?"

"*Certes* with Bran. I see several other dogs inside, so it's clearly not a rule of the house."

Conan led the way to the door through which Ursula had entered the day before. There was a great deal of noise and chatter, the rattle of cutlery, and the smell of food as waiters and maids scurried to and from the dining room with fully laden trays. Fewer people were in the taproom, however, and there were a number of empty tables. Conan chose one in a corner, and he and Theo took their places. Bran sat on the floor, still on his very best behavior. Conan glanced around and saw the squirrel. "Well, well, look at that. Clearly friend Taynton doesn't object to all white creatures, just wolfhounds. Mind you, there are times when Bran the Pest drives me to full agreement with him."

"Don't call him that when he's being a model of good conduct."

"It won't last," Conan replied dryly. He glanced at the squirrel again. It gazed mournfully back at him with eyes that were almost human. He brushed such a notion aside. It was just a rare, almost albino squirrel, no more, no less.

The passengers from the *Arrow* crowded in, and the last places were taken, although no one presumed to join the two gentlemen in the corner. In spite of the new clamor, Bran's arrival in the room had not gone unnoticed. Taynton happened to be drawing two tankards of perry from one of the barrels near the squirrel, and he was so startled to see the enormous white wolfhound that he overfilled one of them. He pushed the tankards into Vera's hands, then hurried to the corner table, wiping his hands on a towel. A fresh nosegay, wallflowers and heartsease, adorned his lapel, and his gold pin caught the light as he beamed at them both.

"Good evening, sirs."

"Good evening," Theo replied, bridling in readiness for more awkwardness.

"May I inquire which of you gentlemen owns the wolfhound?"

"I do," said Theo.

"May I know your name, sir?"

"You may. I am the Honorable Theodore Glendower, and my uncle is Lord Carmartin of Carmartin Park," Theo supplied impressively. Throwing in his uncle's name always added clout.

Taynton gazed at him without a flicker. "Welcome to the Green Man, Mr. Glendower."

"I trust my wolfhound is welcome too?"

"Oh, yes, indeed, sir," Taynton replied, although Bran had begun to growl deep in his throat, and Theo was obliged to put a warning hand on his collar. The wolfhound clearly did not like the landlord at all.

Conan had been surprised to discover that the landlord of such a hostelry was slightly younger than himself, for it was more usual for older men to take on such ventures. There was also something disturbingly familiar about him, although Conan was sure they hadn't met before. Still, that was of no consequence; it was accommodation and food that mattered now. "I trust you have rooms for us for the night?"

"We do indeed, sir. Only the very best."

"And dinner?"

"Naturally."

"Good. Our carriage is in the yard. If you could accommodate our coachman as well, I'd be much obliged." Conan gave him a bland smile.

Taynton turned and snapped his fingers at Vera. "The two best rooms at the back for these gentlemen," he ordered.

"But, sir, I have dinner orders for the *Arrow* to attend to."

"Do as your master tells you!"

"Yes, sir." She flinched, then hurried out.

Conan was a little surprised at the antiquated terminology. Master? The fellow sounded positively medieval!

Conan was struck anew by the feeling they'd met some- where before. 'Are we acquainted, sir?" he asked.

"I think not, sir. If I could perhaps know your name. . . ?"

"Sir Conan Merrydown."

Something unidentifiable flitted across the other's eyes. "Er . . . no, sir, we are definitely not acquainted. I'm sure I would remember. Perhaps I merely resemble someone."

"Perhaps." Conan didn't think so somehow. They *had* met before.

"On reflection, sir, I think maybe the accommodation here may not be to the standard you require."

Conan looked at him in astonishment. Why the change of heart? "I'm sure it will do very well," he replied.

"Possibly, sir, but—"

Conan interrupted by speaking to Theo. "Theodore Maximilian, I rather get the impression Mr. Taynton dis- approves of us, don't you?"

"Yes, I do," Theo replied. Bran growled again, baring his teeth at the landlord.

Taynton had gone suddenly very pale. "No! You can't have come here! Not at this eleventh hour!" he gasped.

Conan looked askance at him. "I beg your pardon?"

The innkeeper stared at them both, so shaken by something that for a moment he seemed almost to faint. His eyes slid to Theo, then to Bran, then back to Conan. "This is far too modest a house for you, sirs," he said then.

"Modest? It's very prosperous and comfortable, and my friend and I are of a mind to stay. Now, you have rooms, and you have already informed us that dinner will not be a problem, so let us leave it at that, hmm? Before I get a little annoyed."

Taynton backed down. "As you wish, sir," he mur- mured, then walked away, his face still quite ashen.

Theo gaped after him. "What in heaven's name is the matter with them all here? Have we sprouted tails and cloven hooves? I hope not all the inhabitants of Elcester

are like this, or saints preserve me from Ursula Elcester!"

Five minutes later, Vera came to take their order for
the meal—a choice of boiled round of beef, roast loin of
Gloucester Old Spot pig, boiled hand of ham, and roast
goose. They chose the roast pork, which she promised
had excellent crisp crackling. With it there would be
spring greens and boiled potatoes, and afterward they
would have Double Gloucester cheese and savory bis-
cuits. It would all be washed down with a jug of the
inn's own mead, which Vera vowed was very cold, dry,
and sparkling.

Conan smiled up at her. "You must bring three meals,
of course."

"Three?"

He indicated Bran. "He eats as much as we do."

She managed a smile. "Very well, sir."

Conan noticed she kept well away from the wolfhound.
She was not nervous of dogs, just of this particular dog.
"What is your name?" he asked her.

"Vera Pedlar, sir."

"Tell me, Vera, does the landlord always behave in
such a tyrannical way?"

"Tyrannical, sir?"

"Does he always remind you that he is your master?"

"Oh, yes, sir. Because that is what he is."

"I see. Another thing, to whom does the white squirrel belong?"

"Belong, sir?"

"Yes."

Vera gave him a reluctant look. "Why, I-I suppose I
don't rightly know, sir."

He frowned. "You don't know?"

'No, sir. The master brought it here with him when he
took over at Im— I mean, at the beginning of February."
Vera corrected herself awkwardly.

"He has only been here that long?"

She smiled. "He has indeed, sir, and a poor place it
was before then. He has made it into the best inn in all
Gloucestershire."

"In two months or so?" Conan raised a doubting eyebrow.

"The master can do anything he wishes, sir." Vera bobbed a curtsy, then hastened away to the kitchens.

Conan pursed his lips. "Well, Theo, my friend, I think this is an amazingly fascinating place. I believed I could sit here with a good wine and observe for hours."

"Each to his own."

"For instance, there is someone hiding behind that curtain at the far end of the tapped barrels."

"Eh?"

Conan nodded toward the curtain. "It's a woman. I can just see the hem of her cloak. Clearly she is not a lady of fashion, for it's quite a drab old garment. She's been lurking there ever since we arrived."

Theo stretched his neck to see. "A thief, do you think?"

"Maybe. I reserve judgment."

Their dinner was brought, and they all three ate it with relish, especially Bran. Theo was just reaching for his pewter tankard when he heard a whisper in his ear. *"Eleanor."* He paused and glanced at Conan, who continued eating without seeming to have heard anything. Theo sipped the mead, trying to control the trembling of his hand. *"Eleanor."* He put the tankard down with a bang.

Conan looked curiously at him. "Is something wrong?"

"Er, no. I'm just tired, that's all." Theo dabbed his lips with his napkin. He felt he must be going mad. What other explanation was there?

"We'll sleep well, I fancy."

"Yes." Theo's appetite had dwindled to nothing. He was definitely hearing voices. But then, no doubt all the inmates of Bedlam thought the same thing!

Bran, who had long since gulped his own dinner and licked the platter clean, was now sitting meekly by Theo's chair, his eyes fixed upon the unfinished meal. He licked his lips and shuffled closer. Theo took no notice. The wolfhound glanced slyly around, then stretched over to gobble what was left. Theo didn't care, and Conan was still intent upon the lurking lady behind the curtain.

In a moment the plate was empty, and when this sin brought no retribution, Bran's glance slid pensively around the rest of the room. There were other unfinished meals, admittedly some of them still being consumed, but nevertheless— What was a healthy hound supposed to do? Leave it to waste? Of course not. Getting up, he sauntered to the next table and blatantly stole a slice of ham. The owner of the meal, a fat wine merchant out of Bristol who was about to spear the very same morsel with his fork, was incensed and began to make a great noise. Taynton came running, and in a moment Theo was being respectfully but firmly requested to remove Bran the Blessed, Son of Llyr, to the stables.

This time Theo knew Bran did indeed warrant banishment, so with a murmur he got up from the table. As he did so, he caught a coat button, which was wrenched off unnoticed. Taynton noticed, however, and swiftly retrieved it. He did not return it to Theo, but slipped it into his own pocket. Bran's tail drooped as he sensed he wasn't everyone's favorite dog, and he made no murmur at all as Theo led him out into the yard.

Left alone at the table, Conan was more interested in the figure behind the curtain. He had now glimpsed the woman's face, for she had been so bold as to peep around. She was young and rather lovely, if he was not mistaken, and she did not look like a thief or pickpocket, but who could tell these days. Her attention was on the squirrel's cage, and in a flash Conan realized she wished to set the animal free. Well, he approved of *that*! But Taynton was standing close by, and if she made a single move, he would see her. "Very well, let's make sure he's otherwise engaged," Conan muttered, and got up to take the now empty jug of mead to the landlord to be refilled. "Some more, if you please," he requested, and placed the jug down in front of Taynton.

11

"I trust your meal was to your satisfaction, sir?" Taynton inquired of Conan as he filled the jug.

"Oh, indeed it was. I, er, understand you haven't been here long. . . ." Conan proceeded to engage the man in idle conversation.

Behind the curtain, Ursula was now becoming desperate to act. She had left Miss Muffet tethered secretly in the field behind the inn, and did not know how long she had been hiding like this, just that it was too long. Unless an opportunity presented itself soon, the *Arrow* would depart again, and she would have lost her chance. Her hair was tied with a fresh length of the lilac ribbon, and over her riding habit she wore a shabby old cloak that always hung in the Elcester Manor stables. Its hood was raised to conceal her identity from the casual glance, for it wouldn't do for anyone to recognize her. She didn't realize that Conan had already seen her, because she had not really seen him. She had observed two gentlemen arrive with a white wolfhound, but had not taken all that much notice of them because she was too intent upon keeping a watchful eye upon the taproom in general, waiting for an opportune moment.

She peeped warily out again. Taynton was occupied with one of the gentlemen who'd come in with the wolfhound. Still she did not look at Conan's face. For the first time the significance of the wolfhound's breed and color struck her. The Emperor Macsen had been hunting with a white wolfhound. No, it was just another foolish coincidence. She glanced around the room again. Vera was scurrying from table to table, as were two other maids. The travelers were all engrossed in their meals, except for the gentleman with Taynton, and *he* was too interested in what the landlord was saying to notice her. As for the landlord, his glance followed Vera's dainty ankles. So Ursula knew the moment was there at last. All she had to do was slip out, open the cage door, then run. Swallowing, she slowly held the curtain aside.

Conan watched her from the corner of his eye. "Which rooms have Mr. Glendower and I been provided with?" he inquired of Taynton.

"As I said, the two best rooms at the back of the house. The second floor, turn right at the top of the stairs, the second and third doors on the left. Your coachman gave us your overnight luggage, and everything is in readiness. Oh, here are your keys." Taynton slid them across the trestle.

"How long have you been an innkeeper?" Conan went on, determined to keep the man talking for as long as he reasonably could.

As Taynton proceeded to tell him how he had become interested in the business, Ursula darted to the cage, but the handle wouldn't work! She fumbled with it, and her hood fell back to reveal her silvery hair and large lilac eyes—and the length of ribbon in her hair.

Conan stared at her. The woman in the square! The woman in the woods he had dreamed of!

Ursula's glance suddenly flew to his face as she continued to struggle with the handle. Her eyes widened. The man in the carriage! The gentleman on the path in the woods! At last the cage door opened. The squirrel leapt down and fled beneath the curtain to freedom. Ursula fled too, not stopping for anything until she was in the field, fumbling again as she unlooped Miss Muffet's reins. She hauled herself awkwardly up onto the saddle and urged the mare away, out of the field and down through the village on the road to Stroud.

Conan rushed from the inn in time to see the white horse leaving the field. Its hooves drummed upon the road, and that was the last he saw of his mysterious Lady of Ribbons. Angry that she had gotten away, he looked at the gate through which she had gone. "Damn you, gate, why couldn't you have stayed closed?" he breathed. To his amazement, the gate swung on its hinges, then clanged shut firmly.

Startled, Conan stared at it, but shook his head. An idle whim of the wind, he decided, and went back inside.

Things had taken another astonishing turn for Theo as well. He had taken Bran to the stables, where the head groom, who seemed very uneasy indeed about the wolf-hound, showed him an empty stall where Bran could be tied to an iron ring set in the stone wall. The stall was clean, with fresh straw on the floor, but Bran was not at all pleased. Humans confused him. Why was it all right to help one man finish his dinner, but not another? He was merely tidying up. Why, when he'd finished, the plates did not even need washing! Yet he'd been banished out here in the cold and dark. He lay down on the straw with a very hangdog expression, then heaved a huge sigh, and turned his head away from Theo.

Theo glanced around as he waited for the man to bring a bucket of water for Bran to drink. Like everything else at the Green Man, the stables were in tip-top condition, and so were the horses in nearby stalls. Several lanterns hanging from beams cast a good light over most of the stalls, and he could hear the murmur of men through the door that led into an adjacent coach house. There was no laugher or jocularity, just low, earnest conversation. He caught the word "wolfhound" and knew they were speaking of Bran. Just why were they all so concerned about a white dog? It didn't make sense. Perhaps Conan was right, and it was superstition, although such things seemed very out of place indeed in a thriving coaching inn where the modern world passed constantly through.

He glanced around a little more. The village maypole lay in the straw against a far wall. It had obviously been freshly painted, and new ribbons had been tied to it in readiness for May Day in a few days' time. Then he saw something hanging on the wall above the maypole. It was as handsome a set of antlers as he'd ever seen. Im-

mediately recalling what had happened on the road just
outside the village, he was too puzzled as to why such a
magnificent trophy should be relegated to the stables. He
went to examine them and saw that they were indeed
very fine. They were also very highly polished, and
scented with something herbal! His lips parted in surprise, but then he glanced down at the maypole. Of
course, they were for the May Day festivities. Morris
dancing, no doubt.

The main doors of the stables were open to the yard,
and Theo turned as he heard someone leaving the inn.
He saw a hooded figure—a woman, he guessed—hurrying toward the little gate into the field at the back of
the stables. Then he heard hooves and glimpsed her urg-
ing a white horse away. Conan ran out of the inn as well,
and halted as the sound of hooves told him she had gone.
Theo was about to go see what had happened when
something made him glance up with a start. A pair of
squirrels chased each other along a beam. Then he saw
more—indeed they seemed to be everywhere! Theo
didn't quite know what to think. He wasn't all that *au
fait* with the habits of red squirrels; perhaps they were
always to be found in places like this.

He glanced outside again, but Conan had gone back
inside, so Theo returned to Bran's stall, expecting to find
the wolfhound still in a sulk, but instead Bran was standing with his front paws on the wooden partition between
his stall and the one next to it, into which very little of
the lantern light penetrated. The hound's tail was wagging, and he whined a little.

What was there? Theo leaned over to look and was
startled to see a young woman dressed entirely in white
pressing back into the darkest corner. There were squirrels at her feet, and they were facing Bran defiantly, as
if protecting the young woman.

"Who on earth—?" he began, but then the man returned with the bucket of water. The young woman
shrank back in terror, and Theo turned quickly to take
the bucket. "Thank you," he said, and tossed the man a
coin. The squirrels melted back into the shadows.

The man touched his hat, then glanced curiously at Bran, who was so eagerly intent upon the next stall. "What's he seen?" he asked.

"Oh, a mouse in the straw, that's all," Theo said quickly.

The man accepted the explanation. "That durned cat don't earn its keep," he muttered, then walked off to join his fellows in the coach house.

Theo immediately went around into the other stall. "Who are you?" he asked the young woman.

She took a hesitant step forward, her squirrel escort accompanying her. Her white gown was made of costly satin, with pendulous sleeves and a long train that dragged over the straw. It was richly embroidered—with squirrels, he thought—and was totally unlike any gown he had ever seen before. The lantern light fell across her face, and he recognized her sweet, heart-shaped face, big green eyes, and mane of loose red-gold curls tumbling to her shoulders. His heart turned over at her beauty. She was the face of his dream, the face in the fire. She was also transparent. He could see right through her!

"I am known as Eleanor Rhodes," she said. Her voice was gentle and soft, yet with a frightened undertone.

Theo stared at her. His uncle's long lost ward? Was it possible? "Eleanor Rhodes?" he repeated. "Are-are you Lord Carmartin's Eleanor Rhodes?"

"Yes." A sound distracted her, and again she glanced at the doorway to the yard. "Please help me," she begged.

"I will do anything you wish," he breathed, falling so hopelessly in love in those few seconds that he would have laid down his life for her.

Just then an uproar arose in the yard. Taynton ran out of the inn, shouting that the squirrel had escaped. The men in the coach house dashed out to him, and the innkeeper ordered them to search everywhere. Eleanor gave a terrified cry, and before Theo could do anything, she gathered the folds of her white gown and fled into the coach house. Bran began to bark furiously and strained to break free of the rope that tied him to the wall. He was beside himself with fury, snapping and snarling as if he would tear limb from limb anyone who harmed her.

Fleeing to the coach house was a fatal error of judgment on Eleanor's part, for directly she passed from Theo's sight, she ran right into some of Taynton's men. Theo heard her cry out, and ran to rescue her, but when he arrived, she was nowhere to be seen. The men were going out into the yard by another doorway, and Theo saw them go to Taynton, who waited by the entrance to the inn. Something was handed to him. Theo could not see what, and then Taynton went back inside. The men dispersed, and calm was restored, except for Bran's continuing noise from the stables. Of Eleanor Rhodes there was no sign at all. Even the squirrels had gone.

Theo halted in the middle of the yard and glanced all around. She *had* been here, he *had* spoken to her! He ran his hand through his hair.

12

When Conan's Lady of Ribbons made her getaway without him discovering her identity, he had returned a little disconsolately to the taproom. He longed to know exactly who she was, for shabby cloak or not, the rest of her clothing he'd glimpsed was of good quality. He regarded himself as her accomplice-in-crime, and as such would at least have liked to know her name.

He took his refilled jug of mead back to the corner table, and watched Taynton continuing with his landlordly duties. It wasn't long before the squirrel's disappearance was noted, and to Conan's amazement it was as if someone had stolen the crown jewels! The landlord was beside himself, and every traveler in the room watched openmouthed as he sent maids and waiters scurrying in all directions to look for it. Then he himself dashed outside, shouting to the rest of his men. There were curious murmurs from the diners, and after a minute or so Taynton returned with the squirrel firmly in his grasp. He shoved it angrily back into the cage and closed the door tightly. He checked the catch several times, and then took a length of string from a shelf and tied the door closed as well.

Conan was disappointed to see the creature restored to captivity. He and the Lady of Ribbons had labored in vain. Well, he for one was not defeated. He sipped the mead, a faint smile on his lips. He would wait until the small hours of the night, then set the squirrel free again.

Taynton was at pains to behave as if nothing untoward had happened, but he was considerably rattled. He made much of hanging some tankards on the hooks on a beam, but his glance darted suspiciously around the taproom. Someone had released the squirrel, for the catch was too complicated for the creature to have done it. His eyes went to the corner table, and Sir Conan Merrydown. Oh, yes, *there* sat the culprit, Taynton thought. The landlord's eyes hardened. He had already vowed to keep a very sharp eye on his two unwanted guests; from now on they would not be able to move without him knowing all about it. Taynton put his hand in his pocket, where Theo's button lay hidden. All he needed was something belonging to Sir Conan Merrydown as well. The rest would be simple.

Theo returned from the stables and resumed his seat with Conan, who immediately noticed the missing button. "You've torn a button off somewhere," he pointed out.

"Mm? Oh, I-I hadn't noticed. . . ."

Conan's brows drew together in concern. "Is something wrong?"

"Yes, as it happens." Theo poured himself a large measure of mead and drank it in quick gulps.

"Steady, for it isn't lemonade," Conan murmured.

"Can we go up to one of our rooms? I need to talk in private before I burst."

"Of course. You bring the tankards." Conan got up, took the jug of mead, and led the way out into the hall. Remembering Taynton's directions, he led the way upstairs, and then to the first room the landlord had indicated. It proved to be his own, for his was the valise standing on the floor at the foot of the capacious four-posted bed. He set the jug down on a table, then went to the window to look down into the yard. The *Arrow* stagecoach was preparing to depart, late as it happened, and the coachman was shouting into the inn for the passengers to make haste or he'd lose his job. In the stables, Bran's barking had now subsided into the occasional mournful howl.

After drawing the curtains and lighting a candle from the fire, Conan took off his boots, poured two more drafts of mead, then sprawled on the bed. "Right, what's wrong?" he asked Theo, who stood with a hand on the mantel, looking down into the fire.

"I don't know, and that's a fact. But *something's* wrong, very wrong indeed. Things have been happening, weird things . . ." Theo gulped some more mead.

"Begin at the beginning," Conan advised. Weird things? He had a few of those to relate himself!

"The beginning? Well, that would be the night of February the first, when I reached London after journeying from Naples. I dreamed of a young woman." Theo went on to relate how he'd seen the same woman in the fire, how he associated the face with the name Eleanor, and now how he'd actually met Eleanor Rhodes.

"Eleanor Rhodes?" Conan sat up slowly. "She actually said that was who she was?"

"Yes. And there were squirrels everywhere, like attendants. Oh, Lord, it sounds so foolish, but that's exactly how they behaved. Conan, it was if I were seeing something that wasn't really there. I could see through her."

Conan's mind flashed back to the incident in St. James's Square, when his Lady of Ribbons had appeared and then disappeared. There had been a squirrel then too. . . .

Theo continued, describing how Taynton raised the alarm about the missing squirrel, and then Eleanor had fled into the coach house and disappeared.

These ethereal young women had a habit of disappearing, Conan thought, except that his Lady of Ribbons now turned out to be very much flesh and blood. A very real hand had released the squirrel, and a very real horse had galloped away.

Theo pressed a log down with his boot. "It makes no sense, Conan. I *heard* them catch her, yet when I looked, they didn't seem to have her with them. They gave something to Taynton, and that was that."

"Taynton came in with the squirrel," Conan said quietly.

"That's as may be."

"Theo, the caged squirrel has a red head, green eyes,

and a white body. According to you, Eleanor Rhodes has red hair, green eyes, and a white gown."

Theo stared at him. "Are you suggesting—? Oh, come now!"

"Is it so preposterous? You seem able to accept that voices talk to you, that a young woman can disappear into thin air, and that she has a bodyguard of squirrels!"

"Exactly." Theo gave a wry laugh. "Don't you see? It's because I am losing my mind. I'm seeing and hearing things and that makes me a prime candidate for a lunatic asylum."

"Then we must both be candidates," Conan replied.

"What do you mean?"

"You aren't the only one to see and hear things of late." Conan told him all *his* mysterious happenings, and then placed the roll of ribbon on the bed as proof that he had not imagined it all.

Theo's eyes widened. "Why didn't you tell me about all this?"

"Why didn't you do the same thing?"

Theo managed a small smile. "Touché," he murmured.

Conan drew a long breath. "Theo, I have a feeling that all this is fate."

Theo straightened. "I just wish it would all go away."

"Even your beautiful Eleanor?"

"Well, maybe not." Theo lowered his eyes. "Except that I am here to dance attendance on Ursula Elcester!" Something struck him then. "I've just remembered. There was a set of antlers in the stables. They were polished and rubbed with something herbal. I thought they were for May Day dancing because the maypole was there too, but now—"

"The figure Gardner saw?" Conan broke in.

"Yes, although why anyone should dress up like that and appear in the middle of the road, I can't imagine."

"Nor can I, except . . . Well, Taynton and his minions aren't very happy about poor old Bran, are they? And my name seemed to affect Taynton himself. Come to that, I am still convinced I know him from somewhere. He says we've never met, but it's niggling away at me."

Theo reached for the jug of mead and filled his tankard again. "This is going to be my last. I'm fuddled and agitated enough, without making it any worse."

"What are we going to do?" Conan ventured.

"Do? I don't know. I don't even want to think about it anymore. Maybe in the morning, when I've slept and sobered up." Theo placed the tankard on the mantelshelf untouched. "Let's face it. I must forget it all if I can."

"Forget it? But—"

"I can't afford to err from my uncle's straight-and-narrow path to Elcester Manor." Turning on his heel, Theo strode from the room.

Conan gazed after him, and then at the roll of ribbon. Sober or not, everything would still be the same in the morning. Except that the caged squirrel would be free again. Or was it Eleanor Rhodes who would be free again . . . ?

He leaned his head against the back of the bed. Theo was right about one thing—it *was* preposterous. All of it. Yet he, Conan Merrydown, knew he must accept it all as fact. Maybe it was his Welsh heritage, a spark of fatalism handed down to him from his distant ancestors. Whatever it was, he would let everything take its course. But he wouldn't say anything more to Theo for the time being, for the poor fellow was obviously very upset by the whole thing. As well he might be, for his feelings toward the ethereal Eleanor Rhodes placed another great strain upon the intended match with Ursula Elcester. Perhaps an insurmountable strain. Heaven alone knew what Miss Elcester's feelings were toward the union, but from the outset Theo's had left a great deal to be desired.

If Eleanor was singling out Theo, as seemed to be the case so far, that gentleman showed every likelihood of straying from the all-important straight-and-narrow path!

13

The inn was quiet, and Conan was lying fully dressed on his bed, waiting for the right moment to slip down and attend to the releasing of the squirrel. He heard the church bell strike eleven, and then the longcase clock in the inn hall chimed as well. He had ascertained from a waiter that the last stagecoach of the night departed at half past ten, and there wouldn't be another until five in the morning, when a by-mail would arrive. Outside the night was cold, with a clear sky and waxing moon, and down in the stables Bran had at last given up howling. But even as Conan noticed this, the wolfhound suddenly began to bark furiously, as if raising the alarm.

Conan quickly left the bed and went to the window. He expected to see an empty yard, but a group of cloaked figures was gathered there with a muted lantern. About a dozen he reckoned, but Taynton wasn't among them. Most of them were men Conan had seen working at the inn, but one was a woman. Vera Pedlar stood a little apart. Her head was bowed, and she seemed more subdued than the others, among whom there was a detectable air of eagerness. They were all carrying something that looked like white clothing draped over their arms, and their breath was visible in the light from the lantern. He saw nodding heads and the occasional gesture. Their manner was that of men about to embark on something they found exciting. Something sat on the ground beside them. It was covered with a cloth, but its shape was very much like that of the squirrel's cage.

Bran's barking was silenced on a yelp, then Taynton emerged from the stable with a short leather strap in his hand, which he casually draped over a nail on the wall. The innkeeper was also carrying white clothing, as well as a long staff or shepherd's crook and the set of antlers Theo had mentioned. So Gardner *had* seen a figure on the road! Bran could still be heard, growling more ferociously than Conan had ever heard him before. If the wolfhound could get at Bellamy Taynton right now, he'd tear him limb from limb!

"If I don't do it first," breathed Conan furiously, for he could not abide cruelty to animals! He turned to grab his greatcoat, then strode from the room, meaning to confront the innkeeper. He hurried downstairs, pausing only briefly by the open door of the taproom. The squirrel and its cage were no longer by the barrels. Conan strode out into the yard, only to find it suddenly deserted. He paused in surprise, for he had fully expected to tackle Taynton about Bran, whose angry growls were again beginning to swell into the occasional bark. Then he saw the lantern. It bobbed briefly beyond the coach house and stables as the innkeeper and his companions crossed the field that descended into the valley.

Conan decided to follow them, for they were clearly up to something out of the ordinary, but first he went to see that Bran was all right. The wolfhound did not seem to have come to much harm, and gave delighted yelps and whines, sensing release was at hand. But Conan had to disabuse him of that notion, for the last thing he required right now was the company of a large, barely controllable hound with a grievance. Bran seemed dismayed that he was going to remain in the stables. His tail sank, and he assumed a look of mournful, dejected reproach that revealed Bran the Blessed, Son of Llyr, to be the Edmund Kean of the canine world.

As Conan left the stable, Bran directed a disgusted wolfhound snort after him. Then a look of bright determination gleamed in his canine eyes, and he set to gnawing the rope that tied him to the hook in the wall.

Ursula simply did not feel able to sleep, and was sitting up in bed with her mother's manuscripts spread before

her. She was still flustered by her unorthodox visit to the
Green Man, and shocked to have recognized the gentleman speaking to Taynton. There was no doubt this time
that she really had seen him. He hadn't been perceived
in a brief flash of hallucination or witnessed in a haze of
dreamy sleep; he was only too clearly living flesh and
blood. Who was he? she mused. Maybe she would be
able to find out somehow, for Vera would know, if only
because of the fuss about the wolfhound—the wretchedly
white wolfhound. Why couldn't it have been brown, or
gray? She didn't know whether to be apprehensive or
invigorated by the bizarre events of the last day or so.
Maybe she had been delving into ancient Celtic lore for
too long and was beginning to let it creep into her every-
day life as well! Still, at least she had the consolation of
knowing that the squirrel had been set free. She felt good
about that—very good.

   The eleven o'clock bell at Elcester church drifted
across the valley outside. By this time tomorrow night
she hoped her first meeting with the Honorable Theodore Glendower would be over. She hoped too that the
dinner she and the cook had decided upon would be a
success. There would be Severn salmon, for which a man
would ride to Gloucester early in the morning, guinea-
fowl, and roast leg of local lamb. She knew that many
people regarded the latter as a pale shadow of mutton,
but she preferred it, and with all the trimmings considered it to be a very tasty and handsome joint. All these
would be accompanied by salad and asparagus from the
stove house, and various vegetables from the kitchen garden or store cupboard, followed by bottled peaches in
champagne with cream, then cheese, nuts, liqueurs, and
so on. Maybe it wasn't fashionably French, she knew,
and maybe the country cooking would be looked down
upon at places like Grillion's in London, but it was the
best Elcester Manor could manage, especially at such
short notice.

   If only the next twenty-four hours were over and done
with. At eleven o'clock tomorrow night she would sleep
like the proverbial log! At least, that was what she

hoped. With a sigh she collected the manuscripts carefully together, and laid them on the table by the bed. But instead of snuggling down to try to sleep, she got up and went to the window. She was in time to see the lantern bobbing down toward the valley again.

In the space of a heartbeat common sense had departed. She flew into the dressing room to don footwear and the first ordinary gown she came to, a simple dove gray fustian. She tied her hair back with the length of lilac ribbon she had discarded earlier, then left the room with her hooded cloak. But a vestige of common sense remained, for this time she took one of her father's pistols with her, knowing she'd feel safer that way. He kept two loaded pistols in the drawer of his writing desk in the drawing room, in which room he also kept his glass cabinets of treasured archeological finds, including the recently found gold solidus of Magnus Maximus.

Her heart was beating swiftly as she checked that the pistol was safe, then put on her cloak and hid the weapon in the inside pocket. There wasn't a sound in the house as she slipped out onto the upper terrace, then hurried down the steps toward the door in the wall of the rose garden. Within a few minutes, as she was making her way along the path across the lower park, it came as hardly any surprise when she discovered two squirrels were bounding along with her. It was as if they had been waiting to escort her.

She entered the woods, where the bluebells were again silver in the light of a moon that would be full in a days' time. Their haunting scent seemed to draw her farther and farther along the path toward Hazel Pool, and she could hear the gentle burble of the little stream. A snatch of voices carried on the air, and she halted, remembering what had happened before. There was no gentleman coming toward her this time, but was Taynton nearby? She turned nervously, but the path was clear that way too. Nevertheless, she felt doubtful about remaining on the path. Another path to the right, little used and occasionally overgrown, actually led more directly to Hazel

Pool, but wasn't favored because it did not enjoy the prettiness of the stream. She decided to go that way.

Conan had followed Taynton and his companions to Hazel Pool, which he knew from his dream. It was a small circular lake edged by coppiced hazel trees and surrounded by open glades. Not in the dream were the life-size wooden figures someone had set to guard the approaches. Possessed of leering, grotesque faces like that on the inn sign, they were intended to frighten intruders away, but Conan was not so easily deterred. They made him shiver, though.

He hid among the hazels, where dog's mercury and moss grew in the center of the stools. Water trickled softly by his feet, and he slithered a little in the mud and moss. It was when he glanced down to be sure of his footing that he realized the pool wasn't natural, but formed in the distant past by the deliberate damming of spring water with a low stone wall that was now so overgrown it seemed like a natural bank.

The moon shone on the expanse of water, the surface of which was disturbed now and then by the plop of a fish. And in all the glades around were bluebells. He had never seen a wood so full of them as this. It was very beautiful in the moonlight; in daylight it must be magnificent. There was no mistake it was the place he had dreamed of and where he had seen someone creep up behind his Lady of Ribbons to place a harsh hand upon her shoulder.

For the moment, however, his attention was on Taynton and his friends, who had gathered by an old hollow oak tree on the far side of the water. It was the only oak in a wood that was predominantly beech. The lantern had been hung upon a low branch, and the squirrel was in its cage on the grass among the flowers. Conan knew it was the squirrel's cage now, because the covering cloth had been removed, and he could see the little creature—or was it Eleanor Rhodes?—cowering inside, clearly terrified. What had it been brought here for? A sacrifice? He hoped not.

14

The white clothing Taynton and his accomplices had carried from the inn had proved to be long, loose robes, which they all donned with care. Taynton himself wore the antlers, which were somehow fixed to a metal circlet adorned with mistletoe and oak leaves. He also wore a golden torque around his throat, and held the staff, which he raised before him as the others began to form into a line. Vera was reluctant to join them and had to be pulled into place.

Conan watched carefully from the other side of the pool. Thirteen, including the innkeeper. A coven, maybe? He glanced up as the hazels trembled suddenly. Many squirrels had joined him, and were quivering fearfully as they too watched what was happening across the pool. Were they really Eleanor's attendants? Theo certainly seemed to think so, and their presence here now suggested they were definitely connected with her in some way, or at least with the white squirrel in the cage. But Conan knew there wasn't any "or" about it! The two were one; he was more sure of it with each passing moment.

A magic ritual of some sort commenced as Taynton used his staff to knock a nail into the oak's gnarled trunk. Then his companions began to weave a serpentine pattern through the bluebells, chanting the old ring game that Conan also knew from childhood. They would have looked rather laughable if it were daylight, he thought, but in the moonlight they were rather eerie. It was Taynton alone who uttered the words "I am your master," and when he said it, he touched one of them with his staff. This was repeated until all twelve had been touched. Then they fell still and silent, and he spoke on his own.

Conan couldn't fully understand his words, but they sounded like "Loo-nass-ah, Sow-inn, Im-olk, and something, may all the secrets be known to my might. Loo-nass-ah, Sow-inn, Im-olk, and something, by the turn of the last may it be mine by right." A spell had been cast, Conan thought, shivering. Then the staff was stretched forward again, this time to touch the squirrel's cage. As it did so, a shooting star suddenly curved brilliantly across the sky, clearly an auspicious sign, for Taynton gave a triumphant cry and spread his arms to the heavens as if giving thanks to the gods.

The squirrels in the hazels became agitated, flicking their tails and making angry little noises. Then Conan suddenly heard a twig snap nearby. He whipped around to see his Lady of Ribbons creeping toward the pool to spy on the goings-on by the hollow oak. Her hood was raised, but he knew it was she. In the same split second he realized she was too intent upon the other side of the pool to notice one of the fearsome wooden guardians a few feet in front of her. Before he could whisper a warning, she suddenly saw it. She wasn't prepared, and a terrified, only too audible cry escaped her lips as she instinctively stumbled backward.

Ursula had never been filled with more dread in her life. In the moonlight the awful figure seemed somehow to move, as if it were alive. Suddenly, she knew only too well what had frightened Rufus Almore so much.

Somehow she gathered her wits. Taynton and his companions had heard her, and most of them were already running around the pool, so she turned and fled the way she had come. She left the path, running headlong through the bluebells, trees, and undergrowth. But after going less than fifty yards she caught her foot in a protruding root and pitched forward into an old badger set. It was a heavy fall that winded her to the point of losing consciousness, and as she lay there in the darkness, the

last thing she heard was the distant baying of a wolfhound.

Conan gave no thought to running after her, for other
things were now happening at the pool, and anyway he
thought she had gotten away safely. Taynton and his
robed friends did not run far around the pool, for Bran
suddenly appeared from nowhere in front of them,
crouching down and growling with such menace that now
it was their turn to stumble backward in fear. As they
edged away, the wolfhound leapt forward, barking at the
top of his lungs as he singled out Taynton, upon whom
he meant to wreak full revenge for the leather strap.
Then the squirrels poured from the hazels as well, dart-
ing in all directions at once to cause as much disruption
as possible.

Chaos soon reigned at Hazel Pool, and Conan could
only watch, helpless with laughter, for it was the most
comic spectacle he had ever seen. Most of the white-
robed figures scurried everywhere, holding up their skirts
like startled matrons, but one or two had wit enough to
throw missiles at the wolfhound, or try to kick him if he
came near, which wasn't often. And all the while the
squirrels ran under as many feet as they could, managing
to topple more than one white-robed figure.

However, some of the squirrels had other goals, such
as trying to open the cage to release the captive. With
all the dexterity and ingenuity of their kind, they
swarmed over the metalwork, scratching and scrabbling
at the handle. This they did as Vera Pedlar watched. She
was the only one of the thirteen who had not left her
place beneath the oak, and she made no move to prevent
the squirrels from trying to open the cage. Neither did
she assist them, although Conan felt that was what she
really wished to do. Perhaps she was afraid. Yes, that
was probably it, he decided. She was fearful of doing
anything that would be against her master's wishes.

Then his attention was snatched back to the Pandemo-
nium Bran was causing. The wolfhound worried joyously
at Taynton's robe's hem, trying to get at the legs beneath.

He relished the innkeeper's panic. *Let that be a lesson! Snap, snarl! And that! And that!* At last the gnashing jaws found a soft calf, and with a howl of pain Taynton flung himself in the pool to escape. But if he thought that would rid him of his canine pursuer, he was very much mistaken, for Bran leapt in after him. There were two tremendous splashes, causing ripples that spread rapidly to wash against the bank where Conan was hiding.

Taynton floundered around, hampered by his cumbersome robe, but soon began to swim when Bran followed him into the pool. He wasn't very good, and was hard put to stay out of the wolfhound's reach. The men on the bank still threw anything they could find in an effort to drive the hound away, but it wasn't until one of them was toppled into the water by the milling squirrels that they lost all courage. Robes flapping, they scurried back to the oak to start grabbing their belongings, and were only halted from fleeing together by Taynton's bellow for help. He had managed to reach the bank, but couldn't haul himself out because his wet robe was too heavy. Bran was bearing down on him at a spanking paddle, his teeth bared in readiness just as two of the men managed to pull the bedraggled innkeeper to safety.

Bran knew when to call it a day—or night—and veered hastily away, paddling for all he was worth toward Conan. The twelve men and one woman had now had more than enough of the situation. Everything was hurriedly collected, including the still unopened cage, then they all disappeared along the path toward the field and safety. All that remained to show they had been there at all were the nails in the tree and the horrible wooden figures. The squirrels had disappeared too. There wasn't one to be seen, not even in the hazels.

Conan emerged from hiding as Bran neared the bank. He reached down for the wolfhound's collar to help him out of the water. "Well, my friend, you were certainly a fox among *those* chickens," he said, stepping out of the way as Bran shook himself. Droplets of water showered everywhere. Bran was delighted with himself, wagging his tail and panting. He seemed to be grinning, for his mouth was turned up at the corners, and his eyes bore a wickedly pleased look that was clearly visible in the moonlight. Revenge was very sweet, and he had savored the moment he sank his teeth into Bellamy Taynton.

Conan bent to pat him. "I'm sorry I left you behind, and glad that you managed to get out anyway. It was a rout, was it not? And in the nick of time," he added, thinking of the Lady of Ribbons.

Bran whined, stood up on his hind legs, put his wet paws on Conan's shoulders, and licked his face.

Conan managed to ease him to the ground again, for it wasn't exactly pleasant to be leaned on and slobbered over by a very large, very wet wolfhound. "Come on, let's take a look at what's been going on here." He began to walk toward the wooden figure that had frightened Ursula into revealing her presence. It was as tall as he was, and roughly but cleverly carved to appear only too real to someone who came upon it without warning. He himself had been given a start when he saw the first one, so he could only imagine the dread it must have struck through his Lady of Ribbons.

Conan studied it dispassionately. He remembered reading somewhere that the ancient Druids had protected thier sacred groves with figures like these. Was that what Taynton and his cohorts imagined themselves to be—Druids? Anything was possible, he supposed.

Bran growled again suddenly, looking intently in the direction Ursula had taken. Conan turned warily, although he didn't think Taynton and his crew would be back tonight. Nevertheless, the wolfhound had heard something. "What is it, boy?"

Bran set off into the trees, and Conan followed, remaining very much on his guard, for after all that had gone on so far tonight, who knew what might happen next?

The sound Bran had heard was Ursula's slight groan as she regained consciousness in the abandoned badger set. She sat up dazedly as fearsome memories returned. Realizing the danger she had been in before she fell, she glanced back toward the pool. Fresh fear settled coldly over her at the sight of a large white dog running toward her through the moonlight. She fumbled in her cloak for the pistol, cocked it, and aimed with both hands. She was trembling so much that the pistol wobbled visibly, but if the hound made to attack her, she would not hesitate to shoot.

"Hold your fire! Bran won't hurt you!" cried a man's voice.

Her breath caught anew as she saw someone pushing past a low-growing holly tree. Who was it? One of Taynton's men? She leveled the pistol at him. "Stay where you are!"

"I want to help you. I saw what happened back there."

She knew the voice, but couldn't remember whose it was. She didn't lower the pistol. "Who are you?" she demanded.

"Sir Conan Merrydown. Your servant, madam." Conan sketched a bow. As he straightened, he looked intently at the pistol, for there was something very alarming indeed about the way the muzzle wavered in his direction!

Ursula's mind was still upon Conan's name, which meant nothing to her. "What are you doing here in my—" She broke off quickly, for she had been about to say that the woods were her father's, which would have given away her identity. "Are you one of them?" she asked then, still very suspicious.

"Them? The precious thirteen, you mean? Certainly not. If I were, do you honestly imagine I would have helped you try to free the squirrel?"

With a shock she realized who he was. "No, I-I suppose you wouldn't," she conceded, then lowered the pistol.

15

Ursula was covered with confusion as she set the pistol aside and then looked at Conan. The night was suddenly more fey than ever, and all the eerie events of the past day or so flooded over her anew. Yet, if she was honest, might everything not still be coincidence? Or daydreaming? Or—as she had wondered earlier—that her absorption with ancient myths about sorcery and the Otherworld had finally taken over completely!

Suddenly, his words nudged her. "But what do you mean '*try* to free' the squirrel? I did free it," she said.

"Only briefly. It was recaptured within moments. You'd barely ridden off before it was back in the cage."

"Oh. I-I did so hope . . ."

"I know. They had her with them tonight, didn't you see?"

"Her?"

He felt a little foolish, for he had almost referred to the creature as Eleanor! He didn't know anything for certain; he was simply guessing. And a very outrageous guess it was too! "I wasn't thinking. I meant to simply say 'it.' "

Ursula could not ignore the implication of the squirrel's presence at the rites. "You don't think it was there as a-a—?"

"Sacrifice? I don't know. If they did, your arrival put paid to their plan. They took it with them and fled. It's probably back in the taproom now. Don't worry, if there's a chance to release it again, I won't hesitate to do it."

She gave him a shy smile. "We are strange allies, are we not, Sir Conan?"

"We are indeed." He went over to the set. "I didn't realize you'd only come this far before hiding. I thought you'd long since gone," he said, scrambling down to her and dislodging earth and stones, which rolled away into the darker recesses of the hole.

"I should have been, but I tripped and fell. Then I fainted." She glanced uncertainly back toward the pool. "Have they really gone?"

"Oh, yes, with no little help from Bran here." He decided not to mention the squirrels, for that would require the suspension of common sense, and he did not know her at all. Just because he had experienced apparently supernatural events, it did not mean she had too.

Ursula looked at the wolfhound. "I-I heard him barking just before I lost consciousness." She shivered as she remembered what had sent her into such reckless, headlong flight. "Do you know what was going on by the pool?" she asked then.

"No, just what appeared to be sham magical rites. To be honest, I was rather hoping you might have some idea."

She shook her head. "All I know is that it isn't the first time they've met. I heard them last night as well. From what I saw tonight, I can only imagine they are Druids of some description."

"That crossed my mind too. Here, let me help you up. There's a grassy bank just over there." He held out a hand.

She hesitated. She knew he was real, for an apparition could not have scattered earth and stones as he just had, but nevertheless . . . If she touched him, would he suddenly vanish? Would she find herself alone in the woods with her fear?

He smiled, then stretched down to actually take her hand. At his touch a sensation engulfed her that was unlike anything she had experienced before. It was as if a part of her awakened that until now had been deeply asleep. She felt a beguiling warmth spread across her skin, an erotic warmth that was tinged with a need that ached sweetly

through her veins. There was something wanton too, a desire to seduce, to surrender, to give herself completely . . .

Covered with confusion by the sheer force of these new
emotions, she snatched her hand away. "I-I can manage,
thank you," she said, and avoided his eyes by making much
of getting out of the set by herself. Then she shook her
cloak a little, and took a long steadying breath in a vain
effort to compose herself, before going to sit on the grassy
bank. Bran promptly joined her. She could smell his wet
coat, and the herbs Theo had used to rid him of unwel-
come guests.

Conan had not survived the moment unscathed either.
Touching her had aroused desires so strong that he had
wanted to pull her up into his arms in order to taste her
lips, feel her body against his. He wanted her so much that
it was all he could do to suppress the imperative craving
that excited his heart. And his loins. He had wanted many
women, and possessed most of them, but nothing could
compare with the almost primitive passion he fought
against now. He could feel his whole body trembling, and
when she snatched her hand away, he was almost relieved,
for if they had touched for much longer, he did not know
if he could have contained his base male instincts. Dear
God, he thought, what was happening? What forces were
at large in these woods that he could come so close to
forgetting every rule of conduct? He took a moment to
control himself before he too climbed out of the set.

When he joined her on the bank, he hoped his voice
sounded relaxed. "How are you feeling now?" he asked
her.

"I-I'm still a little shaken, that's all." Shaken? She was
in such a state of secret disarray that she hardly knew what
to say or do. Never had she imagined such feelings existed
as she had felt a few moments ago. In a heartbeat her
whole existence had been turned upside down, nothing was
as it had been, and her quiet existence was in turmoil. And
all because this man had taken her hand!

"Are you quite sure you're all right?" he asked, de-
tecting the quiver in her voice. Had she realized how he'd

felt? He prayed not, or she would be terrified all over again!

She summoned a wan smile. "Yes, I simply need a few moments to recover. It was alarming enough to see those robed figures, without the fetish, or whatever it was. Something about the moonlight made the horrid thing seem to move! I almost passed out with fright, but somehow found the strength to run. And then to come around only to see your wolfhound coming toward me, all white and super—" She didn't finish the word.

"Supernatural?"

"Something of the sort, although of course that would be silly." She wasn't about to elaborate on the supernatural, for she did not know anything about him. *She* may have had several strange things happen to her, but it wouldn't do to assume he had as well. Besides, the strange things could not be proved to have happened. She could have imagined every one. Drawing another deep, steadying breath, she went on. "Whatever all this is, Taynton, the landlord at the inn, is involved, isn't he?"

"Yes. He was the one wearing the ridiculous antlers."

"So I saw. Most of the others are from the inn as well, although one or two are villagers. And there's Vera Pedlar, of course." Ursula shivered again, for it was as she realized Vera was there that she had seen the terrifying wooden figure. She wished the blacksmith's daughter wasn't involved, for it would break Daniel Pedlar's heart more than ever if he discovered she was involved in things like this.

Conan realized she knew and liked Vera. "Well, if it's any consolation, I don't think Vera is a very willing participant. I think she's frightened of Taynton."

"I think so too. The way he speaks to her—"

"About being her master?" Conan interrupted.

"Yes. You've noticed that as well?"

"It's hard not to. He really is a rather obnoxious fellow, isn't he?"

Ursula nodded. "Yes, although apart from my father and me, only Vera's father seems to think so."

"Which brings me to an obvious point. You now know who I am, but I have no idea who you are."

"I-I'd rather not say, if you don't mind." Ursula didn't want to tell him because she was on the eve of her first all-important meeting with Theodore Glendower, and the last thing she wanted was to jeopardize the manor's future because tonight's excursion got out. Her instinct was to trust handsome Sir Conan, but tonight she had discovered how treacherous and seductive instinct could be! If Lord Carmartin were to find out that the prospective bride had been alone in the woods at night with a gentleman like Sir Conan, she doubted if even the acquisition of Elcester Manor would convince him to proceed with the match. The future Lady Carmartin, like Caesar's wife, must be above suspicion.

There wasn't much Conan could say, for he could hardly *force* her to divulge her name. So, the Lady of Ribbons she would have to remain. He was very curious, though. Her cloak was definitely a shabby old thing, much worn and washed, and never expensive in the first place, yet the gown underneath it was of fine quality, as were her shoes. She spoke like a lady, and he was sure that was what she was. Oh, how he longed to press her, but he wouldn't. He had almost forgotten he was a gentleman once tonight!

She knew he had noticed the contradiction in her clothes, and felt she had to offer an explanation. "I am a lady's maid, and my mistress gives me her unwanted clothes. I don't wish you to know my name, because I should not be out here like this, and fear for my position." That last at least was true!

"Ah, that would explain it," Conan murmured. A lady's maid? Aye, and pigs were given to flying! She was the lady herself. He found her utterly fascinating, both because he desired her, and because she was a woman of mystery. It didn't for a moment cross his mind that she might be Ursula Elcester, because she did not seem at all like a stuffy bluestocking. Quite the opposite, in fact, for a bluestocking wouldn't be out and about after midnight, poking about in woods where quasi-Druids were performing weird rites!

16

Ursula thought she had convinced Conan with her fib about being a lady's maid, and was now thinking again about the rites by the pool. "It's strange how a childhood game can suddenly seem diabolic, isn't it? When I was small, it never occurred to me that 'In and out the dusky bluebells' was anything other than what it seemed. Tonight, though . . ."

"Well, it's as well that children don't know the origins of most nursery rhymes. If they knew about the plague, they wouldn't enjoy 'Ring o' roses.' "

"I suppose not."

He went on. "I couldn't understand the words Taynton said just before you alerted them. Could you?"

"I was too intent on creeping forward to listen properly. It sounded like gibberish to me."

"Not quite. It was something like 'Loo-nass-ah, Sow-inn, Im-olk, something, may the secret be known to my might. Loo-nass-ah, Sow-inn Im-olk, something, by the turn of the last may it be mine by right.' "

It signified nothing to Ursula, except that if it was another childhood game, she did not know it.

"Whatever it meant," Conan went on, "the shooting star seemed to please Taynton greatly, as if his desire had been granted."

"Yes, that's what I thought too," Ursula replied. "But what can that desire be? Taynton is at pains to keep people away, which I suppose is understandable if he and his friends are going to behave as they did tonight. The local poacher, Rufus Almore, was terrified almost witless in the woods recently, so I imagine he saw one of those figures.

And Taynton has gone to the length of warning people to stay away because of an escaped prisoner he says is hiding here. He claims to have alerted the authorities, but I don't believe he has done any such thing." It occurred to her suddenly that if Conan asked the innkeeper about her, described her maybe, he would soon find out who she was. "By the way, you won't mention me to Taynton, will you? I-I mean, he could cause a great deal of embarrassment for me, especially if he realized I was the one who tried to let the squirrel go. I-I wouldn't like my employment to be at risk."

Conan smiled. "In other words, don't try to trace you through him. That's what you're really saying, isn't it?"

She colored and didn't respond.

He exhaled. "You have my word that I will not pry further." They were difficult words to say, for he wanted so much to know all about her.

"Thank you." She studied him.

"And my friend and I are leaving in the morning, so you need not fear that I may be staying long enough to discover your identity anyway."

She felt dreadful. "I-I know you must think me—"

"I don't think anything, for it is your prerogative to remain anonymous."

She still felt dreadful, but then another thought crossed her mind. "What will you do when you return to the Green Man? I mean, there aren't exactly a plague of white wolfhounds in the neighborhood, so Taynton is bound to know it was Bran by the pool."

"I'll cross that bridge when I come to it," Conan replied. He had already thought of that himself. Taynton had been handy enough with the strap *before* the business by the pool; now he had a bitten calf and a drenching to add to Bran's sins.

"Why did you come down here tonight?" Ursula asked then.

"I could ask the same of you," he countered.

"I saw a lantern from my window."

And where exactly was that window? he wondered. It *had* to be the large house he had noticed from the other side of the valley. Then it struck him for the first time that there could not be many such large houses near Elcester. Might it be Elcester Manor? A glimmer of realization began to light the mystery of his Lady of Ribbons. Was she Theo's intended bride, Ursula Elcester? Oh, he hoped she wasn't, for he didn't want his friend to have her. This last thought took him completely by surprise, for there was nothing idle about it. He really meant it.

Ursula saw the expressions flitting across his moonlit face. "Is something wrong?" she asked.

"Mm? Er . . . no," he replied, but it was reassurance born of guilt. Suddenly, he noticed the ribbon in her hair. Now *there* was a puzzle he had to clear up if he could. "Have you lost a length of ribbon like that recently?" he inquired.

She was a little surprised. "Why, yes, as it happens I have. Why do you ask?"

"Because I have found one."

"Really? Where?"

"Yesterday in St. James's Square, London," he replied, watching her face very closely in the moonlight.

Ursula stared at him, recalling the moment she'd discovered the ribbon to be lost. That had been the first time she'd "seen" him. If ever she had needed proof that these occurrences were occult in some way, this was it. It was physically impossible for him to have actually found her ribbon in London; but not *meta*physically impossible. The same applied to her having observed him in his London carriage when she had been standing on Hatty Pedlar's Tump! She longed to tell him the truth, but did not wish to be thought unhinged, so all she said in reply was, "Then it cannot be mine, for I was here in Elcester yesterday, and anyway I have never been in St. James's Square." She met his eyes as levelly as she could, then got up quickly. "I-I think I ought to go home now," she declared in a tone that completely closed the subject of ribbons.

Conan rose to his feet as well, wondering from her reaction if there was more to it than she was admitting. He was quite prepared to believe she hadn't been to St. James's Square, for he hadn't been in these woods before,

either, yet he knew them from a dream. He knew he had
seen her in London when she had been here in Gloucestershire, and then when their eyes had met at the Green Man
tonight, he was sure he'd seen a spark of recognition in
hers. Had she "seen" him before tonight as well? Did they
both have what were known as "fetches"—other selves?
He too longed to confess the truth, but decided against it
for the same reason she had. So all he said was, "Allow
me to escort you safely to your door."

"No. Thank you." She declined very firmly.

"But—"

"No, Sir Conan, I would really rather you didn't," she
insisted. Then before he realized it, she had turned to hurry
away. She didn't use the path for fear he would follow; instead she ran past some more of the holly trees that flourished among the much taller beeches, then changed direction
when she was out of view. In a moment she had reached
a dip in the land, where more bushes soon folded over her,
as did the mysterious and evocative scent of bluebells.

Conan went after her, but when he reached the holly
thicket, she had already disappeared. He considered
using Bran to pick up her trail, then thought better of
it. After all, he was now fairly sure he knew who she
was, and that he would meet her again soon. Tomorrow
night at dinner, if he was not mistaken. Although how
he was going to be able to let the match with Theo
proceed unchallenged he did not know. How was any
man supposed to behave when he wanted his friend's
bride for himself?

It was with very mixed feelings indeed that he returned
to the Green Man, and the dark clouds that suddenly
obscured the moon did not help. He had to put his Lady
of Ribbons to the back of his mind for the moment in
order to consider more immediate problems. To wit, Bellamy Taynton. The innkeeper must by now know it was
Bran who had ruined his woodland ceremony. Even
allowing for another white wolfhound somewhere in the
vicinity, there was the empty stall to give the game away.
Conan decided that Bran would have to spend the rest
of the night with him in his room, for whatever Taynton

might risk in the stables, he was unlikely to do anything in the inn itself. Least of all with a gentleman who for all he knew might be very handy with his fists or a pistol. Bran would soon be out of danger at Carmartin Park, at which point Conan would consider what to do next. He didn't intend to leave this mystery unsolved. He would winkle out the whys and wherefors of Taynton's dubious activities and put a stop to them.

The inn was quiet as he reached the yard, with no sign of Taynton or any of his band. Conan thought he felt a raindrop on his face and glanced up at the sky, now covered with thick clouds, without a star to be seen. Another raindrop touched his hand as he looked around the yard. The only sign of anyone being up was a glimmer of candlelight from a small window in the farthest corner of the inn itself, which Conan guessed to be part of the innkeeper's private quarters. Curiosity got the better of him, and with a warning hand on Bran's collar to keep the wolfhound silent, he went across to the window. It belonged to a small whitewashed storeroom, empty except for a dilapidated chest of drawers in a corner. The door was ajar, and the candlelight shone through. He could see into the comfortable parlor beyond. Taynton was leaning on a table with his back to him while Vera attended to the bite on the calf that Bran had left. Taynton was in long shirttails, *ohne* breeches, and he was not a brave patient, for he hopped around, winced, and made such a general fuss that Vera was taking twice as long to dress the injury than she would have otherwise. Conan smiled to himself, for it was most satisfactory to see that the master was not so masterful now!

There was a noise from the stables, only a restless horse, but it drew a short warning bark from Bran. Both Taynton and Vera turned, and Conan drew back hastily from the window. He had to think of something! The obvious came to him in a flash, and he began to call the wolfhound. "Bran? Here, boy! Bran!"

The wolfhound looked up at him as if he had gone mad. Why call me when I'm here already? his expression inquired, but Conan kept calling. Sure enough, a moment

or so later the door of the inn opened, and Vera looked
out cautiously.

Conan led Bran toward her. "Did I disturb you? I'm so
sorry, it's just that I looked out of my window a few minutes ago and saw Bran wandering loose. He must have
chewed through his rope. Anyway, I have him now. Perhaps it would be best if I took him up to my room for
what's left of the night. Will that be in order?"

"Why, I-I . . . Yes, sir, I'm sure it is all right."

"I have no idea how long the old reprobate has been
on the loose, but by the look of him he's been across half
the county," Conan said lightly. "I'd swear he's even been
in a river, for he's quite damp."

Vera gave a weak smile. 'Well, he's safe now."

"Yes, and that's all that matters, hmm?" Conan beamed
at her and patted the wolfhound.

She clearly believed his tale as she stood aside for him
to enter the inn. He led Bran past her as nonchalantly as
he could. But the wolfhound growled softly at her, and had
to be silenced by a gentle tug of the collar. Conan glanced
into the taproom as he passed the open door. There was
no sign of the squirrel or its cage.

When he at last reached his room and wedged the back
of a chair beneath the handle, he gave a long sigh of relief.
Bran wagged his tail and promptly jumped up onto the
bottom of the bed, turned around a few times, then
sprawled out to sleep, damp coat and all. Conan was too
tired to move him. It wouldn't be all that long before the
five o'clock by-mail arrived, and after that there would be
inn noise aplenty, so he'd have to snatch what rest he could.

He began to undress, satisfied that his own involvement
in the night's events would remain undetected. As he
closed his eyes, his Lady of Ribbons filled his thoughts. As
he sank into sleep, she filled his dreams. Outside it began
to rain properly, a steady downpour that augured ill for
the coming morning.

17

It was a dismal Monday morning par excellence, with gray clouds scudding low over the hills, rain that seemed without end, and a blustery breeze that lent an echo of winter to the hitherto glorious spring. The gutters and drains at the Green Man ran with water, and those who had to venture out into the yard did so well wrapped against the weather. It was a sharp and unpleasant change from the previous day, and proof positive that one could never trust April to be clement.

The people of Elcester looked out at the rain-swept village green and hoped things would improve for the May Day celebrations the day after next. A wagon containing the merry-go-round for the fair had arrived just after dusk the previous evening, and as breakfast was being served at the Green Man, two more wagons lumbered onto the green with the cumbersome parts and seats that would be assembled into the great wheel.

Soon there would be booths of all sorts, from fortune tellers and puppet shows to purveyors of gingerbread and questionable gin. Acrobats would perform, and musicians would play, especially the one-legged fiddler who had come every year for the past fifty. There would be halfpenny showmen, waxworks, clowns, fire-eaters, and even a tooth-drawer. The man with the performing bear might be bold enough to come again, although he had been expelled the previous year by Mr. Elcester, who thoroughly disapproved of dancing bears, bear-baiting, cockfighting, dog-fighting, prizefighting, and all else of that ilk. Numerous other attractions would compensate, especially the stagecoach races that promised a thrilling spec-

tacle as they dashed through the village. To crown it all
there would be free food and drink at the Green Man.
Crowds were expected from far and near for what was
set to be a memorable day for all concerned, but everything would be ruined beyond redemption if the weather
was anything like today's.

Conan and Theo breakfasted at the same table they'd
occupied the night before, and Bran sat on the floor at
their feet. He was behaving very well, except for growling
every time Taynton limped even remotely near. The innkeeper's calf was evidently very sore indeed this morning,
for he frequently rubbed it and then cast dire glances in
Bran's direction. He had also acquired a chill from his
soaking in Hazel Pool, and sneezed at regular intervals
into a large handkerchief. In fact, the master was a rather
sorry sight this morning, even to his nosegay of apple
blossom, which looked rather crushed. All in all he did
not look worthy of the fine antlers and solid gold torque
he'd preened in the night before. He was also in a sour
mood because, rain and injuries notwithstanding, he had
to drive the pony cart to Dursley that afternoon to pur-
chase various provisions in readiness for the lavish hospi-
tality he had promised for May Day.

A master's life was certainly not all sweetness and light
this wet Monday morning, Conan thought. Nor was it
filled with a comfortable feeling of safety, for the sacred
grove had been violated the night before, and this morning the innkeeper had dispatched half a dozen men—
presumably from the thirteen—to bring the wooden
guardians back to the Green Man. To leave them there
would be proof of strange activities. Conan had seen the
men's return from his window. They carried the figures
wrapped in old sheets, took them into the stables, and
emerged several minutes later with just the sheets.

The squirrel cage was still absent from the taproom,
and Conan guessed it must be in Taynton's quarters,
where it would be rather difficult to get at. An escape
plan of some sort would have to be hatched. But what?
Daylight was a little public, and the innkeeper was

clearly taking no chances. Conan mused upon the matter as he ate his breakfast.

Theo, meanwhile, knew nothing of the night's goings-on, and had been told the same story as Vera regarding Bran's presence in the inn instead of the stables. Conan had even made sure Taynton himself was within hearing when he related it, knowing that Theo's genuinely dismayed reaction to the wolfhound's escape would convince as nothing else could. Theo was sunk in gloom and despondency, having awoken in the knowledge that everything he recalled about the previous evening really had happened. His mind was full of beautiful, mystical Eleanor, but his life was about to be filled with bookish, awful Ursula Elcester. He felt sure a communication from Elcester Manor would be waiting when they arrived at Carmartin Park, and that as a consequence dinner with Ursula was bound to be uncomfortably imminent. He had hoped that the cold light of day would dispel Eleanor from his mind, but that had not happened. He was still entranced by her, and still unable to cope with the stranger aspects surrounding her. So he didn't want to speak about her, or about Conan's mysterious ribbon lady either. In fact, he didn't want to speak about anything at all! Therefore he scowled at the world in general, and ate his breakfast in heavy silence. This suited Conan, who had enough of his own to think about. Theo's attitude merely confirmed his decision the previous night not to say anything more about Eleanor Rhodes and other such things. It would be far wiser to keep the matter to himself until something *had* to be said.

Stagecoaches came and went at regular intervals, and the dining room was very busy as passengers consumed their breakfasts hastily because the weather was hampering times, and coachmen didn't dare to dally. The Green Man's breakfasts were as excellent as its dinners. The tables all had fresh white cloths, and a choice of beefsteak pie, ham, a round of cold boiled beef, as well as kidneys, steaks, eggs and bacon, toast and muffins was offered. Coffee and tea were brought whenever another cup was desired. The quality of the cooking was as high as ever; evidently Vera Pedlar's culinary skills were not impaired by lack of sleep, Conan thought.

Theo was about to spear a kidney with his fork when suddenly he heard the mysterious voice again. *"Eleanor."* He turned quickly, and saw that Vera had just put the cage back by the barrels. The squirrel's emerald eyes gazed at him, soft and pleading. *"Eleanor,"* the voice repeated, and he had the most uncanny feeling it came from the caged creature! Oh, no, he thought, please don't let this be happening. . . .

Conan glanced up at that moment and followed Theo's gaze. His brow cleared. The squirrel was accessible again. As both men watched, Taynton limped up to the cage. His manner was taunting and unpleasant, not at all that of a man with a much loved pet! He jabbed a finger between the slender metal bars. Conan willed the squirrel to bite it, and to his immense satisfaction the creature did just that. Taynton gave a yell of pain that silenced the taproom, and he was about to dash the cage to the floor in a fury when Vera hurried over to prevent him.

"Remember, master, no harm must befall her yet," she said in a low tone that carried only because of the hush that had descended over the room. As Taynton hesitated, and then heeded her words, she smiled at him. "Come, let me dress your finger." The innkeeper allowed her to lead him into the passage beyond the curtain where Ursula had hidden.

Conan and Theo exchanged glances, then Theo scowled again. "Don't say a word, not one word, for I do not wish to hear it."

Conan hadn't been about to say anything anyway; he was too disturbed by what Vera had said. *"No harm must befall her yet."* Yet? The implication was only too plain; sooner or later harm would indeed befall the unfortunate squirrel. It had to be freed without delay. One thing was certain—Taynton and his cronies wouldn't return to the woods until nightfall, which meant the squirrel was safe for the rest of the day, especially as the master himself had been heard to say he would be absent in Dursley this afternoon. Conan decided to find an excuse to return to the inn at that time in order to do a little squirrel freeing, and some snooping at the same time. He'd do it right under everyone's nose by leaving something behind and then saying he must look for it. A seal from his fob, perhaps. Yes, that would do nicely.

Half an hour later, Conan, Theo, and Bran set out from the Green Man en route for Carmartin Park. Conan's fob had been carefully "lost" in the stable where Bran had been kept, and all was set for a speedy return to look for it. But one mystery that Conan *had* solved was that of the large house across the valley. When he asked a groom what house it was, his worst fears were realized when he was told it was Elcester Manor. His Lady of Ribbons was almost certainly Ursula Elcester. His heart was very heavy as the carriage drove out beneath the inn archway onto the rain-drenched road. It would be impossible not to meet her again at some point, if only because Theo would be obligated to invite her and her father to Carmartin Park. When that moment came, Sir Conan Merrydown would have to try very hard indeed to hide his desire.

At the crossroad Gardner turned the horses west onto the road to Gloucester. The beginnings of the May Day fair looked very sorry indeed on the village green. Makeshift tents of canvas and tarpaulin dripped and flapped, tethered horses huddled with their heads low, and fair people sat in forlorn groups around cooking fires, the smoke from which was torn away and dispersed by the wind. Anything less like May Day would be hard to imagine.

Once the village was behind, Gardner brought the team of white horses up to as smart a pace as practicable in such conditions, and the passengers looked out at the rain-distorted countryside. A stagecoach dashed past in the other direction, the key-bugle blaring advance warning to the Green Man, and Bran directed a volley of barks at it until Theo managed to settle him again. The road led over the edge of the escarpment, and then steeply down toward the vale of the Severn. On a clear day they would have seen the same wonderful view that

Ursula and her father had admired from Hatty Pedlar's Tump, but today it was lost in the waves of cloud and rain that swept inland on the wind.

The descent was steep and none too safe in such conditions, but Gardner knew his business and managed the team like the expert he was. At last the escarpment was behind them, and the road began to level out on the floor of the vale. Carmartin Hill loomed through the haze ahead, with Carmartin Park presiding gloriously on the summit. The armorial gates stood at the foot of the hill, with twin lodges on either side, and the lodge-keeper swung the gates open as the carriage approached. Gardner flung the horses forward to gain a little momentum for the climb through the deer park to the house.

Carmartin Park was formed of a pedimented central block with two flanking wings, and was built of Cotswold stone that had once been golden but was now aged to a mellow gray. Four stories rose from the basement to attic, the latter being marked by a line of handsome dormer windows that pierced the chimney-studded roof. A stone balustrade encircled a flat area at the very top, from where the view could be admired, and where a central cupola provided seats and tables for the enjoyment of summer meals. The main entrance, approached by a grand flight of steps, faced the escarpment as if awaiting their arrival, and indeed as the carriage drew near, the great main doors were flung open and four of Lord Carmartin's brown-and-gold-liveried footmen hastened down the steps to attend it.

Conan and Theo, who had a close hand upon Bran's collar, entered to find themselves in a square, very grand hall with oak-paneled walls and black-and-white marble tiles on the floor. Fine seventeenth-century chandeliers were suspended from the ceiling, and twelve high-back chairs stood against walls hung with twenty-eight half-length portraits of kings and queens of England, from William the Conqueror to William III. Two fireplaces at the far end flanked the double doors that led into the heart of the house. It was all very impressive, very impersonal, and far from welcoming. Theo's spirits plunged even lower. Was *this* what he was marrying Ursula Elcester for?

The housekeeper, Mrs. Anthony, small, slight, and silver-haired, came to greet them. Her bunch of keys chinked pleasantly against the gathers of her dark blue silk gown as she sank into a respectful curtsy before Theo, whom she seemed to know was Lord Carmartin's nephew, even though Conan might as easily have been. "Oh, Mr. Glendower, sir, I'm so relieved to see you at last! I was becoming quite concerned, for his lordship told me to expect you yesterday," she said, her glance sliding uncertainly to Conan, whom she definitely had *not* expected, either yesterday or any other day.

Theo warmed a little. At least *she* wasn't cold or impersonal. "We had a bad journey and stayed overnight at the Green Man in Elcester. Oh . . . this is Sir Conan Merrydown. I trust you will be able to provide him with suitable rooms?"

"Oh, yes, sir. By the way, my name is Mrs. Anthony," she explained.

Theo nodded, then looked puzzled. "Mrs. Anthony, how did you know *I* was Mr. Glendower?"

"Because you are so like your dear mother, sir.'

"Ah."

She searched in her pocket and drew out a sealed note. "This came the day before yesterday from Elcester Manor, sir," she said.

Theo gazed at it as if it were venomous snake. He took it very unwillingly and broke the seal to read. Then without a word he trust it into Conan's hand. It was an invitation to dine at Elcester Manor that night!

Conan smiled and returned it. "You'll have to go," he said.

"I know, I know." Theo breathed out heavily. "I want you to come with me," he said then.

"You can't invite me to someone else's dinner party."

"I intend to send a note to Mr. Elcester, explaining that you are with me, and trusting that it will be in order for you to accompany me. It will be quite all right, I'm sure. One more or less at the table isn't going to make much difference."

This one will, Conan thought. He'll make all the difference in the world! "Look Theo, it's bad form to impose me upon them as well. I'll stay here."

"I need you there."

"You don't," Conan insisted.

"Yes, I do," Theo replied equally emphatically.

"But—"

"Please, Conan."

Conan said nothing more. He'd have to go too, and that was that.

Theo was relieved. "It's settled then. I'll write the note as soon as I can."

18

As Conan and Theo were arriving at Carmartin Park, Ursula and her father were almost at the end of breakfast. Ursula was very tired, for she had now had two broken nights in a row. She had managed to creep back into the house undetected, and had hidden the old cloak at the bottom of her wardrobe, meaning to return it to the stables later. But when she tried to sleep, it again proved impossible because her mind was far too active. The moment her eyes closed, flashes of the night's events kept returning, like a portfolio of watercolors. Now that it was day, albeit a miserably wet Monday that would culminate in the dreaded dinner with Theodore Glendower, she could scarce believe what she had witnessed in the woods overnight; or whom she had met.

Sir Conan Merrydown. His name was sweetness to her; *he* was sweetness to her. She could not forget those moments when he held her hand. Her body still recalled the amazing feelings that had almost swept her inhibitions away. It was a seductive recollection, warming, aching, compelling. If such a moment should happen again, would she be able to resist? Would she even *want* to resist? Ah, she mused, that was the question. And if she gave in to temptation, what then of the slings and arrows of outrageous fortune that would follow? She had too much to lose and very little to gain from wanting him, so he had to be banished to the distant corners of her mind. And there he must stay.

She wore her emerald-and-white-checkered seersucker morning gown again, but it did not make her look as bright and fresh as usual. It was doubtful if anything could have made her bright and fresh as she toyed with her plate of cold scrambled eggs. It was all very well to tell herself what she must do, to *know* what she must do, but that was to ignore the less worldly aspects of it all. She wished she knew what was going on in Elcester, but she didn't have the slightest idea. If she were to suddenly awaken and discover that *everything* had been a dream, she would feel vastly relieved. As it was, there was no such reassurance, and she was left to conclude that either it really was happening, or she was rather less sane than she had always believed.

Mr. Elcester watched her. "You seem very preoccupied this morning, m'dear."

"Mm?"

"Is something on your mind? If there is a problem, perhaps I can help?"

"No, I'm quite all right," she replied quickly, and with a shameful lack of honesty. She could hardly tell him what she was really thinking about, not only because it was all so preposterous, but because relating any of it would mean confessing she had disobeyed him a second time where the woods were concerned. On top of which, this time she really had been in danger! And then there was the added embarrassment of being alone with Sir Conan, whom she would probably never see again anyway. Besides, what was there to really say? She had been having hallucinations, and Bellamy Taynton and twelve others liked to dress up in Druidic robes and carry out peculiar ceremonies in the woods. Her father would be appalled, but if such a story were to reach the local newspapers, she could just imagine the mirth with which it would be read in every drawing room in Gloucestershire. Oh, no, she realized for the sake of Elcester Manor and her reputation, she had to hold her tongue.

Mr. Elcester poured himself a final cup of strong black coffee. "I have to ride into the village later to see the Reverend Arrowsmith about some parish matters, and before returning here I might call at the Green Man to see Taynton."

"Oh?" Ursula looked up quickly.

"Yes. It's a curious thing, but after going to Fromewell Mill yesterday, I made a point of riding into Stroud itself to make inquiries about the escaped prisoner who is apparently taking refuge in the woods. No one knew anything about it."

What a surprise, Ursula thought wryly.

"Anyway, it could be that it wasn't the Stroud authorities Taynton alerted, but Nailsworth or even Dursley. I mean to find out."

Ursula felt guilty for not telling him she was sure there had never been a prisoner; it was just that Taynton *et al.* required the woods to themselves, but she couldn't bring herself to do it. What Taynton's explanation would be remained to be seen. No doubt it would be suitably smooth and convincing.

A maid tapped at the door and entered with a sealed note on a little tray. "Begging your pardon for interrupting, sir, but this has just been delivered. The messenger says it's important, and that he will await your reply."

"Who is it from, I wonder? Ah, I perceive the paper to be Lord Carmartin's," Mr. Elcester murmured, taking the note and breaking the seal to read it. "Oh, this is a little unexpected," he said then.

"What is?"

"The note is from Mr. Glendower. He accepts the invitation to dine tonight, but respectfully requests that he may bring his friend with him."

"Friend?"

"A fellow by the name of Merrydown."

Ursula stared at him. "Merrydown?" she repeated faintly.

"Yes. Sir Conan Merrydown. It seems he has accompanied Mr. Glendower from London. Well, no doubt the cook can manage another setting."

"No doubt." Ursula struggled to reply levelly, for she was on the verge of panic. This could not be happening to her! It was too unfair for words. How on earth was she going to carry *this* off? Sir Conan might not know who she was at the moment, but he would the moment he entered the house! What if he should regale Mr. Glendower with her nighttime adventures? What if he should paint a scarlet picture that ruined her good name?

To her relief her father tossed his napkin onto the table and got up. "It's stopped raining, so I'll order Lysander to be saddled, then I'll be off on this wretched parish business. Oh, I do so loathe going over church matters with Arrowsmith. The fellow is dull to the point of tedium. Blunted by his atrocious wife, no doubt."

As he left the room, Ursula closed her eyes for a long moment. If she had to make a prediction at this moment, it would be that her match with Theodore Glendower was doomed. Of course, Sir Conan *might* be the soul of discretion; indeed he had given every sign of being just that, but she would be very ill-advised indeed to bank upon it. There was nothing for it but to face up to the situation and keep her fingers crossed that somehow she would retire to her bed tonight without even a tiny scratch on the surface of her respectability.

She glanced out of the French windows, which opened onto the terrace. The cloud was breaking up a little, with here and there a patch of blue to relieve the hitherto uniform gray. Sky shadows swept across the valley, scudding over the Green Man and allowing a brief shaft of sunlight to lighten the church tower beyond. As she looked, a squirrel ran up to the glass and peeped in at her. It looked at her long and hard, twitching its beautiful tail. Then it turned away and ran a few yards, before looking back at her again. It was almost as if it were trying to make her follow it. Suddenly, the head groom's terrier appeared from nowhere, yapping excitedly. The squirrel fled.

Ursula rose from her chair and went to look out properly. The squirrel had gone now, and the head groom had called the terrier back to the stables. She looked across the valley at the inn and saw Taynton setting off in his pony cart. He was dressed in his best clothes, which meant he had some business to conduct, and by the road he took she guessed he was going to Dursley. Her father would not be able to speak to him after all.

She glanced at the inn again. If Taynton wasn't there,

she might be able to see Vera. Maybe a little information could be wheedled. Maybe, too, she would be able to free the white squirrel. It was worth a try. And it would help to temporarily banish thoughts of the coming evening. She would ride there directly after she had changed.

At Carmartin Park Conan was talking to Theo in the grand hall. He was dressed in his pine green riding jacket and cream breeches, and a handsome gelding, the only white horse in Lord Carmartin's stables, was saddled and waiting outside. A folded cloak lay in readiness on one of the twelve chairs against the paneled walls, together with his top hat, gloves, and riding crop.

Theo could not believe he wished to go riding. "Haven't you had enough of being out and about? Right now I can't think of anything I'd rather do less than ride."

"You have no stamina, my friend."

"Perhaps I have more sense," Theo retorted.

"Perhaps." Conan smiled, and went to get his things from the chair. "I hope I won't need the cloak, but it's better to be safe than sorry."

Mrs. Anthony hurried into the hall. "I'm sorry, sir," she said to Theo, "but I'm afraid the wolfhound is nowhere to be seen."

Theo sighed and ran agitated fingers through his hair. "Where on earth has that wretched hound gone?"

This was the first Conan had heard of Bran being missed. "When did you last see him?" he asked.

"When we arrived. Now I seem to have . . . mislaid him."

Conan raised an eyebrow. "How does one *mislay* something as large and noisy as Bran the Blessed, Son of Llyr?" he inquired dryly.

"With consummate ease, as it happens," Theo confessed. "Oh, he'll turn up when he's hungry."

"That at least can be relied upon." Conan laughed, then turned to go out to the waiting horse. It was admirably white, and quite clearly a prime animal. Whatever one might think of Lord Carmartin, he had an eye for blood aniamls.

Conan rode down through the park to the double lodge, then east across the vale toward the escarpment, which seemed very green and close after all the rain. The air was cold and invigorating, and filled with the scents of spring. Hawthorn petals flew on the breeze like snow, the creamy lace of cow parsley already flourished abundantly on the verges, and the air was alive with birdsong. It was good to be out, Conan thought, as he brought the gelding up to an easy canter.

All of a sudden he felt as if someone were following him, and he glanced back, but the road was empty. He rode on, and the feeling swept over him again. This time he reined in to turn and look back. Once more the road was empty, but the sensation of being stalked was uncomfortably strong. After a moment he rode on.

He was right to suspect a follower, but it was only Bran. The wolfhound slunk close to the hedge, where his white coat blended with the hawthorn and cow parsley. Two squirrels made their way through the hedge beside him.

19

As Conan urged his mount up the steep climb to the top of the escarpment, Ursula was already alighting from Miss Muffet in the yard of the Green Man. She had not taken any chances with the mare this time, and had come by way of the road, pausing at Hatty Pedlar's Tump on the way to make sure it had not suffered any further damage. She was dressed in her lilac riding habit again, with her hair contained as neatly as possible in the black net to which she had pinned another bow of the lilac ribbon.

By chance she had managed to pick a quiet time at the inn. There was a private traveling carriage drawn up in a corner, and a post chaise was about to continue its journey to Gloucester, but apart from these the yard was clear. A Stroud stagecoach had not long departed, and the *Meteor* wasn't expected for another half an hour, so most of those employed at the inn were taking advantage of the lull—and of Taynton's absence in Dursley—to enjoy a little time to themselves.

After tethering Miss Muffet to the post, Ursula raised the veil on her little black hat and went inside. The murmur of voices in the dining room revealed the whereabouts of the party from the traveling carriage, and when she glanced around the door, she saw them seated at a table at the far end of the long, low room. They had finished a meal and were being served coffee by a maid, but it wasn't Vera, so Ursula crossed the hall to the taproom, where the squirrel was hunched unhappily in its cage, its tail drooping, its whole demeanor one of wretchedness. Vera was laying the tables for an expected

rush toward the end of the afternoon. Her hair was
pushed up beneath a mobcap, and she wore a dull green
linen dress that did nothing for her coloring. She looked
less than lighthearted, and as Ursula watched, she suddenly burst into tears and hid her face in her hands.

Concerned, Ursula hurried to her. "Vera? Whatever
is it?"

Startled to realize she had been seen crying, Vera
struggled to give a falsely bright smile. "Oh, i-it's nothing, Miss Ursula. I have been slicing onions, and they
always affect me."

"You haven't been doing any such thing, Vera Pedlar.
You were laying these tables and just started weeping. I
saw you from the doorway."

Vera avoided her eyes. "I'm foolish, that's all."

"Allow me to be the judge of that. Come and sit down
here." Ursula ushered her to a settle by the inglenook.
"Now then, what's wrong?" she asked when they were
both seated.

"Nothing, Miss Ursula."

"Don't fib, Vera. Is it Taynton?"

Vera drew away. "No, of course not," she said quickly.

Ursula glanced across at the squirrel, which was now
alert and quivering, its astonishing green eyes imploring
her across the room. She longed to release it right there
and then, but couldn't do that with Vera watching. It didn't
matter that Sir Conan thought the blacksmith's daughter
had participated only reluctantly in the night's ceremony,
she had still been there. Vera was Taynton's lover, and
sadly could not be trusted. "Vera, something must be
making you unhappy. Is it because of the rift between
you and your father?"

Vera's eyes filled with tears again. "I-I'm so miserable
about it all, Miss Ursula. I want to be my father's little
girl again, but I can't."

"Because Bellamy Taynton is preventing it?" Ursula
ventured.

"Maybe."

Encouraged to probe a little more, Ursula asked another question. "Why have you come here to the Green Man, Vera?"

"There was no other way."

"What do you mean? Is it because you love Taynton so much?"

Vera gave a wan smile. "Oh, I love him with all my heart, Miss Ursula, but even if I did not, I would still have had to come here. It is something that must be."

"*Must* be? I don't understand."

"Mr. Taynton is my master, Miss Ursula."

Ursula held her breath for a moment, then said, "That's a very unusual way to refer to one's lover, Vera."

"Lover? Oh, he isn't my lover, either, Miss Ursula. I only wish he was, for I would be more than willing."

Ursula stared at her. "I really don't understand. You have cast aside your reputation and the respect of your father for *nothing*?"

"If you loved someone as much as I love him, Miss Ursula, you would not be so surprised. Besides, you don't know him as I do. He can be so kind and gentle, and he can make me laugh as no one else can."

Ursula blinked. Were they talking about the same Bellamy Taynton?

Vera smiled. "Oh, you may look like that, Miss Ursula, but it's true. There are two sides to him, the one you know, and the one I know. I would do anything to spend the rest of my life with him."

Ursula simply could not believe Taynton was such a paragon. "What is going on here, Vera? How can you possibly expect me to believe what you say about him? And what of that poor squirrel? Why is it so important to him? I want to help you if I can, and to start with I'd like to understand."

Vera became guarded. "Don't ask me more, Miss Ursula, for I must not say."

"Vera, it's wrong to keep a squirrel caged like that. It ought to be set free and—" Ursula broke off as one of Taynton's grooms appeared in the doorway. His shrewd gaze rested on her for a moment before he addressed Vera.

"The *Meteor*'s on its way, I heard it a moment since."

Vera got up quickly. "I'll go to the kitchens presently," she said.

"Do you know when the master will return?" he asked them.

"No, but I imagine it will be before nightfall," Vera replied.

He nodded, gave Ursula another long look, then hurried back to the yard.

Did they *all* refer to Taynton as "master"? Ursula put a hand on Vera's arm. "What's going on here, Vera?"

"Nothing that need concern you, Miss Ursula."

"It concerns me if it takes place on my father's land."

"I-I must not—" Vera broke off as hooves sounded in the yard. She gave a sharp intake of breath as she saw Conan dismounting outside. "Why has *he* come back?"

"Who?" Ursula turned, and dismay struck through her as she recognized him. Flustered, she rose sharply to her feet. "If you speak to this gentleman at all, please don't mention me, Vera, I beg of you!" she whispered, then fled out of the taproom and across into the dining room, where to the bemusement of the traveling carriage party she pressed back out of sight behind the door. It was only then that she realized she had once again lost her hair ribbon. She knew it had been in place when she entered the taproom, so it must still be in there somewhere. Please don't let it be too easy to see! her thoughts begged. She heard his footsteps in the hall, and closed her eyes tightly.

The key-bugle of the *Meteor* stagecoach sounded from the village green as Conan paused by the dining room and glanced in just as Ursula had done minutes earlier. He had seen Miss Muffet tethered outside and wondered if his Lady of Ribbons was here, for he was sure the mare was hers. He wondered if Taynton was around anywhere, or Vera perhaps. As he looked into the dining room, he was a little disconcerted to see the few diners who were there gazing at him as if they found him of intense interest. At least, that was what he believed, but actually they were staring at Ursula, who was only inches away from him behind the door. He doffed his top hat politely, and the carriage party inclined their heads in patently puzzled response.

Turning, he went into the taproom, which seemed so invitingly quiet that he thought his rescue mission was about to be accomplished without even the tiniest of hitches. Still no sign of Taynton, he thought, or of Vera, who had now hurried through to the kitchens in readiness for the imminent stagecoach. But the moment he crossed the threshold he saw a telltale bow of lilac ribbon on the floor. As he bent to retrieve it, he heard the rustle of a woman's skirt behind him, then straightened in time to see Ursula dashing for the door into the yard.

"Hey!" he cried, and left the ribbon on the floor in order to pursue her.

Wishing she had stayed where she had been, she slammed the yard door behind her to gain a few seconds, but knew she could not hope to untether Miss Muffet, mount, and ride away before he reached her. So instead she ran across the yard into the deserted stables, where she crouched behind a pile of straw in an empty stall. As she made herself as small as possible, she found herself staring into Bran's startled eyes, for the wolfhound had chosen to hide in the very same place! She put a finger to her lips. "Shh, Bran," she whispered.

The wolfhound cocked his head on one side and looked askance at her. His expression was eloquent. What a very odd woman, he seemed to be thinking. First she hid in badger sets, and now behind piles of straw. Wherever next? Perhaps she was a little touched in the head.

By now Conan had wrenched open the inn door and caught a glimpse of lilac riding habit as she fled into the stables. He ran after her just as the *Meteor* stagecoach swept beneath the archway and grooms and ostlers hastened from all directions to go about their duties. No one even noticed him hurrying into the stables, and he didn't think anyone knew Ursula had preceded him.

20

In spite of the racket in the yard, on entering the stables
Conan distinctly heard a rustling sound from behind
the pile of straw in the stall. He strode over to it and
was startled to find Bran with Ursula. "What in God's
own name . . . ?" he began, then folded his arms to
survey them both. First he addressed the wolfhound. "It
was you following me, eh, sir? You're supposed to be at
Carmartin Park, not here."

Bran hung his head, sensing full well he was in trouble.

Then Conan addressed Ursula. "As for you, Miss Elcester—it *is* Miss Elcester, is it not?"

She sat up slowly, feeling very foolish, and very apprehensive. She hadn't anticipated meeting him until this
evening, and having the moment thrust upon her now
denied her the opportunity to prepare herself. Her wits
seemed to have scattered to the four corners of the stables, and all she could think of saying was, "How did
you find out who I was?"

"Oh, I worked it out for myself, so please do not ac-
cuse me of breaking my word about making inquiries."

Finding herself alone with him again, and in questionable circumstances, she looked uneasily toward the door.
"Perhaps we should go outside, Sir Conan. I don't wish
to be discovered alone with you in here."

"No one knows we are here."

"Are you sure?"

"As sure as I can be. We are private enough, and if
anyone should come, you have only to dive down behind
the straw again."

She had to remove her hat because it had been knocked

sideways and was tugging at its pins. "Are you going to tell Mr. Glendower about me?"

"Tell—?" A frown darkened his brow. "What do you take me for, madam?"

"I don't know. I hardly know you, so how can I possibly guess what manner of man you are?" she retorted. *I only know that when I look into your eyes, I feel more alive than ever before. . . .* Hot color warmed her cheeks, and she made much of brushing bits of straw from her hat.

"Well, I know as little about you, Miss Elcester," he declared, although it wasn't strictly true. He knew about the marriage that was being foisted upon her, about her interests, her desire to stay in Elcester, her contentment with her father. He knew there was far more to her than Theo believed; and he knew that he desired her to the point of lunacy. Just to look at her now was to want her with a passion so fierce that it almost overrode restraint. She looked so lovely, her riding habit crumpled, her hair barely contained by the net at the nape of her neck, a fragment of straw clinging to her cheek. . . .

"Sir Conan, I rather think you know much more about me than I do about you. You have had time to speak to Mr. Glendower concerning me, whereas until last night I did not even know you existed."

They gazed at each other, both trying to conceal their feelings, then for the second time since meeting her, he stretched down a hand to help her to her feet. And for the second time the physical contact engulfed them in a tidal wave of erotic sensations that warmed and quickened their hearts, then dragged at their guilt with an undertow of unconsummated desire. They both knew they shouldn't feel the way they did; and both knew they would strive with all their might to deny the craving that ached through their bodies and very souls.

The moment was broken when Bran whined suddenly and sniffed the air as if an intriguing scent of some sort had just reached him. Conan took no notice, but glanced back toward the yard, where the passengers from the *Meteor* had now disappeared into the inn. "Look, I don't know why you're here now, but I came here to pry a little, and to try to release the squirrel."

"So did I."

"I fancy this might be a case of too many cooks. Leave it to me. If *I* get caught meddling, it isn't so bad, but it wouldn't do for Taynton to catch you." Conan couldn't resist brushing away the wisp of straw that clung to her cheek.

"Taynton isn't here. I saw him leaving earlier, so I came while I knew he was out. I think he's gone to Dursley."

Conan looked down as Bran suddenly tugged at his cuff. "What is it, boy?"

The wolfhound whined, left the stall, then turned and whined again before padding toward the other end of the stables, where the antlers hung on the wall above the maypole. Freshly heaped straw aroused Conan's curiosity, and he brushed some of it aside and found the wooden guardians lying there as well.

Bran began to scratch at some more straw nearby. "What's he found now?" Conan murmured, and bent to push the maypole aside and clear the straw away. "There are some loose boards here," he said, getting his fingers around the nearest one.

Ursula bent to help him, and in a moment they had lifted the boards away to reveal a sizeable hiding place underneath. In it lay the folded robes that had been worn in the woods, Taynton's staff and torque, the circlet of mistletoe and oak leaves to which the antlers could be attached, and a jar of strong-smelling herbal balm. It was the latter that Bran had detected. There were also three six-inch squares of yew bark, some long iron nails like those that had been driven into the hollow oak, a very old tinderbox, some short, squat candles, and the chalice that had been stolen from the church.

Ursula gasped. "The chalice! The theft must have something to do with Taynton!" She briefly told Conan about the missing goblet and the mystery of the yew tree. "He's probably responsible for breaking into Hatty Pedlar's Tump as well."

"Hatty Who's What?"

She explained about the long barrow and that it was named after one of Vera's forebears. "What with that, the chalice, the disfigured yew, the squirrel, last night in the wood, and so on, some very odd things have been happening in Elcester of late," she finished.

He smiled. "I rather think I already know that."

She smiled too, and again they gazed at each other, struggling to stifle the forbidden need that consumed them both. She tore her eyes away first and tried to sound level as she again looked down into the hiding place. "Well, whatever lies behind it all, I think from the mistletoe and oak leaves that we can now make a very informed assumption that there is a Druid connection of some sort."

"Yes, but what are they trying to achieve?"

Ursula breathed out slowly. "I've tried to ask Vera, but she became very wary. She kept saying 'it must be,' and similar phrases. One thing, though, she isn't Taynton's lover yet, but she'd like to be. He doesn't love her, but she loves him."

"Let's leave everything as we've found it, for I'd rather like to keep a sly eye on Taynton and his happy band." Conan bent to start replacing the boards. "Miss Elcester, there are things I haven't told you, and things I suspect you haven't told me either. It's time to lay our cards on the table and discuss all this in detail, but we ought not to do that here, in the lion's den, so to speak. Can we meet somewhere?" he asked as he pressed the boards down with his foot, then scattered the straw over them again.

"Meet? Oh, I-I . . ."

"If nothing else, we have to clear the air properly before tonight, I fancy," he pointed out.

She knew he was right. "Yes, we do. All right. I'll leave now and let you do what you can here. I'll wait for you outside the village. Do you know the crossroad on the green?"

"Of course."

"Turn right for Stroud as you leave the inn. In about

a quarter of a mile, where the road bears around the line of the escarpment, you'll come to an area of level land on the left, with Scots pines. That's where Hatty Pedlar's Tump is. I'll wait there."

He nodded. "I will try not to be long." He went to the door and looked out at the yard. The bustle around the *Meteor* was at an end for the time being, and the traveling carriage was just leaving. The grooms and ostlers had retreated into a coach house, where he guessed they had a corner to themselves, and there wasn't anyone by the inn entrance. He beckoned quickly to Ursula. "Leave now, when there's no one around. I'll get the mare for you. Stay, Bran."

She nodded, then paused a moment to look up at him. "I wish—"

He put a finger to her lips. "It doesn't do to wish," he murmured, then hurried across the yard to untether Miss Muffet. He led the mare back to the stables, and quickly helped Ursula into the saddle, then handed her the reins. "*À bientôt,* Miss Elcester," he said softly, and slapped the mare's rump to make her move off.

As soon as Ursula had gone, Conan again bade Bran to stay where he was, then went into the inn. The passengers from the *Meteor* were talking and eating noisily in the dining room, but only two elderly clergymen sat in taproom, sipping tankards of mead by the inglenook. There was no one behind the trestle, and only the squirrel saw as he slipped around to the row of barrels and opened the cage door. "Don't be afraid, Eleanor, for I'm here to help you, not harm you," he breathed as he reached inside to take the trembling little creature and push it safely inside his coat. It nestled there as still as a mouse as he casually walked from the taproom again. He walked right into Vera, who nearly dropped the tray of food she was carrying to the two clergymen. "Steady!" Conan said with an easy smile as he took the tray from her.

She summoned a grateful smile. "Why, thank you, sir."

"I came back to see if you'd found a fob seal that I seem to have mislaid. I hoped it was here somewhere."

"A seal, sir? Nothing has been found that I know of."

"Oh, dear. Well, if you find it anywhere, perhaps you could send it to Carmartin Park?"

"Certainly, sir."

He smiled again, and returned the tray to her. "By the way, unless the squirrel has been removed elsewhere, I fear it has escaped again," he said.

The tray fell with a crash.

Vera's face changed, and she hurried away calling for a search to be made. Conan, cool, calm, and collected, strolled out into the yard to get his horse. The grooms and ostlers had emerged from the coach house again and were hurrying hither and thither to look for the squirrel. As Vera's cries of alarm continued to echo from the inn, Conan needed no further proof of the squirrel's importance to Taynton's plans. "We're almost away now, Eleanor," he murmured, casually untethering the horse and mounting, the squirrel cowering so close inside his coat that he could feel its little heart beating.

Suddenly, Bran erupted from the stables, barking ferociously. He had spotted a man who'd given him a savage kick by the pool and wanted revenge. The man concerned, a wiry little ostler, began to run away in alarm, but Bran bowled him over like a skittle, then pinned him facedown in a steaming deposit left by a kindly horse. Taynton's head groom ran across to grab the wolfhound's collar and try to pull him off. Bran gave his victim a sharp nip on the backside, then jerked around to try to get free of the head groom. His collar broke in the brief struggle, and he was able to run away beneath the archway.

Conan hid a grin as he followed.

21

Conan had to laugh as he urged his horse away from the Green Man, for Bran loped ahead of him, tail wagging, ears pricked, well pleased with the summary justice he'd dealt at least one of the disagreeable robed figures from the woods. The squirrel ventured to peep out of Conan's coat, its big green eyes wide and nervous.

"You're free now, Eleanor," Conan said gently. He did not hesitate to use the name, because he was so certain he was right. It no longer occurred to him to even question the sanity of this conclusion, because his Welsh birthright told him the Otherworld really existed. He must do what fate expected of him, and he felt now that it was expected that he confide everything to Ursula. Well, perhaps not quite everything, for he suspected the desire he felt for her had more to do with his own sensuality than with fate!

Elcester disappeared in the dip as he rode up onto the escarpment ridge. The only other travelers on the road were a small band of jugglers and acrobats on their way to join the May Day fair. They shouted greetings to him as he passed by, and he replied in kind. To his right lay the leafy depths of the hidden valley, and to the left was spread the magnificent view of the vale, with Carmartin Park so prominent on its outlier. This must be one of the finest panoramas in the whole of England, he decided.

The fair performers were well behind him when the squirrel suddenly leapt from his coat, darted beneath a field gate, then bounded down the cowslip-sprinkled slope into the hidden valley. Taken completely by surprise, Conan reined in to watch the little creature vanish into the woods. That Eleanor Rhodes would want to flee from him as well simply had not crossed his mind. "Oh, well, no doubt we will meet again," he murmured philosophically, and moved his horse on again.

He found Hatty Pedlar's Tump easily enough, and Ursula was waiting for him as promised. She had secured Miss Muffet on the far side of the barrow, out of sight from the road, and was pacing anxiously among the primroses. His heart seemed to tighten within him as he looked upon her again. Maybe fate *did* have a hand in his feelings for her, because those feelings were so strong and potent that it was as if he had been waiting all his life to know her.

She turned as Bran dashed up to her to cover her hand with licks, and she smiled and fussed with the wolfhound as Conan dismounted. "Did you free the squirrel?" was the first thing she asked him.

"Yes, but not five minutes since it chose to escape from me as well, and ran down into the woods," he replied, tethering his horse beside Miss Muffet, then removing his top hat. "Still, this time it really is free, and therefore cannot be of further use to Taynton and his crew." He glanced at the two white horses, then at Bran. "White animals appear to be a feature of this situation, do they not?" he observed.

"Yes, but I have always preferred white horses."

"So have I."

Their eyes met, and she looked quickly down to pat Bran again. She wanted to run to this man, put her arms around him and kiss him on the lips. Not just any kiss, but a declaration of the incredible emotions he had aroused in her. Mortified, color stained her cheeks. She had never been this shameless before. . . .

Conan watched her. "Well, our partiality for white steeds gives us an affinity." He smiled a little. "Did you know that white animals are supposed to belong to the fairies?"

She straightened. "Yes, at least, I know they are supposedly from the Otherworld."

"Ah, the Otherworld." How strange that she should

use that word so soon after it had also passed through his mind, he thought. Then he smiled. "There doesn't seem to be much of the fey about Bran the Blessed, Son of Llyr."

Interest sparked in her lilac eyes. "Is that his full name?"

Conan nodded. "And a mouthful it is, too."

"Bran the Blessed, son of Llyr, is a famous mythical character."

"He is indeed. You are not alone in being well acquainted with Welsh myths, Miss Elcester, for I too was raised upon such tales. My family home is on the Welsh border, and my Welsh nurse used to tell me stories every night before I went to sleep. I had nightmares after some of them, I can tell you."

"I imagine you would." Each word he said drew her to him more and more. He spoke of a shared affinity, but as far as she was concerned it was far more than that. They were kindred spirits, and the thought of him walking out of her life was quite unbearable.

He hung his top hat on the bush to which the horses were tethered, then unstrapped his rolled-up cloak from his saddle and spread it on the bank of the barrow. "We have much to discuss, and may as well be do it in comfort," he said.

Ursula sat down, and when he joined her, they were both silent for a few moments. He spoke first. "I haven't been entirely honest with you, Miss Elcester, in that I have omitted to mention certain things, and as I said at the inn, I believe you have been doing the same."

She nodded.

"Well, one doesn't like to admit to strangers that one has been seeing things, does one?"

She smiled ruefully. "One certain doesn't."

"But we aren't strangers now, are we, Miss Elcester?" he said quietly.

Warmth touched her cheeks again. "No."

"I'll tell you what has been happening to me." He explained about the vision he'd had of her in St. James's Square, and the way her ribbon really had been tied to the railings. He related the strange appearance and disappearance of a hooded, antlered man in the road in front of his carriage, and the squirrels that seemed to be everywhere. Then he spoke of the dream he had had before leaving London. "I dreamed of the bluebell woods here in the Gloucestershire countryside, Miss Elcester, yet I had never been here before. I recognized them last night. What I dreamed was that someone came up secretly behind you, and I couldn't shout out a warning."

Ursula had been listening in growing amazement to all he said, but at this she gasped aloud. "I really was in the woods at that time, and thought I saw you coming toward me, holding out your hand. Then Taynton put his hand on my shoulder." *Tipper-ipper-apper—on your shoulder, I am your master. . . .* The words came unbidden into her head.

"It would be good to have at least some inkling of what he's about, but I haven't a clue." He gave a wry smile then. "At least, there are clues aplenty, but right now they seem unsolvable. Why, for instance, does he require pieces of bark and a church chalice?"

"Except that it isn't a *church* chalice at all, but a very pagan thing."

"Pagan?"

"Yes. You couldn't see in the stables, indeed most people couldn't even see when it was on the altar, but in fact the design upon it is very . . . shocking."

"Really? How very interesting. But what of the pieces of bark?"

"Yew bark is just yew bark, as far as I know. Oh, it's a tree that has always been planted in churchyards, and that particular example is reckoned to be over two thousand years old, but more than that I cannot say." She thought of the damage to the barrow as well. "And why, if Taynton is the culprit, would he wish to break into a prehistoric burial chamber like this? Did you notice how the door is only hanging on its hinges now?"

"Yes, I saw as I rode past." He thought for a moment. "You say you've tried to speak to Vera about it all?"

"Yes, and she probably knows a little, but I doubt if Taynton has confided all that much. To be truthful, she seems more interested in him personally than in what he's up to."

Conan plucked at the grass. "I find friend Taynton of personal interest too, although not in the same way, I hasten to add. He seems familiar to me. I'm sure I know him from somewhere, but I cannot recall where. I'll remember sooner or later." He glanced at Ursula. "Miss Elcester, there is more I have to tell you. It concerns Theo."

"Mr. Glendower?"

"I do not know if I am doing the right thing by mentioning this, but I must if we are to be completely frank about this whole business." He explained about Theo's "voices" and the meeting with Eleanor Rhodes in the stable, and his own conviction that Eleanor and the caged squirrel were one and the same. "Theo is . . . entranced by Eleanor Rhodes, Miss Elcester," he added at the end.

As I am by you, Ursula thought, but she smiled and said, "I cannot lay claim to his heart, Sir Conan, for I do not doubt that he is as reluctant to have me as his wife as I am to have him as my husband." She looked away. "Our personal preferences have little to do with it, Sir Conan. The match will proceed anyway."

"Yes." He had to look away as well, for fear his eyes would display his secret inner truths.

After a moment she spoke again. "You say that Taynton was most reluctant to have you stay at the Green Man?"

"My name seemed to upset him, and *no one* at the inn liked poor old Bran. The fact that he is white definitely counted against him. They were even a little unsettled by my white carriage horses." Seeing the look in her eyes, he smiled. "Oh, yes, my preference for equine white extends to *all* my animals. However, I don't think Theo chose Bran because he is white, rather that Bran chose him, just turning up one day out of the blue and deciding to stay."

Suddenly the words she had translated from *The Dream of Macsen Wledig* came to her.

One evening early in February a long, long time ago, after a day's hunting near Rome with his favorite white wolf-hound—Macsen, the emperor, dreamed of a Welsh princess called Elen, who lived beyond the north wind. . . .

"What is it, Miss Elcester?" Conan asked, observing the hints of emotion on her face.

"I . . . Nothing. At least, I don't think it's anything. No, it *can't* be anything . . ."

"Why? Please don't say it's because whatever it is is too ridiculous, for after the conversation we've had up to this point, I fail to see how anything in the universe can be deemed too ridiculous," he remarked wryly. "So please enlighten me with whatever is on your mind."

She exhaled slowly. "I'm translating a Welsh myth at the moment, and I suddenly recalled how it begins." She repeated the opening sentence.

Conan didn't respond at first. "So what is your conclusion, Miss Elcester?" he said then.

"Conclusion? Oh, I don't know that I would say it's that exactly, just that there are one or two, er, coincidences, wouldn't you say? For white wolfhound, read Bran. For Elen, who incidentally was known as Elen of the Ways, read Eleanor Rhodes. Then for the Emperor Macsen, read Theodore Maximilian Glendower, who like the emperor happens to have Spanish ancestry," she added. Then something else occurred to her. "Elen of the Ways had two male cousins, the brothers Kynan and Cadfan. Is it too great a leap to link Kynan with Conan?"

The more she thought of it, the more certain she seemed. *The Dream of Macsen Wledig* was somehow connected with present-day events here in Elcester!

22

Conan ran a hand through his hair. "Slow down a little. I'm having a little trouble grasping this. Tell me again."

Ursula repeated everything she'd said, but he pulled a doubting face. "Well, given the outlandish happenings so far, I suppose it's more than feasible. Except that I don't have a brother at all, let alone one with a name that might sound like Cadfan."

"I don't know the rest of the story—well, not in detail anyway—so I can't say if there are other coincidences."

"And let us be honest, Miss Elcester. What possible connection could there be between Macsen's tale and the Druid nonsense in the woods?"

"I don't know that either," she admitted. "Maybe if I translate the whole myth, there will be an answer."

"And maybe there won't."

She glanced at him. "Taynton is very interested indeed in the Roman period, and hopes to help my father search for a villa they both think was once in the woods. Why, he even uses the Roman calendar! And recently my father found a coin, a gold solidus of the Emperor Magnus Maximus."

"Who is your Macsen, I suppose?"

"Yes. Macsen is Welsh for Maximus."

Hooves clattered slowly along the road behind them as a string of packhorses made its way to the village, laden with yarn from Mr. Elcester's mills. Ursula sighed, and for a moment her thoughts moved away from myths and puzzles. "I fear packhorses carrying yarn up here may soon be a thing of the past, for my father may have to start weaving at the mills."

"He must be one of the few clothiers still using the old ways."

"And it has cost him dearly so to do. There is no profit in the old ways, Sir Conan, and for some time now he has been bolstering this community with his own money. Now, however, thanks to the despicable activities of Mr. Samuel Haine—" She realized how indiscreet she was being, and broke off abruptly.

"Go on, Miss Elcester."

"I-I shouldn't say anything more."

"Why?"

"Because it wouldn't do for Lord Carmartin to learn too much," she replied candidly.

"Don't you trust me even now, Miss Elcester?"

She blushed a little. "It's not that, it's . . ."

"It *is* that," he retorted. "I promise that whatever you tell me will be held in the strictest confidence. Now then, what were you about to say?"

"That a villain called Samuel Haine swindled my father out of a lot of money, and that is the reason why this match with Mr. Glendower is going ahead. Elcester Manor needs the money Lord Carmartin is offering, both to keep it going and to make sure it stays in Elcester hands for the time being. If Lord Carmartin were to discover the truth about my father's finances, he would insist upon much harsher terms."

Conan gazed at her. "So *that's* why your father has agreed to marry you off to Theo."

"Yes, just as I imagine Lord Carmartin has linked Mr. Glendower's inheritance to agreement to a match that will place most of this escarpment and vale in Carmartin hands. I make no bones about my opinion of Lord Carmartin, for he is a miserly and ruthless man who will not like it at all when he discovers that Elcester Manor is not so profitable as he believes. I am sure he thinks he is acquiring a thriving estate that will not only provide another piece for his grand jigsaw, but will help to swell his already overflowing coffers. The latter could not be further from the truth. Still, my conscience is clear about keeping such a circumstance quiet. The manor and its people are what matters, and this is the best that can be done for them."

Conan grinned. "Well, I think it fair enough. *Caveat emptor,* as they say."

"They do indeed." She took off her hat and laid it beside her on the cloak.

Conan picked a primrose and twirled it between his fingers and thumb. "Do not fear that I will impart any of this to Theo either, for I will not. Actually, speaking of Theo, perhaps you should know that I haven't told him anything about last night, not even that *I* was there, let alone you. He has become somewhat upset by events, so I deemed it best to say nothing more to him. Nor will I mention that I have met you, so at dinner tonight, if you—"

Ursula gave an incredulous laugh. "Sir Conan, do you imagine I am going to sip my soup and say, 'Will you please pass the salt, and oh, by the way, I've been keeping clandestine assignations with your best friend, and seeing supernatural things from time to time'? I can just imagine how well *that* would go down with my father! You may rest assured, sir, that not word of any of this will pass my lips to anyone except you. I do not wish to be consigned to a Bedlam, thank you very much."

Conan smiled into her eyes, adoring her sense of humor; adoring absolutely everything about her. "Miss Elcester, I envy Theo his bride," he said softly, and before he knew it was even in his mind, he leaned forward to put his lips to hers.

She knew she should pull away from the kiss, but that was the very last thing she wished to do. He had spoken of her lack of trust, but at this moment she trusted him implicitly, his motives, his intentions, everything, so her lips yielded beneath his, and she closed her eyes as a current of desire began to rise through her. Wild joy sparkled over her body, a hungry, warming, sensuous joy that bewitched her senses as surely as any spell, and she linked her arms around his neck and lay back on the cloak. It was the act of a wanton, but not even that seemed to matter. Sweet temptation beckoned, and willingly she followed.

Conan's die was cast. The honesty of her response fanned an already kindled flame, and the needful heat burned through his loins. He was conscious of an arousal that was infinitely more intense than any he had experienced before, and as he pressed her to him, he knew how very close he was to making ardent, complete love to her. He held her body against his, and as his kiss became a confession that needed no words, it took every last vestige of his self-control not to take her right there among the primroses.

She clung to him, still aware of how very wrong this was, but unable to help herself. She hardly knew him, yet she felt she knew all there was to know. It was as if in him she had found her other half, and all that was needed now to make those two halves whole would be complete surrender. All thought of her betrothal to Theo slipped away into a wonderful, voluptuous oblivion, and it seemed that the earth itself was no longer of substance. She could feel his masculinity, so close and yet so far, so exciting and yet so dangerous, and tumultuous sensations ran riot within her, taking her to what seemed the very edge of consciousness. If this pleasure could be enjoyed from a single kiss, how much more must there be from the act of love itself? Oh, to know the answer now, to share it with this man above all others . . .

Conan had to force himself back from the brink. He couldn't do this, he *mustn't* do this! Cold reality stung him, and he scrambled to his feet and walked away a few steps as he tried to gather his senses. He ran a shaking hand through his hair and gazed at the vale, which now seemed to shimmer with colors more vibrant than before, then he turned back to look at her. "Please don't cry," he pleaded softly, for she was sitting up in mortified confusion, her eyes bright with unshed tears.

She turned her head away. "What must you think of me? That I have no morals? No honor?"

He went to take her hand and pull her into her arms

again. "I think the world itself of you, Ursula," he breathed, his lips against her hair. "I want you so much that I can hardly bear it, and now I know you want me too . . ." He couldn't finish the sentence, for knowing that his feelings were reciprocated increased the dilemma of wanting Theo's intended wife.

"I do want you too, oh, how I do," she whispered.

"If the saving of Elcester Manor were the only purpose of your betrothal to Theo, I would not hesitate to go to your father with a better offer than Lord Carmartin's, but I have to consider Theo. His uncle has made it clear that inheritance hangs upon this marriage to you."

The jarring reminder stabbed painfully into her heart, and she drew back immediately, her illusions shattering like glass. "Consideration of Mr. Glendower's position has come a little late, sir," she pointed out as she faced up to a chill new reality. He wasn't to be trusted after all, for having lured her into breaking the rules by sharing tender intimacies she had never shared with anyone before. He now mocked her by taking refuge in the arranged match with his friend.

"Please, Ursula . . ."

"I think Miss Elcester would be a more appropriate address, sir. I also think it best if we forget the last few minutes ever happened."

"*Forget*? How can we possibly forget?" he cried.

"It's all we can do if Mr. Glendower's expectations are so important, Sir Conan. I am sure we are both adult enough to know how to behave from now on." She retrieved her hat and pinned it in place again. "I think this conversation is at an end, don't you? Please rest assured that when you and Mr. Glendower come to dinner tonight, I will be all that is civil and agreeable."

"Please don't leave like this," he pleaded, for once in his life unable to handle a situation with any composure at all. He tried to take her hand again, but she snatched it out of reach and walked quickly over to Miss Muffet. She was so hurt and humiliated that she couldn't bear to look at him. She had made a fool of herself, and had done it with a vengeance! Now all she wanted to do was escape to a small corner somewhere, so that she could weep away the wretchedness.

She untied the mare's reins, and suddenly Conan was there with her again. He tried to clasp her hand, to make her look at him, but she wouldn't. She struggled to mount, and in the end he lifted her up onto the saddle. Then he held Miss Muffet's bridle. "Ursula, you wrong me greatly by what you believe of me now."

"I think not, sir. You have a way with you, Sir Conan Merrydown, and I doubt if I am the first or last who has suffered the consequences of your astonishing charm. But that one kiss is all you will ever share with me!" she cried tearfully.

Kicking her heel, she urged the mare away from the barrow, and as Conan gazed helplessly after her, there were tears in his eyes too.

23

Bellamy Taynton was already in a foul mood when he returned from Dursley, because his chill had worsened, his sore leg had not benefited at all from the jolting of the pony cart, and he'd had to pay more for his purchases than he liked. On top of that the petals had all fallen off his nosegay, and he'd lost his fine gold pin. His foul mood turned to incandescent fury when he learned the squirrel had gone again, this time without a trace. He vented his spleen upon Vera, who promptly burst into tears and ran to her room, leaving the remaining kitchen staff with the problem of feeding the *Age* stagecoach passengers, who would shortly arrive. The innkeeper knew he needed Vera's sure touch with the cooking, and so gritted his teeth to speak sweetly to her through her locked door. She was eventually persuaded to come out again, but only after he promised not to shout at her for the loss of the squirrel. This he did, although with shamefully bad grace.

After a while his temper calmed a little, and he assessed the situation as he sat in his private parlor with his feet in a bowl of hot mustard water, drinking a posset cup of hot gruel laced with rum. The squirrel had been present in the woods last night when he had performed the first, most essential, incantation, and the shooting star had been a sign that the gods were with him, so if he stayed calm and clear-headed he was assured of victory. Yet while the squirrel remained at large—and if Glendower was who he seemed to be—the entire strategy might still be vulnerable. Recapturing the runaway now was out of the question, so the only alternative was to eliminate Theo.

Taynton sipped the gruel, wishing Vera had been more liberal with the rum. Then he fell to thinking about Eleanor again. It was tedious that his only attempt at causing someone to shift shape had gone so horribly wrong. Eleanor Rhodes would have been a conveniently inanimate porcelain figurine if that damned red squirrel had not scampered past just as he pronounced the magic words! The presence of another living thing at that crucial second had altered the spell, turning Eleanor into a squirrel that mirrored her actual coloring and clothes. A red head for her chestnut curls, green eyes, and a white body because she had been wearing a white muslin gown. He supposed he could be thankful the gown had not sported a blue sash as well, for how he could have explained away a squirrel with a band of blue fur around its middle he really did not know! For the moment, however, she wasn't a squirrel, because once she was physically free of him she could be *almost* herself, an ethereal being who could walk and talk, but never touch or feel anything. To become fully herself again, he would have to be completely defeated, and the wheel of history would have to turn full circle once again.

He glowered at the sun patterns on the parlor's stone-flagged floor. The setback to that initial shape-changing spell had been the beginning of a series of infuriating obstacles. Next had come the sudden and awful realization that time was running out, which had forced him into precipitate action. Gaining possession of the manor hadn't proved possible in spite of his activities in the guise of Samuel Haine, and then Lord Carmartin had made the marriage offer that let old Elcester cling to residence. The rest of the magic depended upon being here, so when the manor could not be acquired, he, Taynton, had forced Jem Cartwright to sell the inn instead. After that it ought to have been plain sailing, even with time so short, but now had come the London carriage and its fancy occupants.

The innkeeper finished the alcoholic gruel, then

reached for the bell that Vera had placed on the table beside him. He rang it irritably, but she did not come, so he rang it again, and added a peevish yell at the same time. "Vera! I require you here!"

After a moment she looked around the door.

"I want some more of this," he said churlishly, waving the posset cup at her.

For once she wasn't prepared to humor him. She was run off her feet with mouths to feed, and attending to her kitchen duties was all she had in mind. "I haven't time, I'm busy with the *Age*. It was full inside and out, and they all want everything."

"But I need some more now," he whinged.

"I will do it as soon as I can."

"I am your master!"

"Yes, and I will obey. But not right now." With that she closed the door again and went away.

Taynton was thunderstruck. He had been defied! For a moment he didn't know what to do, because boldness from Vera was not something he had encountered before. Well, not in this life, anyway. He scowled at the closed door. He would have the last laugh where she was concerned. Severa may have become his wife fifteen hundred years ago, in a ceremony officiated over by her own father, the Black Druid, beneath that very yew that still shadowed the church lych-gate, but she wasn't about to be his wife again now! Oh, no. Not that she or her fool of a father knew anything about all this anyway, for he certainly hadn't enlightened them concerning the past. His purpose now was to *undo* most of what had happened before, not repeat it, and that meant no wife or Black Druid. Taynton smiled contemptuously, for all that appeared to remain of Daniel Pedlar's previous role was his cavortings as a black-clad figure with the Elcester morris dancers. As for the wife, in some ways it was a pity, for Severa was a splendid cook, and her figure was just as he liked best. Taynton gave a wistful sigh.

If he had but known it, Vera was just on the other side of the door, rigid with shock at having been so impertinent to him. She almost expected a magic dagger to fly through the door and stab her between the shoulder blades, but nothing happened. She walked on hesitantly, then gathered her skirts to hurry back to the kitchen. There was a smile on her lips and a glint in her eyes. Why had it taken so long to realize she could stand up to him after all? His wedding band would grace her finger yet; she was now more determined than *ever* that it would!

In the parlor the innkeeper had already put her to the back of his mind as he mulled over the circumstances that now prevailed where his great goal was concerned. He had made it his business to find out exactly what had happened at the inn during his absence in Dursley, and knew that Ursula had called, and that Conan had returned as well, bringing Bran too. What further confirmation was needed that a combined force was working against him, a force that was powerful enough to hinder his labors, maybe even overturn them? They were *all* thorns in his side, and he would have to pluck them out completely now that time itself was at such an unexpected premium.

Time. Oh, how could he, Cadfan Meriadoc, the only one who had remained true to his birthright, have made such an elementary and enormous blunder in his calculations? He had been so *certain* the relevant period ended on May Eve, 1819, instead of which it was tomorrow night! Now he was forced to resort to desperate spells and charms in order to be ready for the pivotal moment. If he failed, another thousand years and a disagreeable number of boring existences would have to be endured before he had his next chance to find a treasure more fabulous and plentiful than most men could even dream of. So he couldn't afford to let the reins be snatched from him at this late stage.

He picked up the empty posset cup, remembered it was empty, and slammed it down again petulantly. When all this was over and done with, he was going to be waited on hand and foot by a veritable seraglio of fawning maidens who would pander to his every whim! See how Vera Pedlar liked *that*! She wouldn't, and that was a fact. But he would. Oh, indeed he would! The sorcery he had acquired during various lives over the past one and a half millennia had won him the favor of the gods, and all he needed to do now was wait for riches to fall into his hands. Then there would be just luxury, without a single cloud to darken his horizon. No more chicanery and swindling the gullible, no more false names and hasty departures, no more bowing and scraping to fools at a country inn, just privilege of the sort that should have been his by right; privilege such as the likes of Sir Conan Merrydown had always known, and Theodore Glendower wished to know.

The path to the site of the treasure had been a winding one, and had to be discovered anew every five hundred years. It had taken him some time to realize that Elcester was the site he sought, and then more time again to work out where exactly in Elcester Eudaf Hen's old summer house had been. At first he'd wondered if Hatty Pedlar's Tump held the key, but had soon been persuaded it didn't. He'd even wondered if the old yew was an indicator, because it too had been in place fifteen hundred years before, but now he knew beyond all doubt that the valley would yield the harvest. He had cast the necessary magic and would clear his way of eleventh-hour enemies, then discover all that he sought.

Taynton inhaled with anticipation. If only they all knew the truth! If the High-King Eudaf Hen had followed the traditional ways by the male line of succession, the throne and treasure should have gone to Kynan Meriadoc—or Sir Conan Merrydown, as he now was. But Kynan had so cravenly accepted the old man's decision that Elen of the Ways should marry the Roman emperor, that he was owed no allegiance now. As for Theodore Maximilian Glendower, he might be Macsen Wledig returned, but he had never and would never possess the moral right to the throne, the bride, or the treasure. None of them deserved anything. Only Bellamy Taynton, Samuel Haine, Cadfan Meriadoc—three names, one man—was worthy of the heritage. He would teach them all the error of their ways, past and present. They were about to be trounced, every last one of them, including the infernal wolfhound and the Elcester woman, who had both been in the woods when they shouldn't have been. Those woods were *his* domain now, and by the magic he had cast, all else would soon be his as well.

Taynton smiled coldly, for his foes were almost in his grasp already. He possessed items that belonged to each one of them, except Conan, but the inn and its outbuildings would be ransacked from top to bottom until that missing fob seal was found. Tonight he would cut more squares of bark from the yew and go down to the woods to cast the dark ritual spell that was necessary to nullify those who would set themselves against him. He would go alone and take everything he needed with him, including the pieces of bark, Ursula's ribbon, Theo's button, Conan's seal, and Bran's collar. Would that he could enchant them all tonight, when midnight marked the beginning of May Eve, but the moon would not be full until tomorrow night, so it would have to be then. When the last chime of twelve had died away, his enemies would cease to be.

"Then I will come into my own, and there will not be a thing that any of them will be able to do about it," he murmured.

24

As darkness fell that night, Taynton left the inn to limp toward the village green. The breeze had died away, and the air was much warmer, almost like summer in fact, but he shivered and sneezed because of his chill. The May Day fair had grown considerably during the day, and people were seated on the grass around fires where stew bubbled in iron pots. He paused to talk to them, albeit with more than a few sniffs and sneezes to punctuate his conversation, then continued to the church.

Daniel Pedlar's forge fire was still bright, and the sound of hammering issued from the brightly lit entrance. Taynton could see the blacksmith inside, his muscles dirty and shining in the flames. The work he was doing was intricate—Ursula's weathercock gift for her father, as it happened— and he didn't look up as the innkeeper hobbled beneath the lych-gate into the churchyard.

A vicarage window was open, and Taynton heard the new twins crying, then Mrs. Arrowsmith's shrill voice called her maid to remove them because her poor head was throbbing with the noise. The innkeeper paid scant attention to her vapors, for he was too intent upon the trunk of the darkly spreading yew tree, where the three scars he'd recently cut into bark seemed strangely bright in the darkness. Three cuts, one to force Elcester to sell the manor, one to do the same to Jem Cartwright, and one for the previous night's incantations. Actually a fourth square, old and worn now, had been taken from farther up the trunk where no one had ever seen. It had been cut when he performed his magic upon Eleanor Rhodes. He glanced around, in case there was someone else nearby, but all was dark and quiet, so he took out a knife and carefully cut four new squares of bark. Shoving them inside his coat, he pocketed the knife again and left the churchyard.

He returned to the inn to collect all the things he would need, and put them in an old canvas satchel. Conan's fob seal had not been found, despite the inn having been gone over with a fine-tooth comb, and Taynton was now suspicious that there had ever been a missing seal. It had just been an excuse for Kynan Meriadoc to return to poke his superior nose in things that had ceased to be any concern of his fifteen hundred years ago! Only then did something else strike the innkeeper. Kynan Meriadoc had taken to wife a princes named Ursula. . . . All the old shades from the Otherworld were now present in the form of modern counterparts. Three couples then, and three couples now; Macsen Wledig and Elen of the Ways, Kynan Meriadoc and his Lady Ursula, and last but definitely not least, Cadfan Meriadoc and Lady Severa. All bridal couples in the past, but not one of them would be permitted to join together now!

The Beltane moon, which would be full the following night, had risen by the time the innkeeper made his awkward way down through the field toward the woods. He was glad of his staff, for it helped him to walk, and his satchel of paraphernalia was heavy. In spite of the warmer temperature, the silvery light was cool and remote, seeming to banish the rest of the world as he entered the trees. The scent of bluebells enveloped him as he approached Hazel Pool, where the water reflected the moon and stars like a perfect mirror.

Beneath the oak tree he put on his robes, torque, the wreath of mistletoe and oak, and then the antlers. After that he emptied the satchel on the grass at the edge of the pool. It contained the stolen chalice, a long iron nail, the tinderbox, four squat candles, the pieces of bark, and the ribbon, button, dog collar, together with a slip of paper upon which Conan's names, past and present, were written. The last would not work as well as an actual item of property, but it was the best that could be done for the time being. He placed one of the candles and a personal item on each of the little bark rafts, lighted the candles using the tinderbox, then placed them in a neat line at the very edge of the bank. Then he paused as a huge sneeze overwhelmed him. It was followed by another, and then another, and when they had subsided for the time being, he rooted under his robe for his handkerchief and blew his nose rather noisily.

Next he took the nail and his staff and hammered the nail into the hollow oak tree with the staff. Then he returned to the edge of the pool and looked down pensively at the chalice, which glinted richly in the moving light from the nearby candles. This was the one part of the puzzle of which he was not sure. He knew from many a dream that the chalice was essential to the whole scheme, but he did not know in what way. It was necessary to guess how to proceed with it, and he was inclined to believe it must be an offering to the Green Man, the god of summer in whose sacred grove both the pool and the oak tree were to be found. The god's special time commenced now, at Beltane, when spring gave way to the long hot months of the sun. At midsummer, he was said to dance through the woods, reasserting his mastery of nature, but if that was so, it was something that no one had ever seen. Taynton wished to see it. Oh, how he did, for he was the Green Man's dedicated follower.

His thoughts moved on. If the chalice was an offering, where should it be offered? In the water, as was the time-honored way? Or perhaps in the revered tree? His glance moved back to the oak, and a part of him decided to hedge his bets. If he threw the chalice into the water, he would find it again only after a great deal of trouble, by which time his hour of opportunity might have passed. But if it was in the tree, easily accessible, its retrieval would not be difficult. Yes, better safe than sorry, he thought as he picked up the chalice and took it to the tree. There he sneezed again as he held it up with both hands and muttered secret words before placing it in the hollow trunk.

Then the most uncanny sensation of being watched

settled over him. He turned sharply toward the spot where Conan had hidden the night before. Was someone there? He took a step toward the clump of coppiced hazels. Nothing moved, so he went closer again, but still there did not seem to be anything. Yet he could not shake off the feeling that someone's eyes were upon him. He glanced all around. "Who's there?" he demanded. "Show yourself!" There wasn't a sound, except the gentle trickle of water where the pool overflowed to form the little stream.

Taynton stood there for a long moment, his ears sharpened for even the tiniest sound, but as the seconds ticked by, he began to think he'd been mistaken. Taking a long breath to compose himself for the magic at hand, he returned to the row of candlelit bark "rafts" on the bank. Once again he spread his arms majestically to the sky, was obliged to quell yet another sneeze, then began to intone. "When May Eve turns to my May Day, when May Eve turns to my May Day, when May Eve turns to my May Day, *I* am your Master. Tipper-ipper-apper—on your shoulder, Tipper-ipper-apper—on your shoulder, Tipper-ipper-apper—on your shoulder, *I* am your Master!" With another very unwizardly sneeze, he floated the first piece of bark, the one with Conan's name, on the water.

He repeated the words—and the sneezes—three times, until all the little rafts were afloat, their flames gleaming on the surface of the pool. A slight stirring of breeze crept up from somewhere, rippled the water, then died away again, leaving the flames trembling for a moment before becoming still once more. To the innkeeper's dismay, the fragment of paper had blown a little way across the pool, out of reach, even with his staff. Conan would have to wait for his moment of truth.

Composing himself once again, Taynton pointed the staff at the raft upon which Ursula's ribbon lay. "Out upon the waiting water, Out upon the waiting water, Out upon the waiting water, I am your Master!" As he finished, the piece of bark slowly capsized and sank, extinguishing the candle and taking the ribbon to the bottom of the pool.

The same words were uttered for the other rafts, and each time the same thing happened. He wasn't to know that Theo's curse was already null and void because before the necessary words had been uttered, the puff of wind that had blown Conan's paper away had also sent the button to the bottom of the lake. As far as he was aware, the three remaining spells had all been successfully cast, and at the stroke of midnight the next night, Ursula, Theo, and Bran would fall into a sleep from which he hoped they would never awaken.

As he straightened a last time, something made him whirl about suddenly. Someone *was* watching him! Was it the Elcester creature? His nostrils flared, and his eyes were iron bright, but then he made out a ghostly figure at the edge of the clearing, where the path he had followed from the Green Man came out of the woods.

He knew that figure. "Eleanor? Elen of the Ways?" he called softly, concealing his dismay that she had not tried to get as far away from him as possible. He had expected her to be long gone while she had the opportunity. Then he remembered that she had heard Theodore Glendower's name mentioned. She knew Glendower was her bridegroom, Macsen Wledig, come again! Taynton's heart quickened uneasily. Plague take the timing of the full moon! It wasn't sufficient that Glendower would fall beneath the spell tomorrow night, for there were hours enough for the chance of the goal to be wrecked.

Eleanor remained silent, so he spoke to her again, still in the same soft tone. "Have you no greeting for your cousin Cadfan, Elen of the Ways?"

She gazed at him, her red hair tumbling over the shoulders of her filmy white gown. Even in the moonlight he could see right through her, as if she were made of gossamer. All around her on the grass there were squirrels, their eyes warily upon him.

He gave a persuasive smile, hoping there might yet be a chance to recapture her. "Come now, Coz, I'm sure you have something you wish to say to me," he said amiably, and took a step toward her.

At that there was a ferocious warning growl from behind him, and with a dismayed gasp he again turned sharply toward the coppiced hazels. Bran was there now, creeping belly low toward him, his teeth bared savagely.

Eleanor spoke. "Bran!"

The wolfhound stopped growling and sat up in obvious disgust. The hated innkeeper was within easy reach. A single leap, a hefty shove with the front paws, and over he'd go into the water again. It was so easy that a mere puppy could have done it. Bran gave an audible sigh of annoyance, but obeyed Eleanor's command.

Taynton breathed out with relief, but when he glanced toward the path again, Eleanor had gone, taking her army of tiny escorts with her. Bran got up again and started to follow her, but as he passed Taynton temptation got the better of him and he darted at the innkeeper. Taynton stepped instinctively away, slipped on the soft earth at the edge of the water, and cried out as he lost his balance and pitched backward into the pool with a tremendous splash. The water was icy, and he was forced to flounder about again until he managed to catch hold of the bank and drag himself out. By then the glade was deserted.

Shortly afterward, dripping and cold for the second time in as many nights and sure in the knowledge that his chill could now only get worse, Taynton made his way back out of the valley toward the inn. He sneezed a great deal and felt very sorry for himself. This wasn't fair at all. Fate was being very knavish treating a great Celtic prince in such a way! Those of the Otherworld shouldn't suffer such undignified Thisworldly things as chills and drenchings! When he got back inside, he would positively insist that Vera prepare him more of the gruel. *And* he would expect to be fussed over as well.

The innkeeper reached the refuge of the Green Man just as a carriage drove past, its lamps cutting through the darkness. It was conveying Conan and Theo to dinner at Elcester Manor, and the two men inside were dressed formally, as befitted such an occasion. Both were sunk deep in thought.

Conan wore an indigo velvet coat and white trousers, with a lace-trimmed shirt and white silk waistcoat. A large sapphire was pinned on the knot of his neckcloth, and a tricorn hat and white gloves lay on the seat beside him. All he could think of was Ursula. She had filled his mind from the moment she left him at the long barrow, and he was miserably aware that he had not expressed himself very well after ending the kiss. With hindsight he could not believe he had been so clumsy. A man of his experience should have known better on every count, but where she was concerned he felt like a fumbling boy in the first throes of manhood. Being with her was so like breathing the air of the gods that he knew he loved her. It was something he accepted as naturally as if it were a fact that he had been aware of all his life, like a sweetly compelling echo that came from he knew not where.

Opposite him, wearing a black coat, frilled shirt, and white pantaloons, and still unaware of Conan's various encounters with Ursula, was Theo, whose thoughts were almost identical, except that they centered upon Eleanor Rhodes. He knew that he wasn't meant to marry Ursula Elcester, and yet here he was, driving to dine at the manor with the express purpose of formalizing the contract! What could he do? It was all so lunatic that he could not deal sensibly with any of it. He needed to assemble his facts, consider them carefully, and then do the right thing. But what *was* the right thing? Marrying Ursula Elcester and suffering in silence? Or proclaiming his fantasy love for the magical Eleanor? The first would see him in misery, the second in an asylum!

"Eleanor."

Both men heard the whispered name and sat up with a start. Conan thought it came from the direction of the hidden valley and quickly lowered the carriage glass to lean out. The moon shone over the countryside, and they were just passing the field gate beneath which the squirrel had slipped earlier in the day.

"Eleanor." Conan's gaze swung toward the darkness of the woods. That was where it had come from! He called to Gardner, "Stop the carriage immediately!"

"Sir." The coachman reined in, and the arc of light from the lamps swung slightly.

Conan and Theo jumped quickly down and went to the gate to gaze down through the moonlight. There at the very edge of the wood, with squirrels in the grass at her feet, was Eleanor Rhodes. She wore a white muslin gown, and her long red hair fell loose about her shoulders. She seemed to be looking up directly at the gate.

It was too much for Theo. "I have to go to her!" he cried, and climbed over the gate to run down the field of cowslips toward her. Conan didn't hesitate to follow, but as they drew near to her, she and her little attendants drew back into the woods. "Stay, Eleanor!" Theo shouted as he flung himself after her, but he had only gone a few yards when he realized she had vanished. The dark trees and bluebell glades stretched away before him, the only sound the pounding of his own heart. He turned back disconsolately to where Conan waited at the foot of the field. "She's gone," he said, shoving his hair back from his forehead.

"So it would seem."

"But you *did* hear and see her, didn't you?" Theo still needed to be certain he wasn't imagining it all.

"Yes, I saw and heard," Conan confirmed.

Theo exhaled slowly. "What shall I do, Conan? I will never feel for Ursula Elcester what I feel for Eleanor Rhodes."

Conan looked away. "I cannot advise you, Theo." Indeed, he thought, I am the last man on earth to do so. . . .

Theo looked up toward the carriage, the lamps of which pierced the night. "Well, I suppose we had better get this wretched dinner over and done with, although how I am going to agree to marriage details I really don't know."

Conan didn't reply, and as they began the climb up to the road, they heard the bugle notes of the evening by-mail in the distance to the east.

As the carriage drove on again, Bran emerged stealthily from the undergrowth by the hedgerow. He did not continue to follow the carriage, but listened, ears pricked. He detected a voice he knew he must obey, and padded back along the road a little way, then pushed his way into the field through a flimsier portion of the hedge. He loped steadily down the cowslip slope to go to Eleanor Rhodes.

25

Ursula was as ready as she ever would be for the awful moment of meeting the Honorable Theodore Maximilian Glendower, to say nothing of the dread with which she awaited seeing Sir Conan Merrydown again. As far as the latter was concerned, she had been wound up to a pitch of nerves ever since the bitterness of the parting at Hatty Pedlar's Tump, for she no longer trusted him. The humiliation endured then, she still endured now, and she felt so sick with trepidation that she did not think she would be able to eat so much as a morsel of food.

Now, after attending to all her duties regarding the preparation and readiness of the meal, she was dressed and sitting in her candlelit room with her mother's manuscripts spread around on the floor. For such an important occasion as tonight she had chosen to wear her very best gown, pale gray satin with a silver tissue overlay. It was a stylish garment, scooped low at the neckline, with little petal sleeves and a silver belt with a diamond buckle beneath her breasts. Her hair was swept up into a loose knot on her head, with a silver satin bow with trailing ends that floated when she moved her head. She was waiting for the maid to knock at the door to inform her the guests had arrived, and it was like anticipating the knell of doom, she thought as she gazed at the ancient, barely decipherable text.

The window was slightly open, and the fire had been allowed to burn very low because the temperature had risen so much since the much cooler morning. She could hear an owl in the woods, and from time to time the screech of a vixen. Across the valley the lights of the

Green Man twinkled through the moonlight, and the bugle call of the nightly by-mail approaching the village sounded along the Nailsworth road.

She gazed down at the yellowed sheets on the floor at her feet and suddenly saw a name that banished all else from her mind, for it was her own—Ursula. A cold finger ran down her spine. *She* had a counterpart in the past as well? She didn't remember her mother mentioning it when she told the story. She stared at the name for a long moment, then straightened in the chair. This other Ursula, whoever she was, wasn't mentioned until further on in the story than had been translated so far. It was tempting to find out who she was right now, but that wouldn't do. To skip the intervening lines might lead to missing a point that was relevant to present-day events.

Taking a deep breath to regain what little composure she still had, she picked up the page she had been working on before and continued the painstaking translation.

"Macsen could not stop thinking about the maiden, and was so anxious to discover where she was that he set out from Rome the very next day." The second of February, Ursula thought. *"He journeyed over mountains, plains, and seas until he came to the island of Britain. There, beyond the north wind, he found the castle of C———."* Again Ursula could not read the name, except the first letter. *"The castle was just as he had dreamed, rising out of the misty sea . . ."* Or it might be *"sea of mist,"* Ursula thought in passing as she read on *". . . as if to beckon him onward. As he and his retinue approached, the High-King Eudaf Hen sent out two of his daughter's ladies-in-waiting on fine white horses to greet him. The first wore an embroidered velvet gown that was the color of a sandy shore beneath the sun, and her hair was as brown as the finest walnuts. Her name was the Princess Severa, and she was soon to be the wife of Elen of the Ways' younger cousin, Prince Cadfan Meriadoc."* Ursula stared Vera Pedlar and Bellamy Taynton! Was the innkeeper Cadfan, the rebellious, resentful prince who would not accept Macsen Wledig as his ruler? If Conan was Prince Kynan returned, no *wonder* he thought Taynton seemed famil-

iar! Of course, because they had been brothers in the past.

After a moment she collected herself sufficiently to read on. *"The second lady wore a jeweled silk gown that was the color of the pale wild violets that grew by the wayside, and her hair was as silver as the moon. Her name was the Princess Ursula, and she was to marry Elen of the Ways' elder cousin, Prince Kynan. She was of the Christian faith, but honored Prince Kynan's faith too, so they would take their vows twice, once before the Black Druid and once in Rome itself. The two betrothed ladies rode at Macsen's side into the castle."*

It was too much for Ursula. The sheet of manuscript slipped from her fingers as she rose hastily from the chair and went to the window. Her namesake in the past had been married to Prince Kynan Meriadoc, who was Sir Conan Merrydown here in the present. She gazed down toward the woods, so mysterious and alluring in the moonlight. Was that why she felt the way she did toward Conan now?

She glanced back at the scattered sheets of manuscript. She had to be objective about this. Something very important was going on, something almost too fantastic to believe, but why was it going on in Elcester? There was no island here, and even at the time of the Roman invasion the sea came little farther up the Severn valley than it did now, so Carmartin wasn't an island either, although it might have been in prehistoric times. But *The Dream of Macsen Wledig* wasn't from that far back, just from the Roman period.

She remembered an old map that had also been among the manuscripts. It was even more fragile than they were, and so she had left it carefully at the bottom of the wardrobe, where it was dark and safe. Maybe it would give her an idea, she thought, the dinner party now completely forgotten as she hurried to the wardrobe. But as she opened the doors and knelt to reach carefully for the map, she noticed the old cloak she had worn the night before. It had slipped her mind completely and was too old and scruffy a thing to leave with her good clothes, especially after its experiences in the badger set! Frowning, she lifted it out and placed it carefully aside, where she would remember it come the morning. As she did so, however, something small and heavy rolled out, closely followed by another. Puzzled, she picked both up. One appeared to be made of blue glass, the other of cream pottery. What on earth were they?

She put them down and lifted the cloak to shake it a little. Half a dozen more of the strange little objects tumbled from a torn part of the hem, where they must have been scooped up during her fall in the set. She laid them all in a row on the carpet and studied them. In a flash she realized what they were—tesserae from a mosaic floor or wall! Her lips parted as the importance of the discovery struck her in full. The Roman villa her father was convinced was in the valley! Had she, quite literally, stumbled upon something he had been yearning to find for several years now?

Excited, she scrambled to her feet to go tell him, but almost immediately she changed her mind. How could she possibly tell him? She would have to say where the tesserae had been, and that would mean admitting she had once again disobeyed his wishes about the woods. She was in a quandary, but then calmed down a little. First she had to be sure the set was indeed where the pieces of mosaic had come from, and then—

Someone tapped at the window, and she spun around with a startled gasp, for her room was on the second floor with no balcony! A young woman gazed in with eyes that were the same astonishing green as the squirrel's. Her cascading red curls floated in a cloud, and her white muslin gown wafted like thick fronds of weed in a gentle stream. Ursula's eyes widened. She knew it could only be Eleanor Rhodes, or Elen of the Ways, because Conan had given her Theo's description of the young woman in the stables.

The apparition—for what else could one call something through which one could see quite clearly?—beckoned to her suddenly. "Help me to be properly free so that I may be with my beloved Emperor Macsen."

Ursula's lips moved, but she couldn't speak.

Eleanor smiled. "We are all here now, and must see that Prince Cadfan does not triumph. You must help me, Lady Ursula, for you have always been my dearest friend."

Ursula found her tongue at last. "I-I have?"

"In our past. Your Prince Kynan and my sweet Macsen were as close as brothers. Never once did your lord look upon my marriage in anger, unlike Lord Cadfan."

"Is . . . is Bellamy Taynton really Cadfan?" Ursula ventured.

"Yes."

"What must we do, and how long do we have?"

Before Eleanor could answer, the maid knocked at the bedroom door. "Miss Ursula, the gentleman guests have arrived, and Mr. Elcester wishes you to go down."

Ursula tore her eyes away from the window. "Yes, I will be down directly."

The maid's footsteps hurried away, but when Ursula looked at the window again, there was no one there. She ran to look out, and saw Eleanor gliding down through the garden, with Bran at her side and the squirrel escort following.

"Eleanor!" Ursula cried, but the apparition did not look back.

Making a superhuman effort to collect her wits, which were now as scattered as the sheets of manuscript on the floor, Ursula turned from the window to steel herself to go downstairs. This wasn't the time to think of myths, mosaics, or mysterious maidens. She inhaled deeply, then went to get the lacy shawl she had draped over the end of the bed. Strangely, she suddenly felt more able to face the hours ahead, although she could not really have said why. Her head was positively spinning with incredible new information, and she had so much to tell Conan that she hardly knew where to begin. She paused. Tell Conan? Yes, of course she would. He was the only one she could confide in, and it no longer mattered that things had gone so horribly and mortifyingly wrong between them at Hatty Pedlar's Tump. She had to put her bruised pride and depleted dignity behind her and get on with what destiny decreed.

It was at the foot of the great oak staircase that she and Theo at last came face-to-face. She was satisfied that she acquitted herself well, all things considered, but she wished Theo made the same effort. She knew he was captivated by Eleanor Rhodes, but thought he should be as capable as she herself of putting on a brave face.

Her hardest moment came when she was introduced to Conan. He had taken her hand and pressed it to his lips, a gesture more warm than was strictly required, and when he had squeezed her fingers briefly as well, she knew she had misjudged him before. A rich feeling of stolen happiness washed through her, closely followed by guilt that they should secretly share such an exchange right in front of her father and future husband. It was wrong, so wrong, and yet she could not help herself, and when she looked into Conan's eyes, she knew his emotions were exactly the same. She longed to be alone with him, not only for the sake of being with him, but to tell him what she had discovered in her translation *and* in the hem of the cloak.

Theo would not have noticed any undercurrents even had he been in danger of being washed away by them. He was still distracted by the incident on the way to the manor, and although he was aware of how poorly he was behaving now, he couldn't pull himself together sufficiently to behave graciously. As a consequence his manner appeared offhand, which dismayed Mr. Elcester considerably. Ursula's father privately paid Theo no compliment by judging him a Glendower by name, but a true Carmartin by nature.

More than anyone, Conan understood Theo. Being in love with the wrong woman wasn't easy, nor was hiding the truth about that unwise love, so even though he would have given the world to be in Theo's shoes as Ursula's husband-to-be, he did his utmost to smooth over any awkwardness. And when Sir Conan Merrydown set out to be charming and entertaining company, he always succeeded. Dinner therefore went unexpectedly well, even allowing for Theo's paltry contribution to the conversation.

The Severn salmon was as exquisite as only Severn salmon can be, and so was the guinea-fowl, while the roast lamb was declared to be the perfect choice for the time of year. By the time the meal had progressed to the peaches in champagne with cream, Theo had recovered his aplomb a little, and felt ashamed of his earlier conduct. He had to concede that Ursula wasn't at all as bad as he had feared, indeed she was really rather pleasing, so at last he made himself agreeable. He too was well able to be charming, so Ursula reluctantly warmed to him a little.

It was while the conversation turned upon politics, a subject from which Ursula usually refrained because it could so easily become heated, that another coincidence of names occurred to her. The gentlemen were discussing the Whigs' latest stratagem, but she was thinking about *The Dream of Macsen Wledig,* and quite out of the blue she remembered that the latinized version of Eudaf Hen's name was Octavius. From that it was a very small step indeed to recalling that Lord Carmartin's second name was Octavius. Then there was Elen of the Ways— Eleanor Rhodes, roads . . . ways.

Mr. Elcester addressed her. "Ursula, m'dear, would you look after Sir Conan while Mr. Glendower and I discuss, er, the minutiae of the contract?"

"Mm?" Her mind was still racing.

"Have you heard a word I've said?"

She colored a little. "You know how I abhor political debate. Tempers are apt to become frayed."

"Not on this occasion, and besides, we have finished that particular topic, and the cloth has been removed in readiness for coffee and liqueurs."

She looked blankly at the table. She had been so lost in thought that she hadn't even noticed!

Her father continued. "Sir Conan has been tactful enough to suggest that you and he adjourn to the drawing room so that Mr. Glendower and I can discuss matters in private."

Ursula was embarrassed to have been caught so obviously daydreaming. "Forgive me, I'm afraid I allowed my attention to wander." She quickly folded her napkin so as to rise, and Conan got up to draw her chair out.

26

Ursula and Conan left the dining room and crossed the hall, where the Tudor wheel-rim chandelier cast a wavering pool of light on the stone-flagged floor. Neither of them spoke as they entered the dimly lit drawing room, where the maid had forgotten to place extra candles. Ursula was about to call for more when Conan closed the door and caught her hand. "No, don't call anyone, for we may never have another moment to be alone like this."

"Please don't say that."

"It has to be faced, for it is the truth. While you and I are here, your bridal agreement is on the table just across the hall. I do not doubt that you are finding this evening as much of a torment as I am, or that you wish to embrace me as much as I wish to embrace you."

She gazed at him through tears. "Oh, Conan . . ."

He caught her into his arms, his lips finding hers in a passionate kiss. Their hearts beat together, their bodies cleaved close, and for a wonderful, weightless, timeless moment they were absolutely alone. Neither of them wished to be the first to pull away, but at last she drew slowly back to look up into his eyes. "I love you, Conan," she said softly.

He put his hand to her cheek and caressed her skin with his thumb. "And I love you, Ursula," he replied, taking her other hand and drawing it tenderly to his lips.

"I wish we could be together."

His fingers tightened over hers. "I would be without honor to my friend, and we break the rules as it is."

"I *do* understand, Conan, for I do not doubt that I

would feel the same way." She moved away, to the tall window to look out at the night. Her face gazed back at her, fractured into diamonds by the leaded panes.

He went to Mr. Elcester's display cabinet and looked at the exhibits inside. The gold solidus she had mentioned lay there at the front. He wondered what was on the other side of it, and then he gave a start as the coin flipped over. He tried to tell himself he had imagined it, but he knew he hadn't. Other odd occurrences flashed through his mind. The inn gate closing of its own accord, the squirrel biting Taynton's finger to order. . . . Were *these* all coincidences too? He closed his eyes for a moment, for what did it matter whether they were or not? The only thing of consequence right now was his love for Ursula Elcester, for it transcended all else.

Ursula glanced at him. "I will always love only you, Conan, no matter how finally I am married to Mr. Glendower."

"I know."

Their eyes met across the room, and he looked away first. "Perhaps we . . . should talk of something else, for our hearts twist with pain enough."

She nodded. "There is another subject we need to turn to."

"Macsen and his myth?"

"Yes. Conan, I've discovered a great deal that you should know." She told him everything that had happened that evening, including her further association of names.

Conan listened intently, then told her about the incident with Eleanor Rhodes on the way to the manor. "Ursula," he finished, "I begin to think that with all these coincidences and repetitions, the myth isn't a myth after all, but fact. And what is happening now is a reenactment of the past."

"A reenactment?" she repeated.

"Yes. Remember that Vera told you Taynton hasn't touched her, and has made no move to marry her, yet we now know they were man and wife at the time of Macsen Wledig. I wonder if Taynton's present abstinence signifies a wish to *undo* what happened in the past?" Conan's thoughts ran on. "Maybe that is what his whole purpose is, to prevent the sequence of events that led to Cadfan's disinheritance. He thinks the wealth and status of Eudaf Hen should have come to him, not to a Roman emperor, and he probably despises me as the elder brother who meekly permitted the usurping of a birthright that he so desperately wanted for himself. Remember what he said by the pool. How did it go now? 'Loo-nass-ah, Sow-inn, Im-olk, something, may the secret be known to my might. Loo-nass-ah, Sow-inn, Im-olk, something, By the turn of the last may it be mine by right.' "

From out of nowhere Ursula suddenly understood words that hitherto had seemed just gibberish. "Of course, why didn't I realize it before!" she gasped.

"Realize what?"

"Loo-nass-ah is how the Celtic festival of Ludnasadh is pronounced. Ludnasadh is August the first. Sow-inn is Samhain, which is November the first, and Im-olk is Imbolc, which is February the first. The one you can't remember must be the fourth main festival, Beltane, which takes place from May Eve to May Day. I think he is trying to achieve what he thinks is his 'by right' at the turn—midnight—at either the beginning or end of Beltane."

Conan was dismayed. "So it could possibly be tonight?"

"Yes, I fear so, although I incline to believe we have until midnight tomorrow as I imagine May Day itself is a far more auspicious time for magic, and this year will see the full moon at that very moment. Oh, and it will be Walpurgis Night as well, for added propitiousness."

"I pray you are right, otherwise we do not stand an earthly chance." Conan managed a wry smile. "Earthly? Perhaps *un*earthly would be more fitting."

Ursula nodded. "And I've realized more, Conan. Ludnasadh, August the first, was when my father first heard of Samuel Haine. Samuel Haine, don't you see? Samhain, the festival when Haine's swindling very nearly brought ruin. Then Imbolc was when poor Jem Cartwright suddenly upped and left the inn after being there as long as I can remember. It was also the date when Taynton came to Elcester, and when Macsen Wledig dreamed his dream."

"And when Theo dreamed his too," Conan added.

"Yes, and if we consider the name Cadfan has given himself now, Bellamy Taynton, we have Beltane!"

"I'll warrant that if we find out when Eleanor Rhodes disappeared from Carmartin Park, it will have been on one of the festivals."

"Ludnasadh, for I remember it was the beginning of August."

Conan drew a long sigh. "We have so little time in which to outwit Taynton and try to save Eleanor, who will presumably remain a squirrel forever unless his magic can be overturned somehow. Maybe we only have as little was as twenty-four hours in which to achieve it!"

"I know."

"All right, we have worked out so much of it, but what *exactly* is Taynton trying so hard to do? We know he wants to reverse or prevent the past repeating itself, but what does he stand to gain now, in *this* century?"

Ursula felt she knew the answer to that as well. "Eudaf Hen's treasure," she said flatly.

"Treasure?"

"Yes. Right at the beginning of the myth, when Macsen dreams of Elen of the Ways, she tells him that he will not only have her, but all her father's treasure, which is kept at his summer house nearby."

"Meaning here at Elcester?"

Ursula spread her hands. "It must be, for why else is he here? Why are we all here? But I don't understand where Eudaf Hen's castle can have been."

"Well, surely it was where Carmartin Park is now," Conan replied. "Carmartin even begins with the correct letter of the alphabet."

"Yes, but it isn't on an island, nor could it have been at the time of the myth."

Conan pursed his lips. "Well, I don't think we need to concern ourselves with the castle, for it's as plain as a pikestaff that the valley here at Elcester is the place where the treasure is. And now that you have found the tesserae, I think we know more than Taynton about its probable exact whereabouts!"

She was bothered. "Look, I can't be sure that the tesserae came from the badger set—it just seems the most likely place."

"We cannot afford to dally. Theo and I will go there tonight, for it is time to confront him with all this. He is Macsen Wledig, after all, and Elen of the Ways needs him."

"I will come was as well."

"Oh, no. Those woods are dangerous, and—"

"I cannot be moved on this. Conan, do you honestly think I can sit here twiddling my thumbs while you examine the set?"

"Ursula—"

"If you won't let me accompany you, I'll go there anyway. Besides, when Eleanor appeared at my window, she asked me to help, remember?"

Amusement tinged with admiration glinted in his eyes. "You are a devilish difficult woman, Ursula Elcester."

"I was also your wife in the past, sir, and no doubt wielded a very large Celtic rolling pin."

He caught her hands and bent forward to brush his lips to hers. "Would that I could remember our, er, more intimate moments," he whispered.

"Would that I could too," she confessed candidly.

"You do realize, don't you, that if I am right about this being a reenactment, it would be in our personal interest—yours and mine—to make absolutely certain Taynton fails?"

"What do you mean?"

"Because if history repeats itself, not only will Theo marry Eleanor Rhodes, but you and I will marry too, and breaking the rules or not, that is something I want more than anything."

She stared at him. "You . . . you do?" Marriage? He was talking of marriage? A maelstrom of confusion and joy began to whirl through her.

Conan smiled. "Oh, yes, as I think you want it too."

"I-I cannot deny it, but my father and Lord Carmartin—"

Conan put a finger to her lips. "They both have their reasons, but those reasons may not signify if we are correct in our deductions. Lord Carmartin is pursuing the marriage between Theo and you because he wants Elcester Manor, but what would his feelings be if when he learns his long-lost Eleanor has not only returned, but that she and Theo are in love? Would *that* not be a far more satisfactory dynastic match for his lordship than any number of manors? As for your father's situation, Ursula, I have more than sufficient fortune to rescue Elcester, and I have no desire to take it from your family. I want you to become Lady Merrydown, and believe me, I will do all in my power to see that you do. The only loser of sorts will be Lord Carmartin, who will be denied this estate, but I'm sure that what he has to gain will more than cancel that out."

Ursula could barely collect herself. "I-I can't believe we are actually discussing marriage. We hardly know each other, and—"

"Hardly know each other? My beloved Ursula, we have known each other for one and a half millennia!"

At that moment footsteps approached as Mr. Elcester and Theo left the dining room to join them, so Conan seized Ursula urgently by the arms. "If we can outwit Taynton and bring this business to a satisfactory conclusion all around, do you promise to marry me?"

"I—"

"Answer me, Ursula," he pleaded.

"Yes. Oh, yes, I will."

"And we will plight our troth in Rome, just as we did before."

Their lips clung together again, but when Mr. Elcester

and Theo entered a moment or so later after shaking hands upon the details of the contract that neither the bride nor groom desired, there could not have been anything more proper than the distance between the two star-crossed lovers in the drawing room.

27

It was nearly midnight—the first turn of May Eve—when Conan and Theo took their leave of Ursula and her father. Theo was still ashamed of his earlier conduct, especially as he had come to like Ursula during the course of the evening, so his natural charm and amiability were brought to the fore as he bowed over her hand and murmured all the usual polite phrases. It wasn't at all difficult to be agreeable toward her, and he only wished he had never set eyes upon his Eleanor, because but for that he knew he would now be entering this arranged match with a much lighter heart. As it was, he could not put Eleanor from his mind. A seemingly irrational love for her consumed him to the exclusion of all else, and he felt as if he had been waiting for her all his life. The very air around him had begun to tingle with magic from the moment he dreamed of her that first night in London, and as he and Conan stepped out of Elcester Manor into the mild night air, he felt as if she were near him now. Maybe if he turned suddenly— But, no, when he did so, there were only the moon shadows of the house and grounds. . . .

He said nothing as the carriage drove up the slope, past the lodge, then along the road toward the village. So centered upon his thoughts was he that at first he hardly noticed when Conan lowered the window glass and leaned out to command Gardner to halt on the grass near Hatty Pedlar's Tump. As the vehicle jolted to a standstill on the uneven surface, he roused himself in surprise. "Why have we stopped?"

"Because I have a great deal to tell you, and I expect you to listen without interrupting."

Theo looked blankly at him. "All right, although I cannot imagine what is so important that it has to be said now instead of waiting until we are at Carmartin Park."

Conan explained everything, leaving out not a single point, even the news that he and Ursula were in love. Theo gaped more and more as the tale unfolded, and when Conan finished, he stared at him without a word.

Conan looked quizzically at him. "Have you nothing to say?"

"I-I don't know. I can't think what . . ." Theo took an enormous breath. "All this has been going on, and you haven't said a word until now?"

"May I remind you of your attitude at the Green Man? You didn't want to even *think* about it, let alone talk about it."

"I know, I know, but all the same . . ."

"I'm telling you now. You, my friend, are Macsen Wledig, Eleanor Rhodes is Elen of the Ways, and you have to marry her again if we are to thwart our genial innkeeper. Now, if all that Ursula and I have deduced is correct, we may only have about twenty-four hours in which to act, so you, she, and I are going to that badger set tonight to see if it is where the tesserae came from."

They both distinctly heard the bell of Elcester church striking the witching hour, and Conan found he was holding his breath. He didn't know what he was expecting, just that the distant bell was possibly tolling away their chance of vanquishing Cadfan Meriadoc. But nothing happened as the last note diminished into silence—no jagged flash of lightning, no resounding thunderclap, nothing that might indicate the onset of Cadfan's victory. Conan breathed out with qualified relief, then gave a sheepish grin. "I half feared Taynton's sorcery would suddenly show itself," he confessed.

"After all that you've just told me, so did I," replied Theo, "but I feel nothing at all."

"Then let us pray that is a good sign. Ursula believes it is more likely to be midnight tomorrow night."

"Yes, for that was when the Black Druid performed my marriage to Elen of the Ways in the shadow of the yew tree," Theo said suddenly.

Conan was startled. "What on earth made you say that?"

Theo seemed to be looking at something no one else could see. "Mm? I just *know* that's when and where we married."

"Who on earth is—or was—the Black Druid?"

"The priest and the blacksmith. It was misty when we returned to Eudaf Hen's castle for the feast."

"Where was the castle?" Conan asked quickly.

"Why, Carmartin Hill, of course," Theo replied in a tone that suggested astonishment that such a question needed to be asked.

"You're sure of that?"

"Absolutely certain. I can remember it quite clearly, rising out of the mist like an island. . . ."

Conan smiled. "So that's it," he murmured.

Theo had not finished. "When the days of feasting were over, Elen and I came here to the summer house, which was named Elcester in her honor, for it was Elen's fort, and I built the finest villa in the whole of Britannia." He pulled himself together with a shudder. "Good God, that was a strange moment. I really felt I was Macsen Wledig again." He gave a self-conscious laugh. "It would seem I'm definitely him, eh? Right down to the Spanish blood!"

"Oh, yes, after all you just said I don't think there's any doubt."

Theo looked at him "Oh, all right, I'll come to the badger set as well. I'll do whatever you wish, Conan, although to be truthful, it's all far too much for me to take in. How can I possibly be an ancient Roman emperor?"

"You think Ursula and I have found it any easier to accept our double identities? It's fantastic and totally unbelievable, and to speak of it at all makes one feel slightly mad, except that none of us *are* mad because it really is happening."

Theo felt a perverse desire to make light of it. "Oh dear, just as I was beginning to think marrying Ursula wouldn't be so bad a thing after all."

"That's what I happen to think too, and I believe I have the historic right to her."

Theo nodded, then looked away. "Conan, what if we don't trounce Taynton, Cadfan, or whoever he is?"

"At least we will have done our utmost."

"But I will lose my chance of inheritance in this life, let alone any past existence, Eleanor will remain enchanted, and Ursula's father will have to sell the manor because he won't be able to afford not to. Now, you may call me a misery, but it seems to me we ought to weigh things up very carefully indeed before we do anything."

Conan sat back. "Theo, when it comes to the very bones of it, you are the only one who stands to be worse off than at present. I will rescue Elcester Manor whether or not Taynton emerges the victor, and whether or not I marry Ursula, but I cannot rescue your chances of inheritance. That is something you have to face up to on your own. Is Eleanor worth risking everything for? If she is, then you have no quandary, but if she isn't, well, it's better you say so now."

"Of course she's worth it!" Theo cried heatedly.

Conan smiled. "Spoken like a true Roman emperor! Come on, let's to it!" He reached under his seat for the pistol, checked that it was in readiness, then opened the door and jumped lightly down. He turned quickly to Gardner. "Just wait here. I'm afraid I don't know how long we'll be, but you may be assured that I will be generous in my appreciation."

"It is my duty, Lord Kynan, and I will wait as long as you wish," the coachman replied solemnly, and raised his hand in a rather odd way, as if giving a salute of some sort.

Conan's wits sharpened, and he looked intently at the man. "What did you just say?" he asked.

"I said, it is my duty, Sir Conan, and I will wait as long as you wish," Gardner repeated, this time touching his hat in his usual manner.

Conan knew he hadn't misheard the first time. He also knew that the coachman had no idea he'd said anything different. It was yet another instance of history coming full circle. No doubt Gardner had been Kynan Meriadoc's man fifteen hundred years before as well.

Theo had alighted without hearing the exchange, and Conan told him about it as they walked quickly along the road to the nearest gate, then down through the fields toward the lower park, where Ursula and Conan had agreed she would wait by the door into the rose garden.

She was still wearing her silver evening gown, and breathed out with relief as the two men hurried up to her. "Oh, I'm so glad to see you both! When midnight sounded, I was so afraid . . ." She didn't finish.

Conan took her hand and raised the palm to his lips. "I feared the same, but I believe your guess to be closer to the mark."

"Tomorrow night?"

"Yes."

She turned hesitantly to Theo, and to her relief he smiled. "Well met, Lady Ursula," he murmured, and sketched a lavish bow.

"And you, my emperor," she replied, returning the smile.

"I know everything now, including about you and Kynan Meriadoc here." Theo nodded toward Conan.

Ursula flushed, and was glad the moonlight hid the fact. "You and I are just not meant to be," she said after a moment.

"Quite right too."

"Do you really mean that?"

"Of course. My destiny lies with Elen of the Ways."

Conan was impatient. "The longer we dither here in pleasantries, the more the minutes tick away in Taynton's favor. Come on, let's get on with things." Still holding Ursula's hand, he led the way along the tiny path toward the woods.

The bluebell glades were ravishingly beautiful in the silvery light, and the scent of the flowers now seemed more bewitching than ever as the three made their way toward the badger set. As they walked, Conan acquainted Ursula with Theo's remarkable recollections from his existence as Macsen Wledig, and Gardner's peculiar response when they'd left him by the long barrow.

Ursula took it all in with increasing anticipation. So clearly could she now feel the past and present intertwining that it seemed almost tangible in the air around her. All the ancient forces were gathering, flowing through her veins and through the very trees around her. The old rhyme came to her again. *In and out of the dusky bluebells. In and out the dusky bluebells . . .* But Cadfan Meriadoc wasn't going to be anyone's master. She would die before she allowed that to happen!

It was fortunate that the moon was so strong, for it allowed them to inspect the old set without too much trouble. Ursula watched as the two men scrambled down into it and began to scrape at the crumbling soil. It wasn't long before objects began to be revealed, although at first nothing that resembled tesserae. To begin with they found some beads made of Baltic amber, then another coin, although of whose reign it was impossible to tell. Next came a tiny blue glass figurine of a squirrel, followed by a similar ivory horse. Conan knew them immediately, and with a flash of insight that was not unlike Theo's earlier, he cried, "The game Kynan and I were playing when he tossed the board aside! The blue glass men were mine!"

Renewed eagerness seized them, and they scraped the soil away all the harder. More ivory and blue glass animals came to light, but still no tesserae. Then suddenly a large portion of earth fell away, and there were pieces of mosaic everywhere.

Ursula pressed her hands to her mouth to quell the urge to squeal with delight, for surely they had found the villa Macsen Wledig built for Elen of the Ways!

28

Finding so many tesserae galvanized Conan and Theo to great effort, although they worked with great care because it had become apparent they had uncovered the outer edge of a beautiful circular mosaic floor. The more earth they brushed away, the more they saw the intricate pattern that had been created fifteen hundred years earlier. There were birds and animals, including white squirrels, horses, and wolfhounds, and a veritable pantheon of Celtic and Roman deities, all woven among what Ursula guessed were the spokes of a chariot wheel. It was a feast of ancient artistic design, yet curiously modern at the same time, for all things classical had been the vogue for some time now. What lay at the hub of the wheel would have to remain a secret a little longer, because there was too great an area for two men to remove. More hands were needed, with spades and brushes to carefully remove the layer of earth that now rested on the remains of the villa.

Ursula examined the deities more closely, and found one that might have been Vera Pedlar, then another that looked like Conan, and even one that might have been herself. Then she noticed that they all appeared to be gesturing toward the unseen hub of the wheel. Yes, she as sure that was what they were doing. But what could be at the center? Probably a likeness of Elen of the Ways, although . . . What if it was something important? Something vital to resolving everything, maybe even lead to the treasure? She moved away slightly, fearing to allow her all too active imagination to run away with her.

It was probably just a sumptuous mosaic floor design, she told herself strictly, no more and no less.

Conan and Theo clambered out of the set, feeling unable to progress any further, but as Ursula began to tell them about the likeness she had perceived among the mosaic deities, a breath of wind sighed through the woods, shivering the bluebells and rustling the trees. Ursula turned and saw Eleanor Rhodes standing there with Bran at her side. Or should she be regarded as Elen of the Ways? Ursula did not quite know how to think of the almost ghostly figure with the flowing red-gold hair and diaphanous robe.

The moment Theo saw Eleanor, he went to her, but as he reached out, his hand passed right through her. "Eleanor?" he said in dismay.

"Macsen, my beloved lord," she replied, and moved close enough to link her otherworldly arms around his neck. As she put her gossamer lips to his, he sensed rather than felt her touch. He longed to hold her, to know she was living flesh and blood in his arms, but she was as insubstantial as a morning mist. But so precious, so very, very precious.

She stepped away then. "I have come to warn you all. Prince Cadfan has cast a spell upon you. I saw him this very evening by the pool. He means you great harm."

"A spell? You mean something new, as distinct from whatever magic he performed last night?" Conan asked.

She nodded. "I do not know exactly what he has done, for I saw him only when he was finishing, but there were four candles, therefore four incantations. With Bran, there are four of you, so I imagine you are his victims. He intends to clear his path to the goal he seeks. You and my Lord Macsen stand in his way now, just as you did fifteen hundred years ago. We are *all* in his way, for if we repeat now the actions we performed then, he knows he cannot succeed."

Theo reached out to her. "Then marry me without delay." It seemed so obvious a solution.

She smiled and closed her eyes as once again his hand passed through her. "Oh, my dearest lord, if only it were that easy, but we can only marry at midnight on May Eve in the shadow of the yew tree, just as we did before. If we do that, I will become a complete woman again, a warm and loving bride to grace your bed."

Conan was more immediately concerned with the timing of Taynton's sorcery. "When will this spell work?" he asked Eleanor.

"The very same stroke of midnight. So you see, we must marry at the very moment we become enchanted. Which will prove the stronger force? I fear it may be Taynton's magic."

Ursula raised her chin defiantly. "There must be *something* we can do to halt him!"

"If there is, I do not know how. Once he has disposed of us, he must find the treasure or lose his chance for another five hundred years. We can only hope that he fails."

"But if we were to find it in the meantime . . . ?"

Eleanor looked helplessly at her. "Maybe. Oh, I cannot say, for I know so little. All I can tell you is that the answer lies at the heart of mosaic floor, and the chalice shows the way."

"The chalice? Do you mean we can tell something from the decorative frieze on it?" Ursula was thinking swiftly, remembering that she and Conan had seen the chalice in the stables at the Green Man.

Eleanor looked close to tears. "Maybe it is the frieze, maybe something else. It should become clear when you expose the floor completely. The treasure was kept safe by my father, Eudaf Hen, so that Cadfan Meriadoc could not lay thieving hands upon it in my lord Macsen's absence in Rome with his friend, Lord Kynan. But Cadfan conspired with others against my father. My dear lord was overthrown and murdered by a rival for the throne of Rome, and Lord Kynan was gravely wounded, only just escaping with his life. After that, my father became more determined than ever to deny Cadfan the succession, for the new heir was the babe I had borne to Lord Macsen, and so small a child was vulnerable to someone like Cadfan. So to protect his infant grandson, my father hid the treasure and guarded it with a powerful spell because he knew Cadfan would learn magic in order to find it. My father always meant to reveal its whereabouts to the true heir, but died quite suddenly before he was able to do so. Thus his safeguard magic worked against his grandchild as much as it did against Lord Cadfan. Now the treasure can be found only once every five hundred years, and whoever finds it becomes the victor. Both we and Cadfan have failed twice now, once in 818 and again in 1318. If we fail this time as well, we will try again in 2318 and so on." She gazed tearfully at Theo. "If I had not fallen into Cadfan's hands, you and I would by now have married and had our son, but he has prevented this. He knows much more magic than he had before, and is able to interfere with the pattern at every turn. I fear he will succeed in his aim, and when that happens, I will remain as I am forever."

Theo could not bear it. "No! *We* will be the victors this time, my love, I swear that we will! Then you will be my bride again, no matter what my uncle may say! But first we have a dragon to defeat, do we not?"

Conan glanced at the floor they had already uncovered. "It's obvious from the curve of the perimeter that the floor is quite large. You and I cannot hope to clear it in time, Theo, but if we had more men to assist us . . ." He looked at Ursula. "I think the time has come to inform your father about all this. We need as many men as possible from the manor, but we must be stealthy about it, otherwise Taynton might be alerted. What we really need is something to keep him distracted at the inn."

"Vera will help," Ursula said. "She loves him and wants to marry him, so if she thinks that helping us will definitely result in her becoming his wife—which it will if history is allowed to repeat itself—she'll do what she can. I'm sure she will be able to create a problem of some sort in the kitchens that will require his full attention. She can cause a fire if necessary!"

"A fire might be just the thing," Conan declared.

"Then the wretched place can be rebuilt and named something more agreeable than the Green Man!"

"It used to be the Fleece," Ursula said.

"Far more fitting for a village that is based upon wool." Conan returned to the subject of Vera. "It won't do to be wrong about Vera's loyalties. If she loves him, maybe she'll want to help *him,* not us."

Eleanor answered, "It is true that for all his wickedness, the Lady Severa loved Cadfan very much, but she always tried to save him from himself. She will be our ally now. Until now she has been unsure about everything, for she senses much yet has no one to speak to about it. She knew there was something that bound her to me, even though I was a squirrel, but she didn't know exactly what that something was. Why else do you think she did not alert him when my squirrel friends tried to release me by the pool? If we tell her the truth now, she will know what her role must be. Once she is his wife again, he will have to comply for another five hundred years."

"She may have loved him, but did he love her?" Ursula asked curiously.

"Oh, yes, but his greed for the treasure always came between them. If my lord Macsen finds the treasure after all, then Cadfan's heart will rule his head once more, and he will be content with Severa."

Conan exhaled slowly. "Right. I think we know what is needed now. Ursula, you know Vera Pedlar better than anyone, so I want you to approach her and tell her what is necessary. Then, when Taynton's attention is fully diverted, with your father's leave we'll set his men to clear as much of the mosaic floor as possible. Once we see what is at the center of the design, maybe we will know what the chalice is for. Anyway, it's all we can do in the time we have left."

"I'm sure my father will gladly help, although what he will make of our, er, fairy tale, I hardly dare imagine."

"Well, if we go to him now, we'll soon find out," Conan replied with a wry smile.

Theo turned quickly to Eleanor. "You will come with us?"

"No."

"But—"

"Please, for I do not wish to appear to anyone but you three."

"Then I will stay with you." Theo looked urgently at Conan. "I cannot leave her. Please, Conan . . ."

Conan nodded. "As you wish, but how will we find you again?"

Eleanor smiled. "I will know when you return, have no fear of that."

Conan nodded again. "Very well. Ursula and I will get on with matters. We will come back as soon as we can, but we need a little sleep if we are to be effective in the coming hours, so do not expect us for at least a few hours."

Theo gave him a grateful smile. Then he and Eleanor walked away into the trees, with Bran padding faithfully at their heels.

Conan held his hand out to Ursula. "Come, we have things to do."

She slipped her hand into his, and they hurried away along the little path they'd followed earlier. They glanced back before the set was lost to view, in time to see Eleanor raising her ethereal lips to Theo's in another kiss that longed to cross the boundary from the Otherworld to this.

Ursula let Conan lead her a few yards more, then halted. "Have you no kiss for me as well, Lord Kynan?" she asked softly.

His eyes were warm and knowing in the moonlight as he pulled her into his arms and kissed her. She savored the taste of his lips and the contours of his body, molding herself to him in a way that knew no shame. But what place did shame have in these ancient woods? The pagan past was the pagan present, and she was no longer bookish, proper Ursula Elcester, but the Lady Ursula in the arms of her lord and husband. She should surrender to

him now, let him take her here among the dusky bluebells; let him be her master . . .

Conan's desire was as fierce, and gratification was
temptingly close, but with a huge effort he held her away.
"We must not succumb just yet, my love. Let us first
have become man and wife in Rome, for then the nectar
will be all the more sweet."

"What if I disappoint you?" she asked then, Ursula
Elcester suddenly very much to the fore again.

He smiled. "Disappoint me? My darling, I have already sampled your kisses, and believe me you have acquired *that* art to the full."

"Have I?"

"Oh, yes, so I anticipate the rest of you with barely
contained ardor." He pulled her to him again and slid
his hands to her waist, then down to enclose her buttocks
through the thin silver silk of her gown. "And you, my
lady, may anticipate eagerly as well, for I know how to
pleasure a woman myself. I have not led the life of a
monk, I fear." He kissed her again, at the same time
pulling her hips to his and pressing her against his
aroused maleness.

Voluptuous feelings swept her to the very edge of consciousness. The moonlit woods seemed to spin, and she
felt as light as air, held to earth only by his embrace.
Her body sang with excitement for a long, long moment,
and then she felt weak and deliciously warm as she sank
against him.

Minutes later, when they at last emerged from the
woods to cross the lower park, she felt stronger and more
invigorated than ever before. While she had Conan, there
was nothing she could not achieve. Nothing.

29

It was just as Ursula and Conan reached the door into the rose garden that she remembered something she had noticed on the mosaic floor. "Wait!" she breathed, and turned urgently to him. "The chalice is depicted on the floor."

"Are you sure? I didn't notice it."

"Yes, I'm certain. Neither you nor Theo uncovered it. Some earth slipped away of its own accord, and I saw what I am sure was the base of the cup, or at least the base of *a* cup. I want to go back and look."

"Ursula—"

"Please, Conan."

"What will it achieve to see if it is or not? There were all sorts of things in that design."

She didn't know herself why she wished to see it, just that she wanted to very much indeed. The desire to rest awhile seemed to have suddenly deserted her, and the need to return to the set was so strong that she began to hurry back across the lower park. Conan hesitated a moment, then followed, soon catching up and taking her hand to retrace their steps into the woods.

The set was deserted when they arrived. At least, not quite, for Bran was there, and Ursula knew he was waiting for them. The wolfhound had been drawn back to the set as surely as she herself had been. More than that, he was seated at the very place where she had seen what she believed to be a portrayal of the chalice. Sure enough, when she scraped away a little more of the earth, the tesserae design was quite clearly what she thought it to be.

"There!" she declared triumphantly. "I *knew* I was right!"

Conan smiled at her. "You are indeed, but I still fail to—" He broke off as Bran suddenly began to whine and scratch at the design. "What is it, boy?" Conan asked then, reaching down to pat the wolfhound.

Bran trotted away a few yards toward Hazel Pool, then turned to look back at them. He moved on another few yards and looked back again. They followed instinctively, and the wolfhound led them steadily toward the pool, and then to the hollow oak, where he got up on his hind legs to paw at the trunk just where he had seen Taynton hide the chalice.

Conan reached up to feel inside the tree, but just as his questing fingers closed over one of the chalice's handles, Ursula heard a sound. "Listen! I think someone's coming!" she breathed uneasily.

Conan left the chalice where it was, grabbed her hand, and ran toward the nearest thicket of bushes. Bran ran with them, and they ducked down out of sight just as Taynton arrived with his companions, including Vera. As luck would have it, Vera came quite close to the bushes to put on her robe, and Ursula hardly knew the words were on her lips before she spoke. "Vera!" she whispered urgently.

The blacksmith's daughter froze. "Miss Ursula?"

"Don't look around. Just hear what I have to say. I can explain a great deal to you, and I can tell you a way to marry Bellamy Taynton."

Vera had to make a huge effort not to turn around toward the whispered voice. "You . . . you can?"

"Yes. Meet me on the village green in the morning. I will await you by the merry-go-round at ten."

"No, not ten, for I have much to do in the kitchens at that time. I can meet you at half past."

"Very well, but be sure to be there. It's very important, and will make much clear to you."

Vera had turned her head just sufficiently for them to see her profile. She gave an ironic smile. "Then I will be very grateful, Miss Ursula, because I sense so very much, yet understand nothing at all."

There was no time to say anything more because Taynton called rather irritably to her, "Don't dally there, Vera!"

"Forgive me," Vera replied, and hurried to join the others.

The ritual was repeated, another nail driven into the oak, and the old ring game performed so that Taynton was able to reassert himself as the others' master. When all was completed, and the thirteen had departed again, the secret watchers came out of hiding.

Conan smiled at Ursula. "That was quick-witted, if a little risky, of you to speak to Vera."

"I know she loves him, and so will do whatever she can to win him."

"I don't think much of her taste in men. However, no doubt even Cadfan Meriadoc has some redeeming features."

Ursula looked at the hollow oak. "What shall we do about the chalice? Take it with us?"

"Oh, yes. I'll feel a great deal easier if it's in our hands rather than his." He hurried to the tree, reached in for the chalice, and then looked at it in the moonlight. "It's a very beautiful thing," he observed admiringly, turning it slightly so that the gold and jewels shone.

"And very unholy indeed," Ursula replied with a smile.

"True." He continued to study it. "Well, if there is a clue of some sort in this frieze, I'm hanged if I can see it. Not that moonlight helps, I suppose."

"Nor does the fact that we are both tired. We've had more than one exceedingly broken night," she said.

"Yes. Come on—we'd better get back to the manor to see your father. If you are to meet Vera at half past ten, and we are to get some sleep, we shouldn't dally."

And so once again they retraced their steps through the wood, then across the lower park to the rose garden. They concealed the chalice in the stables, not wishing to answer questions about how and where they had come into possession of such a notorious stolen object, then crossed to the house itself. But there a shock awaited them, for Mr. Elcester was not there. A sleepy footman informed them that about an hour earlier a messenger had ridden posthaste from Stroud with the news that the River Frome had flooded Fromewell Mill to the possible extent of making the building dangerous. Mr. Elcester's presence had been required urgently.

The footman made little attempt to conceal his curiosity about Conan's presence. It would have been bad enough if Ursula had been out and about alone with Theo, whom she was to marry, but to be with his friend instead raised all manner of scandalous questions. Ursula was past caring about such tiresome matters. "Sir Conan will be staying here tonight, so I wish you to show him to the east bedroom. We are both to be awoken at eight, and breakfast is to be served at half past. Then I wish all the men employed here to assemble in the hall, for there is work to be done. Oh, and I wish my mare to be saddled for half past nine."

The footman was a little bemused to hear that. Sir Conan was to stay. "Er, yes, Miss Ursula," he said, pulling himself together as best he could.

"And nothing is to be said of this. No one, but *no one* is to mention Sir Conan's presence here."

The footman could well understand *that* order! "Yes, Miss Ursula."

"Nor is anyone to speak outside of my order regarding the men. If anyone speaks out of turn, they will be instantly dismissed. Is that clear?"

"Yes, Miss Ursula."

"See to it, then."

The footman bowed, then withdrew, leaving Conan to look admiringly at her. "Oh, I can see what a very splendid Lady Merrydown you will be," he declared.

She flushed. "There is many a slip," she reminded him.

"Ah, but we now have the cup," he pointed out.

"Yes. I only hope we will know how to use it."

The footman returned with the maid, and Conan was led away to the east bedroom. Shortly afterward both he and Ursula were sound asleep in their beds. It was the dreamless sleep of the exhausted, and it seemed to be over all too soon as they were both aroused at eight o'clock.

The morning of May Eve was bright, clear, and sunny, and Ursula found she was surprisingly refreshed. She dressed in her riding habit because she was going to meet Vera at half past ten, then went down to the dining room, where Conan was already waiting. He looked a little incongruous in evening attire, but it did not matter. He greeted her with a kiss, and they both sat down to a hearty repast. When the men were assembled as commanded, she informed them that she believed she had discovered the Roman villa that her father had been seeking, but that in case it was a false alarm, she did not wish the matter to be spoken of outside the manor. That included all family and friends in the village, she added, knowing that Taynton numbered some villagers among his cohorts. She instructed them to bring as many spades and brushes as they could find and told them they were to act under Conan's command.

Then she went outside, mounted Miss Muffet, and rode to the village to meet Vera on the green.

30

The village green was a hive of activity. The maypole had been carried from the Green Man and was in the process of being raised, and the merry-go-round had been almost completely assembled, much to the excitement of the village children. Even greater excitement was caused by the erection of a big wheel, an attraction never before been seen at Elcester. Acrobats and tightrope walkers rehearsed their performances, music played, and there was the smell of late breakfast cooking on various campfires.

Vera was waiting by the merry-go-round. She wore a dark blue mantle over a light blue dress, with a little straw bonnet on her head, and she was very nervous, glancing frequently in the direction of the inn as if she feared to see Taynton coming after her. She came over relievedly as Ursula dismounted. "I cannot stay long, Miss Ursula, for there was very nearly a fire in the kitchens this morning, and now we're all behind."

"I will try to be as brief as possible, but there is a great deal you have to know, much of it that you may not even believe. Come on, let's walk." Leading Miss Muffet, Ursula walked slowly around the crowded green, with Vera listening at her side. The blacksmith's daughter's eyes grew wider and wider as the story of Macsen Wledig unfolded, but gradually their astonishment turned to a more thoughtful glint, and when everything had been related, she halted and faced Ursula.

"Bellamy and Sir Conan were once *brothers*?"

"Yes."

"That means you and I were sisters-in-law?" Vera

clearly had more difficulty accepting this latter fact than she did about the two men being siblings.

"Yes, we were, Vera," Ursula confirmed, "and it's up to us to make certain it all happens again."

Vera thought a moment. "If he loved me then, does that mean he will love me again?"

"Yes, according to Elen of the Ways."

Vera smoothed her skirts with hands that trembled, then glanced toward the church, where she could see the top of the yew tree and the curl of smoke from her father's forge. "And my father is the Black Druid who will marry us?"

"We believe so."

Vera smiled. "I will do whatever I can to help you, Miss Ursula."

"We think that we can stop Taynton by finding the treasure first. At least, we hope that is how it will be. Whatever the way of it, it's bound to be best that he doesn't know we've discovered the villa, or that we've taken the chalice from the oak, so if you keep him busy today while we search in the woods . . . ? I don't know how much magic he's capable of, so the least said the soonest mended, if you know what I mean."

"Oh, I do know, Miss Ursula."

A male voice intruded. "Vera? Miss Hursula?"

"Father!" Vera turned sharply as the blacksmith spoke behind them.

He touched his hat to Ursula as she turned quickly as well. "Miss Hursula," he said again.

"Daniel."

His glance searched their faces. "So 'tis all astirring then?" he said.

Ursula looked at him in surprise. "You know?"

"I do now, Miss Hursula, on account of I 'ad the darnedest dream last night. Longest dream I ever 'ad in all my born days. So I know what 'appened 'ere long back, and what must 'appen again now. The dream even told me I'd find you both 'ere on the green, so I came to let you know I'll be at the yew at midnight in my regalia."

"As the Black Druid?" Ursula asked.

He nodded. "Yes, for that is my place in it all. I am meant to preside over three marriages, yours to Sir Conan, Mr. Glendower to Eleanor Rhodes, and my Vera to that darned varmint Taynton."

Vera's eyes filled with tears. "He isn't a varmint, truly he isn't, Father."

"I'll 'ave to be convinced of that, my girl." The blacksmith looked at Ursula again. "But it ent all cut and dried yet, Miss Hursula. I don't know if I'll preside over any marriages at all, on account of Taynton 'ave done some sorcery . . ."

"I know."

"I can tell you that only part of it 'as taken."

"You know what he's done?" Ursula asked quickly.

"Not really, just enough to know 'e've not been as thorough as 'e thinks. 'E've still done mischief though, and come midnight tonight I can't say 'ow many couples there'll be beneath that there yew tree. 'Appen three, 'appen none at all. I'll be ready and waitin', though, you 'ave my solemn vow on that."

Vera stepped uncertainly toward him. "Father, do you forgive me now?"

He smiled. "Of course I do, you foolish little trot."

She ran to him and flung her arms tearfully around his neck. They hugged each other tightly, then he held her gently away before walking back the way he'd come. Vera gazed after him. "I-I can hardly believe all this is happening, Miss Ursula," she whispered.

Ursula gave her a wry smile. "*You* can't? Vera, we're *all* having trouble believing it. Anyway, you can get back to the Green Man and see that Taynton stays there, and I'll go to the woods to see if anything exciting has been found." She mounted Miss Muffet, then reached a hand down to Vera. "We're going to win, I promise," she breathed.

They clasped hands for a second, then Ursula kicked her heel and urged the mare away from the green.

*   *   *

Taynton was waiting for Vera when she returned. "And where have you been?" he demanded. "There's a stagecoach due any minute, and I'm told the mutton has boiled away to next to nothing!"

"It's not due any minute," she replied calmly, removing her bonnet and mantle and hanging them on the hook on the wall in his parlor. "There's another hour yet, and I have everything in hand. You surely do not imagine I need to scurry around over one stagecoach when I've been preparing for May Day since last week? You've seen fit to grandly tell everyone in creation that there's free food and drink to be had, but you didn't pause to wonder where it was all going to come from, did you? There's a cold ham in the larder, more than sufficient cold meat from yesterday," she replied calmly.

"Well, I'm glad *one* of us is so at ease!" he snapped, then sneezed.

"Is your cold worse? Oh, and I expect your poor leg is still hurting," she said solicitously, and put a loving hand to his cheek.

He stepped hastily back from her. "Don't do that!"

"Do what? Here, come and sit down while I put some more balm on the bite, then I'll make you some more rum gruel."

He looked suspiciously at her. "What's all this? Just before you went out you all but bit my head off!"

"Because you were being a bear. It wasn't *my* fault that the kitchen almost caught fire."

"Well, I had to shout at someone," he replied with the infuriating thoughtlessness of so many men.

"And it's always me you choose," she replied tartly, almost pushing him to sit down in a comfortable armchair. Then she reached for the jar of balm from the nearby table.

Taynton sat back. He was determined to relax all he could today. It was foolish to panic too much. The gods were with him, and that was what really counted. He'd done all that was necessary, and now he only had to wait for the witching hour. He closed his eyes as Vera massaged the balm gently into his sore calf. Oh, it felt good, he thought. Her fingers were warm and supple, and he could smell the rosemary infusion in which she had washed her hair on rising.

He hardly noticed that the massaging had ascended from his calf to his knee, then to his thigh, then . . . His eyes flew open as her fingers moved where they definitely should not be. She was leaning close to him, her brown hair tumbling forward, her soft brown eyes dark with desire, her buxom figure pressing needfully against him. But now was the caster of spells under a spell himself. Her clever fingers knew how to arouse and please, how to banish resistance.

"Make love to me, Master," she whispered, and pursed her moist lips toward his.

The centuries peeled back, and she was his Lady Severa again. Desire flooded through his loins, and he pulled her roughly into his arms. It wouldn't harm his plans if he gave in a little—just a little. After all, he wasn't just of the Otherworld, he was human too. . . .

Ursula left Miss Muffet in the stables, and hurried on foot to the set, where the men had cleared the mosaic floor about half an hour earlier before returning to the manor. Conan was still there, however, and had now been joined by Theo and Eleanor, the latter having kept well out of sight while the men were present. The fully exposed floor was even larger than Ursula had thought, and quite magnificently well preserved.

Conan came toward her as soon as he saw her approaching. "Did you speak to Vera?"

"Yes." She told them all that had happened.

"So we have our Black Druid?" Conan asked.

"So it seems." Ursula surveyed the floor. "Have you found a clue?"

"No."

"Oh." She stepped gingerly onto the close-packed tessarae and tiptoed to the center, where as expected there was a likeness of Elen of the Ways. The figure had its hands cupped before it, as if holding something that was in the geometric center of the floor, but the mosaics depicting what that something was were missing. She glanced at Eleanor. "Have you any idea what was here?"

"No, because a statue of my father always stood there."

Ursula gazed down again at the gap in the tesserae, and suddenly it seemed to her that the hole that they had left was very symmetrical. Too symmetrical to be accidental! She knelt down to scrape the earth away with her fingertips, then her eyes lit up as she realized there never had been mosaic in that particular spot. Rather, they had been set at a lower level, leaving a hexagonal indentation. She knew exactly what that indentation was for, and she turned excitedly to Conan. "Bring the chalice!"

"The chalice?"

"Yes. It is supposed to stand here."

He brought the golden cup, and the others pressed around as she placed it in the indentation. Fifteen hundred years may have passed, but it still fitted snugly. "There!" she cried, scrambling triumphantly to her feet. "Don't you see? It's a huge sundial!"

"You're right," Conan breathed.

"And I'll warrant that it is to be read on May Day morning! When the sun rises tomorrow, the shadow of the chalice will point exactly at the treasure. The valley lies almost directly from east to west, so it must be somewhere between here and Hazel Pool."

But Theo was dismayed. "That's all very well, but we need to defeat Taynton before midnight *tonight*!"

"I know," Conan replied quietly.

"And anyway, where *exactly* must we dig? It must be fifty yards or more to the water, and even if we cut a trench all the way, who is to say how wide the trench should be? Two feet? Three? Six? How can we possibly do that when there are trees in the way that couldn't possibly have been there fifteen hundred years ago? Beeches aren't long-lived like yews!"

Conan nodded. "Precisely. The top of the chalice lid is very like an arrow, so presumably it will mark the spot very precisely, without a tree trunk confusing matters.

But even if we find the very spot, who is to say that is where the treasure itself will be? Maybe we will only find another clue."

"I always hated schoolboy treasure hunts," Theo said wretchedly, and Eleanor smiled wanly at him.

"Do not be defeated yet, my lord," she said gently.

Conan drew a heavy breath. "I don't know what to do next. If the chalice only indicates another clue, that clue might be very small indeed, and we could destroy it by digging hastily. It all depends on the angle at which the sun strikes the chalice, which might have a very short shadow if there is something in the way and the sun has risen a little before it reaches here. Conversely, the shadow might be very long if there is no obstacle and the sun touches the chalice directly it appears above the eastern horizon. I fear we need to know exactly."

Theo's spirits were still low. "It might rain, and we won't get a sunrise anyway! Even worse, we won't be around to do anything because Taynton's damned spell will work at midnight tonight!"

"I refuse to be that much of a pessimist," Conan replied firmly.

Theo could not be encouraged. "Well, we await your inspirational lead," he said a little sarcastically.

Eleanor reproved him. "Do not be so ungrateful, my lord, for everyone wishes this to go well."

Instinctively, they all turned to Conan again, and after a moment he met their gaze. "I have an idea, but I do not intend to share it."

Ursula was alarmed. "Is it something dangerous?"

He smiled and put his hand tenderly to her cheek. "Don't fret, my love, for I know what I'm doing. I'm going to take you back to the manor now, and then I will leave you. As for you two"—he turned to the others—"I suppose you will remain here in the woods?"

They nodded. Then Theo said, "But I think I should be with you, Conan."

"No. I need no help for what I have in mind."

31

It was late afternoon, and Ursula was alone in her room at the manor. She was wearing a peach muslin gown, and her hair was tied up with a light blue ribbon. Her mother's manuscripts were spread around her again as she tried to occupy her mind with finishing the translation of Macsen's story.

She didn't know where Conan had gone, or what he was doing, for he had obstinately refused to divulge what his idea entailed. Such reticence had only fueled anxiety over his safety. Where someone like Taynton was concerned she knew it did not do to take risks. Yet that was what Conan was taking; she knew it as surely as she knew her own self. She wished her father had come home, but he had sent word from Stroud that things were so bad at Fromewell Mill that he needed to stay another night.

There seemed to be worries on all sides, each one with a doubtful outcome, and since dwelling on what might go wrong was never advisable, she forced herself to look at the manuscripts. To her astonishment, after a while she managed to concentrate sufficiently to continue writing the translation in her notebook.

The Emperor Macsen entered the castle with the two ladies, and there discovered the very scene of which he had dreamed. The maiden was more beautiful by far than he had dared to believe, and her elder cousin Kynan did indeed bow his head in resignation. Her other cousin Cadfan, however, was even more angry than Macsen had dreamed, casting the game board aside so bitterly that it

*broke in two. The fallen pieces were scattered to the cor-
ners of the great hall, where they turned into animals,
squirrels, dogs, and horses, that all went to gather around
the maiden. The High-King Eudaf Hen hid his head in
his hands in sorrow as Cadfan ran from the hall, but there
was nothing that could be done. Macsen was enraptured
with Elen of the Ways, but still could not touch her. He
learned that she would become his true bride when he
married her before the Black Druid. The chosen place for
the ceremony was the sacred yew, and the vows were taken
as May Eve turned to May Day. There were three brides
and three bridegrooms that memorable night, and afterward all lived in true happiness together, for there was
great love between them. Only Prince Cadfan cast a
shadow over the land, for he swore to be avenged for the
cruel injustice that had denied him his rightful place in
line of succession. It was feared that he would roam
throughout eternity, seeking his heritage, but never finding it.*

There, it was finished. Ursula pushed the manuscripts
aside and rose from the chair to go to the window. The
May Eve sun was warm, and the valley seemed almost
hazy. She looked toward the Green Man, unable to help
a sneaking sympathy for Cadfan Meriadoc, who by the
standards of his day had indeed suffered a wrong. It
hadn't been his fault that Eudaf Hen decided to import
a fine Roman husband for Elen of the Ways, or that
Conan's previous self had loyally stepped aside in favor
of the newcomer. As far as Ursula could see, Cadfan was
not entirely unjustified in resenting the abandonment of
the true male line of succession. Eudaf Hen had a lot to
answer for.

She stared out of the window, wishing she knew where
Conan was and what he was doing. The hours were tick-
ing relentlessly away toward midnight, when anything
might happen. As she looked, Bran suddenly bounded
up the opposite slope of the valley toward the inn. A
pang of alarm struck through her. What was happening?
She wanted to go see, but had given her word to Conan

that no matter what, she would stay at the manor. The wolfhound disappeared into the inn yard, and it was all Ursula could do to honor her promise.

At that moment Conan was lounging comfortably on a mound of hay in the stables of the Green Man. He had found a quiet corner where a knothole afforded an excellent view of the inn. So far, however, there had been no sign of Bellamy Taynton.

The reason for this was known to one and all, for the innkeeper and Vera had remained tucked away in his private quarters ever since she returned from her meeting with Ursula. The tightly drawn curtains at the window facing the yard had been the cause of much amusement among the men, and much annoyance among the kitchen staff, who seemed to be totally adrift without Vera's confident hand to steer them. But both she and Taynton stayed where they were, regardless of what was going on elsewhere in the Green Man. A number of stagecoaches had arrived and departed, some with regular passengers who grumbled a great deal about having to us wait for food that wasn't up to the usual standard, but even then Taynton did not emerge. For the moment Conan was content to leave them, because while Cadfan Meriadoc was busying himself with the Lady Severa's charms, he wasn't up to mischief elsewhere!

Conan stretched and put his hands behind his head. He was sure he was on the right path with what he intended to do. It was a matter of instinct—of knowing one's own brother. Paws pattered suddenly, and Bran was there, covering his face with licks. "Get off me, you great fool," Conan complained, fending the hound away.

Bran whined, then sat down, tail wagging.

"Why have you come here?" Conan wondered aloud, sitting up and stroking the hound's head.

As he spoke, the shadows of two men darkened the stable entrance, and Conan got up warily, for they clearly knew he was there. "Who are you?" he demanded, reaching for an old coaching whip that must have hung on the wall for an age if its drapery of cobwebs was anything to go by.

"You won't be needing that, Sir Conan," Gardner's voice replied. Then he came farther into the stables so that Conan could see his face.

Conan stared at him. "Gardner? Why on earth—?"

The coachman held up a reassuring hand. "I don't know what all this is about, sir, just that I had to be here. It just came over me, a need to come to this inn, where I knew I would find you. Then I met Daniel, and—"

"Daniel? Would that be Daniel Pedlar?" Conan inquired, looking at the second man.

The blacksmith nodded.

Conan smiled a little. "The Black Druid, I believe."

"That is so, sir, and Gardner 'ere was once your faithful squire."

Well, that explained the coachman's remark the previous night, Conan thought.

Daniel bent to stroke Bran, who had gone to him. "And this 'ere was Lord Macsen's favorite 'unting dog," he said. "Weren't you, old boy? Eh? Eh?" He ruffled the wolfhound's coat, and Bran stood up on his hind legs, looked him in the eyes, and proceeded to smother his face with very wet licks.

"Do you know why you've come?" Conan asked the blacksmith.

"In case that toad Taynton cuts up rough with you." Daniel pushed Bran away and gave a grin. "Oh, I knows your reason for being 'ere, sir."

"You do?"

"Well, I 'ad this dream, you see."

"Not *another* dream . . ." Conan groaned inwardly.

"Shook me up sommat rotten, it did," Daniel said. "Anyway, Gardner and I 'ave just come to 'elp should you need us. This 'ere 'ound's ready too. 'E'd just *love* to take a piece out of Taynton's back end, wouldn't you, boy? Eh?" He ruffled the wolfhound's head, and Bran's tail wagged nineteen to the dozen.

Daniel turned to look across at Taynton's window, and

as if on cue Vera suddenly flung the curtains back. She looked directly at her father and gave a single nod. Daniel glanced at Conan. " 'Tis time to go to it, sir," he said quietly.

Conan dropped the whip and brushed some straw from his clothes, then left the stables.

Vera was waiting for him in the hall. There was a new glow about her and a light in her eyes that certainly had not been there before. "He's still in his rooms," she said, "and he doesn't know you are here."

"He soon will," Conan replied.

Anxiety touched her. "You . . . you will not harm him, will you?"

"He is the one doing harm," Conan reminded her.

"I know, but he has now told me all that happened in the past, and I cannot point a finger at him and say he is wrong. The High-King chose wisely in Macsen Wledig, but might not you or my lord have been as fine a choice? You were both cast aside for a stranger, and although you could accept the king's decision, my lord could not. I do not know that I could have done either. My lord may be the villain now, but the grudge he has borne these past fifteen hundred years was to some extent more than warranted.

Conan hesitated. He had never had to face an arbitrary decision by someone who could make his fortune or ruin him. Maybe Vera was right, poor old Cafan *was* due a little sympathy. Except that it was rather difficult to sympathize with someone who resorted to dark magic!

Vera could read some of the expressions that passed across his face. "Please don't condemn him out of hand, sir," she begged, "for I love him so very much that I could not bear it if anything truly bad happened to him."

Conan took her gently by the arms. "Vera, I will do what I can, but I am not the sorcerer. Believe me, if anyone is in danger now, it's me, not him. Now, which way do I go to find him?"

For a moment she met his eyes with a hint of mutiny, but then gave in. "Go through the curtain at the back of the taproom. His door is at the end of the passage."

32

Taynton lay stark naked on the crumpled bed that was still warm where Vera had lain. He felt better than he had in, oh, one thousand five hundred years! He smiled sardonically, for he had to admit that although Eudaf Hen's decision had been basically wrong, there had been some compensation in the resulting situation. Macsen Wledig had had to go here, there, and everywhere defending his British realm as well as trying to keep a firm grip on the reins of Rome, so much so that the term *being run ragged* occasionally sprang to mind. Taynton smiled again. Serves the usurper right! Still, midnight tonight would be what might be called just deserts. Macsen, Kynan, *et al.* would be brought up sharply for their former misdemeanors. The eyes of the otherworldly innkeeper watered, but not with tears of sorrow for his enemies; instead it was his cold. He sneezed several times, then blew his nose on a large handkerchief. Vera was taking a plaguey long time over that rum gruel!

The door opened without warning, and Taynton sat up with a start, summoning a masterly frown because he expected it to be Vera having the temerity to enter unannounced. Instead, he saw Conan standing there. With a strangled cry, the innkeeper grabbed the sheet and dragged it over himself. "You've no business coming in here!" he shouted, struggling up from the bed, still clutching the sheet in front of him.

"On the contrary, brother mine, I have a great deal of business in here." Conan gave a backward kick to shut the door.

Taynton was regaining his composure apace. "Our

business was over and done with in the time of Eudaf Hen," he said coldly.

"Please don't try to sound dignified, for you look rather ridiculous," Conan replied. "Besides, as I see it, *you* are the one who is bent upon business now."

Taynton flushed. "Mock me at your peril," he warned, and glanced at a vase on the window, which promptly jumped off the ledge and crashed in pieces on the floor.

"Very impressive. One day you must show me how you do it."

Taynton sneered. "One day? You only have today left, brother dear."

"That's why I've come to have a little chat with you," Conan answered, making himself comfortable on a chair in a patch of sunlight. "How is your leg, by the way?"

"Eh? Sore, if you must know."

"Oh, dear. And your cold?"

"Disagreeable. I'm flattered at your interest." Taynton spoke with haughty sarcasm, but spoiled it all by sneezing again.

"Bless you." Conan beamed at him.

Anger stained the innkeeper's face. "Why are you here?"

"To haggle."

"Haggle?"

Conan nodded. "About the treasure."

Taynton stiffened. "What about it?"

"Well, we know exactly where it is."

The innkeeper became very still. "I don't believe you."

Conan glanced at a candlestick on the mantel, wishing he could make it hurl itself obligingly to the hearth below. He was somewhat gratified when it did just that.

Taynton leapt like a scalded cat, his feet became entangled in the sheet, and with a yelp of dismay he fell. Conan went to help him up.

"Don't touch me!" yelled the innkeeper, grabbing the sheet to his loins again and trying to get up.

Conan tried his new skill once more, this time fixing his attention on the sheet, which obediently snaked around Taynton's legs, tying him up a little like an Egyptian mummy. The innkeeper stared up at him, wide-eyed. "You have the power?" he breathed incredulously.

"So it seems," agreed Conan cordially, by now accepting that the closing gate, biting squirrel, acrobatic coin, and suicidal candlestick had all been *his* doing, not the questionable whim of coincidence. "Now then, while you're lying there so neatly, let me put my bargain to you."

"I won't bargain with you, Kynan Meriadoc!"

"I think you will. You see, I happen to think you had good reason to grouse about Eudaf Hen's decision. Not good enough to start throwing your wizardry around now, but certainly some justification for being peeved."

"Peeved?" squeaked Taynton furiously, squirming in his enormous bandage.

"Well, piqued, then."

Taynton gave him a look that should have burned him to ashes on the spot. "Damn you," he breathed, then sneezed violently, which was no easy matter when he couldn't bend. His stomach muscles tugged painfully, and he sucked his breath in.

Conan smiled again. "Look, I'm being very amiable about this, and if you promise to behave yourself, I'll let you out of that, er, winding sheet."

"I promise nothing!"

"Then stay there." Conan returned to his chair, stretched his long legs out nonchalantly, then touched his fingertips before him. "Now then, I have an offer that you might do well to accept. You are to undo all your bad magic, and in return we will forgive you. There, is that not magnanimous?"

Taynton couldn't even bring himself to reply. Magnanimous? he thought. They might take him for a fool, but a fool he most certainly was not!

Conan pursed his lips disappointedly. "Very well, let me put it another way. You undo all your spells, and we will all live happily ever after. *All* of us, you and Vera included."

"And leave the treasure to Macsen Wledig again? Never!"

"By the laws of this day, the treasure belongs to Mr. Elcester because it is on his land, and because it will be impossible to prove who the original owner was."

"Elcester is a nonentity!" spat the innkeeper, squirming again, then becoming rigid as he tensed for another sneeze.

"Bless you," murmured Conan. "Unfortunately, it doesn't matter whether or not Mr. Elcester is a nonentity, the law is still the same. I'm not going to put myself out indefinitely to reason with you. You've been a very bad lad of late, and I do not think the Green Man will be very pleased about it. *He* is the master, my friend, not you. But that aside, for all your machinations, we've still managed to find the treasure before you, and now I want to live a long and happy life, with Ursula Elcester as my bride."

"Ursula Elcester?" Taynton gaped at him. "But she's supposed to marry—"

"I know, and that is just another of my problems at the moment. You have my word as your brother that if I marry her, and the treasure eventually comes to me, I will share it equally with you and Theo . . . I mean, Macsen."

"Your word? Pah!"

"Well, *your* word may not mean much to you, but mine is my honor. If I make such a promise, I mean it. In the meantime, I have more than sufficient fortune of my own to see you and Vera very comfortably off. Just think, man, you could be in legitimate clover for the rest of your life."

"I'd rather be in obscene luxury that has come by illegitimately," Taynton replied candidly.

"Vera wouldn't wish that." Conan looked at the rumpled bed. "Be honest now, haven't you just had the best time of all your lives?"

Taynton hesitated for the first time. Damn it all, he realized, the fellow was right. He *had* just enjoyed the most gratifying few hours he could ever remember. Well, since his original life, anyway. And *that* had been happy in its way because of his Severa. She alone had saved him from complete destruction.

Conan pressed home the advantage he suddenly perceived. "You've been trying to make sure nothing is repeated, haven't you? Well, I'm afraid you fell by the wayside today." He nodded at the bed, and made it shudder slightly, as if two lovers were still engaged upon its downy mattress.

"Damn you," Taynton breathed, giving him a venomous look.

"No, I'm afraid it's damn *you*, my dear brother. After all this time, why can't you just accept that you aren't meant to be master now any more than you were meant to be master then? More than that, why can't you accept that keeping one of the finest inns I've ever been in is clearly your forte? With Vera at your side, you could own more than one inn—indeed you could become the realm's foremost innkeeper."

"Do you really imagine I will settle for *that*?" Taynton cried.

"Why not? Surely there is some satisfaction in doing something you not only like, but you're damned good at? I believe the Duke of Beaufort himself sat down to dine at your Sunday table, and that he sang your praises afterward. An innkeeper such as I envisage you becoming would be a man of great influence, the friend of the nobility, accepted among them. So think well, brother. I can see to it that you never find the treasure, or I can welcome you among us. Which is it to be?"

Taynton gazed at him. Conan felt a disagreeable tingling sensation, and knew that magic was being directed upon him, so he gazed back, simply willing the magic to turn upon its creator. To his huge satisfaction, Taynton gave a cry of pain. "May that teach you a lesson," Conan murmured.

The innkeeper went almost as pale as the sheet that enveloped him. "Where did you learn such things?" he demanded.

"I don't know. Until I confronted you in here, I wasn't

aware I could do anything. Still, I am not as easy a victim
as you may have thought, and I will not hesitate to do
to you what you have seen fit to do to us." Conan folded
his arms. "I'm still awaiting your answer. Can we call a
truce and work together?"

Taynton didn't reply.

"Come on, my patience is running out," Conan
pressed, fixing his eye upon another candlestick and
sending it to join its fellow in the hearth. Lord, this was
really rather fun, he thought, wondering what other
things he might be able to do. Foretell the cards in a
deck? Now *that* would be useful!

Taynton drew a long, resigned breath. "All right, I
accept your offer," he said.

"This had better be the truth, or I vow it will be the
worst for you."

"You have my word, which is as much my bond as it
is yours."

Conan directed the sheet to unwind, and the innkeeper
sat up to grab it quickly before it slithered back to the
bed. His lower anatomy was still rather on display, which
might be all right in front of Vera, who admired his
masculinity, but he didn't particularly wish to brandish
all before Sir Conan Merrydown.

Conan got up from the chair. "Right, it is safe to assume we are now allies?" He extended a hand.

Taynton hesitated, then took it. "We are."

"I'm much relieved to hear it. Now there's just one
more thing. Will you kindly undo whatever it is you've
set to happen to us at midnight?"

Taynton stared at him. "I—"

Conan frowned. "Don't think to trick me now," he
warned.

"I'm not, truly. It's just, well, I don't know how to
undo it."

"Please tell me you jest," Conan replied in dismay.

"No. I know how to cast spells, but not how to undo
them."

Conan felt like putting his hands to the innkeeper's

neck and strangling him, but confined himself to simply saying, "Then you had best look to your arts for some illumination."

"Believe me, if I knew what to do, I wouldn't hesitate." Taynton ran his fingers through his hair in a way that was so like Conan's own, that it would have been amusing had the situation not suddenly become so very serious.

"What exact spell have you cast?"

"That Mr. Glendower, Miss Elcester, and the wolfhound will fall asleep and not awaken."

"*Bran*? You directed your damned powers at a *hound*? How base can anyone be?"

"That white cur has caused me a great deal of trouble."

"Not nearly enough. I've a good mind to set him on you again. He's outside in the stables right now."

Taynton moved backward. "Keep him from me."

Conan looked at him. "Why didn't you include me in your magic?"

"I would have done, but I didn't have anything that belonged to you." Taynton told him about the piece of paper that blew away and about the other items he'd used, then added, "I'd have come to you before long, because that seal you lost must still be here somewhere."

"I didn't lose it at all. I deliberately left it."

"So it *was* just an excuse to poke and pry."

"I fear so," Conan admitted, then drew a heavy breath. "If you don't know how to revoke your evildoing, I don't really know how to proceed from here."

"I've been thinking about that. I may not be able to undo anything, but it seems to me that everything I've sought to do will be overturned if the past is repeated exactly after all. You and Miss Elcester must marry before the Black Druid, as must Mr. Glendower and Eleanor Rhodes."

"And you and Vera," Conan pointed out.

Taynton nodded. "I know."

"And this must be at midnight tonight?"

"Yes. By the yew."

"And provided half of us don't fall terminally asleep before we can make our vows," Conan pointed out bitterly.

"We can only wait and see."

33

The full moon slid from behind a cloud, and the shadow of the yew was very black indeed as midnight approached. The village was very quiet, with hardly a window lit. On the green very few of the fairground people were still awake, and those were seated around a single campfire. An owl hooted from the top of the church tower, and a fox slipped across the graveyard. The air was still, and much cooler than it had been the night before, so that breath hung silver in the darkness. The primitive atmosphere of Beltane filled the night, and in the distance to the east one or two Beltane fires flickered as hamlets and farms more remote than Elcester celebrated the old festival in time-honored manner.

Daniel Pedlar stood beneath the overhanging branches of the yew. He wore his black robes, transformed into his original self, with nothing of the blacksmith about him now, or even the traditional morris man, for which latter role he had often worn his robes before. Tonight he was the Black Druid, high priest of the Green Man, and as such he would officiate at a pagan ceremony within the walls of the churchyard.

Horses snorted and stamped, for Conan's carriage was drawn up near the lych-gate, having conveyed Ursula and him from the manor. Theo and Eleanor had come by foot from the woods, and everyone else had walked as well, including Taynton and Vera. The gathering of people before the Black Druid could not have been more varied or strange, for as well as the three couples he hoped to join in matrimony, there were all those village families who seldom if ever attended the Reverend Arrowsmith's solemn services. Taynton's men from the inn—his "coven"—were in attendance, as well as a number of the fairground folk. Gardner was there, of course, to say nothing of a party of men from Carmartin Park who had ridden the five miles after somehow realizing what was to take place.

However, perhaps the most unexpected person present, indeed the most *astonishing* person, was none other than Mrs. Arrowsmith. When she had first emerged from the vicarage, the others became a little alarmed, fully expecting her to have a fit of the shrieking vapors when she perceived the pagan assembly by the lych-gate. Instead, she dumbfounded them all by taking her place in their midst. She seemed a different woman, no longer a silly goose of a creature, but calm and sensible, almost dignified. It beggared belief what the Reverend Arrowsmith would have said if he'd known his wife was participating in such ancient rites. The only conclusion to be drawn from the radical change in her personality was that although she loved her Christian husband, she was at heart most uncomfortable with his religion. *This* was her true faith, a venerable belief tested by infinitely more centuries than his, and requiring only the elements of nature for its worship. She had clearly found what she had been searching for.

Ursula felt almost faint with trepidation as the seconds ticked relentlessly away toward the first chime of May Day. Like Eleanor and Vera, she wore a white gown, with a wreath of sweet-scented spring flowers in her hair, and she carried a ribboned posy of bluebells gathered from beneath the hollow oak by Hazel Pool. She was arm in arm with Conan, and was glad of his hand resting lovingly over hers. His warmth was a balm to her nervousness, and his calmness more of a comfort than he could ever have begun to guess.

She glanced toward Bran, who stood next to Theo. The wolfhound's tail was still, and he hung his head, as if he knew something bad was about to happen. A pang of alarm struck through her. The wolfhound *knew* all was not well, she thought with a start. This wasn't going to work! Her lips parted to speak to Conan, but at that moment the church bell struck the first note. Ursula heard the collective intake of breath from the gathering. The moment hung, then the second note resounded over the village. Daniel began to speak in Welsh, a language he had no knowledge of at all, yet in which he was suddenly fluent. They had agreed at the outset that the three ceremonies would be conducted simultaneously, and from the first note of the bell Ursula had felt an enervating weariness begin to sweep over her. She was so tired she could barely keep her eyes open. Her legs couldn't support her, and she would have slipped to the ground if Conan hadn't caught her.

Murmurs of dismay came from the onlookers, and Taynton closed his eyes, willing his magic not to tighten its grip. "Go away," he whispered, "please go away." Vera put a concerned hand on his arm and squeezed gently. But when he opened his eyes, Ursula was still sinking beneath his sorcery. So was Bran, who already lay on the ground in a deep sleep. Theo wasn't affected, however. The innkeeper couldn't understand the reason for this, because he still did not know that Theo's button had slipped from its bark raft before the magic spell had been cast.

Theo was filled with consternation, not only for Ursula and Bran's sakes, but because nothing had happened to him. He was exactly the same now as he had been a minute earlier. For him the worst thing by far was the realization that Eleanor was becoming more indistinct. As the magic enveloped Ursula, so it seemed to drain Eleanor as well. He looked urgently at Daniel. "Get on with it, man!" he cried.

Conan nodded as well. "Yes, please hurry!"

Daniel spoke more swiftly, and the three bridegrooms gave their replies as required, but Ursula was already on the verge of unconsciousness. The posy slipped from her fingers, and her head lolled against Conan's shoulders as he continued to hold her upright. She could barely hear what was going on around her. The night seemed to be slipping away, and with it all her other senses too. . . .

Vera and Eleanor answered Daniel. *"Mi derbyn tydi â fy gŵr."* I accept thee as my husband.

Ursula remained silent, and Conan shook her desperately. "Say the words, Ursula! Say them!"

Her eyelids fluttered, and her lips moved slightly, but no sound came out.

He shook her again. "Wake up! If you fall asleep on me now, I'll never forgive you. Wake up, damn it!" After a second's hesitation, he slapped her cheek, then shook her again.

Her eyes opened. "Mmm?"

"Say the words, my darling," he begged, his fingers so viselike he knew he must be hurting her, but he knew he had to do anything and everything to arouse her.

"Words?"

"Yes."

He looked urgently at Daniel again. "Say them again," he ordered.

Daniel did as he was asked, and Conan repeated each one into Ursula's ear. Somehow—ever after she would never know how—she found the strength and will to whisper each one. *"Mi . . . derbyn . . . tydi . . . â . . . fy . . . gŵr . . ."* As the final word left her lips, she felt the overpowering weakness begin to leave her.

The night returned, and her senses became her own once more. She managed to straighten until she was supporting herself again, and then Conan crushed her relievedly into his arms. "Oh, my love, my dear sweet love . . ." he breathed, sinking his fingers into her hair and not caring that several long curls tumbled warmly over his hand because he dislodged her pins.

She heard Theo give a cry of joy, and turned to see that Eleanor was in his arms, her lips upturned to his for their first true kiss. She wasn't ethereal anymore, but a living woman, as real as Ursula and Vera. Only Bran remained motionless, his eyes closed, his long legs stretched out on the ground. Vera knelt to try to awaken him, but he did not stir by so much as a tiny twitch. The magic may have been overturned for its human victims, but for Bran the Blessed, Son of Llyr, it remained only too potent.

Theo's joy over Eleanor gave way to devastation, for he doted on the wolfhound. But despite the valiant efforts of a number of people, including Mrs. Arrowsmith, Bran's eyes did not open. His breathing was slow and regular, and to all intents and purposes he looked as if he were simply asleep. Which, of course, he was; except that it was a strangely deep sleep.

Taynton was distraught, hiding his face in his hands and begging Theo to forgive him. Theo did his best to be noble, because the innkeeper was so evidently overwrought by what had happened, but it was very difficult indeed to forgive the person who caused such a terrible fate to befall poor Bran.

Suddenly, a carriage was heard approaching the village green at some speed from the east. The coachman's whip cracked, and he shouted out to the team as he slowed the pace in order to turn toward the church. Everyone looked in surprise, for who could possibly be arriving at such an hour? And in such haste? The vehicle's lamps swung through the night as it drove into sight. The occupant lowered the window glass and leaned out.

"Damn it, man, you've taken the wrong road!" he cried. It was Lord Carmartin.

The coachman, a new employee who had never driven the route before, reined the sweating horses in and applied the brake. He was a stranger to Elcester village, and he knew he should have driven on, but something had made him take this road instead. It was a whim he could not have resisted even if he'd tried. The carriage halted right by the lych-gate, and Lord Carmartin suddenly realized there was a large number of eyes upon him. He turned his head and looked directly into Theo's startled eyes. "Theodore?" he gasped, taken completely aback.

"Er, my lord . . . ?" Theo was rooted to the spot, for

not only was it a shock to be confronted by his uncle, but he as standing there with his arms wrapped around Eleanor!

Lord Carmartin's gaze slid without recognition to the lady in question, then back to his nephew. "What is the meaning of this?" he demanded, and opened the carriage door to climb stiffly down.

"I . . ." Theo looked helplessly at him, then cleared his throat. "Uncle, may I present my wife, Eleanor?"

"Your *what*?" squeaked his lordship, striding beneath the lych-gate.

"My wife, and, I believe, your ward?"

Lord Carmartin halted. His gaze darted to Eleanor, and his lips moved as if to deny any such link with her, but then his hand crept uncertainly to his heart. "Eleanor?" he whispered. "My little Eleanor?"

She sank into a curtsy. "My lord," she replied nervously.

"Is it really you?"

"Yes, my lord."

He stepped hesitantly toward her. "But where have you been? What happened? How do you know Theodore?"

"It is a very long story, sir," she replied.

Tears filled his eyes. "Oh, my dear, dear girl," he whispered, and reached out to her. In a trice she was in his arms, clutched to his fond breast as tightly as she had been as a beloved child. Lord Carmartin was bewildered. By now he had perceived Ursula holding hands with Conan, and the large assortment of other folk, including Daniel in his black robes. After a long moment he turned to look at Theo. "You and Eleanor are married? But you came here to be betrothed to Miss Elcester!" He was beginning to realize his hopes of gaining the manor would come to nothing after all.

"I know, sir, and for that I can only humbly crave your forgiveness."

Lord Carmartin gazed at him in bewilderment. "What is all this about, boy? I had no intention of leaving London, but earlier today I had the most odd desire to come here. No, desire isn't the word, it was a compulsion!"

"There is a great deal to tell you, sir," Theo replied, wondering exactly how much of such a fantastic story a man as practical and forthright as his uncle would be able to believe.

"Well, get on with it," urged Lord Carmartin.

Conan intervened. "Not here, my lord. I think it best if we all adjourn to Elcester Manor. Theo is right, what we have to relate is a very long tale, one you might not want to believe, and at dawn there is still more we have to do before it is all resolved."

"Before all what is resolved?" demanded Lord Carmartin.

"All in good time, sir. All in good time," replied Conan.

Lord Carmartin wasn't accustomed to following another man's lead, especially a man so much younger than himself, but then he remembered that Eleanor had been restored to him, and nothing else mattered much after that. If he had to wait to be informed, he would wait. What was another hour when it had been so many miserable years since last he had feasted his gaze upon his precious ward? He could not have loved her more if she were his daughter. Nor, if he was honest, could he have chosen a match for her that was dearer to his heart.

The rest of the gathering dispersed as preparations were made to drive to the manor. The only sad thing about the occasion was the ill fate that had struck poor Bran. Conan, Theo, and Taynton carried him gently to Conan's carriage, where he was laid carefully on one of the seats. Then both carriages drove out of the village and along the road to Stroud. They arrived at the manor to find Mr. Elcester just alighting from his carriage.

Half an hour later, both fathers were apprised of the truth, the whole truth, and nothing but the truth. So amazed were they by it all, that when it had been told, neither of them uttered a sound for several minutes. Then, of course, their questions flew thick and fast. But when all was said and done, everyone was delighted with the outcome, excepting what had happened to Bran.

But as the wolfhound slumbered his unnatural sleep on the drawing room hearth, everyone's thoughts could not help turning to the treasure. They awaited dawn with bated breath.

34

Sunrise was imminent, and there was a hush as every-one stood by the mosaic floor. The scent of bluebells was so beguiling and heady that it almost seemed to possess a magic of its own, and the drifts of lilac-blue color reached into the shadowy haze on all sides. The dawn chorus was shrill, echoing with the peculiar clarity of the hour, and tendrils of the mist that had risen from nearby Hazel Pool were already threading away into nothing as the eastern sky turned from crimson to lemon and turquoise.

Conan had placed the chalice in the floor's central in-dentation, and now they could only wait to see how far its shadow would stretch when the sun peeped over the horizon. Ursula clung tightly to Conan's hand. What if they were wrong about this? What if the chalice had nothing to do with the treasure's whereabouts? If that were the case, it would be another five hundred years before this chance returned. . . .

Nearby, Ursula's father was almost overcome by all that had happened. He gazed enraptured at the floor, which was surely one of the most immaculately preserved in the realm. And it was on *his* land! All his hopes and theories had been vindicated, for the villa of the *Dux Britanniarum* had once flourished in this secret Glouces-tershire valley; more than that, it was the villa of the Emperor Magnus Maximus, the legendary Macsen Wledig himself. Had he written his perfect conclusion, he could not have done better.

He wiped a tear from his eye, then glanced at Ursula and Conan. He was glad she was no longer required to make a marriage of convenience in order to save Elcester and its manor. Sir Conan Merrydown was a fine man, worthy of such a matchless bride, and a man whose seemingly bottomless coffers could assure Elcester's future. There were no strings, no unamiable Lord Carmartin always in the offing, just the ideal outcome to a very tricky situation. As for the supernatural aspects of the thing, well, he could not deny their existence. He had never believed in magic—or in fairies, ghosts, and similar such things—but there was no doubt that Ursula and Conan had come together because of something to do with what was known as the Otherworld. The Otherworld was all around him now, touching the valley, maybe crossing over the invisible border into Thisworld. . . .

The sun's rays began to strike above the horizon, driving the night away as they lanced and shimmered along the valley. New shadows came to life, sharply defined shadows that stretched as far as they could from the source of light. The chalice glittered, its gold suddenly brought to life. A shadow suddenly reached out from the base, fingering toward the pool. Farther and farther it crept, and everyone held his breath to see where it would be when at last it ceased to grow.

Ursula's fingers tightened over Conan's, and her lips parted as she watched the tip of the shadow, which pointed like an arrow. Suddenly, the light changed, a breeze disturbed the trees, and Eleanor's squirrels poured across the floor. Bounding and skipping, their tails curled above them, they streamed along the shadow of the chalice, reaching the tip just as it struck the edge of Hazel Pool.

"That's where I hid!" Conan gasped, recalling how his foot had slipped in the soft mud, revealing the low stone wall that lay hidden beneath earth and vegetation. "Hazel Pool wasn't formed naturally, but by a stone dam built centuries ago."

"Fifteen centuries ago?" breathed Ursula.

"Maybe."

The squirrels were not idle, but had begun to dig at the bank as if seeking nuts they had buried. Everyone left the floor to watch, and gradually the ancient stone-work was exposed by countless busy little paws. Water glistened as it seeped through the cracks, and droplets flashed in the slanting sunlight. The shadow of the chalice was already in slow retreat because the sun had risen farther, but the spot had been marked.

Their work apparently done, the squirrels darted away again, melting back into the trees as swiftly as they had come. Theo gazed at the newly revealed wall. "What now?" he asked.

Everyone looked at one another, for no one knew. Then Conan stepped forward, took hold of a piece of stone, and dragged it away. After that he dragged several more, and suddenly water began to pour through the breach.

Lord Carmartin glanced at Ursula's father. "Well, El-cester, it looks as if we will soon be without the reason for our old feud, eh?"

"So it seems," Mr. Elcester replied, watching as more of the wall crumbled away and an even bigger surge of water flowed out, channeling into the little brook, which soon swelled to a narrow torrent that reached almost to the top of its flowery banks. Hazel Pool was draining away, and when the water had gone, everyone believed Eudaf Hen's treasure would come to light again after lying hidden for a millennium and a half. But how long would it take for so much water to pour out?

One thing did not take all day, and a very happy thing it was too, for hardly had Lord Carmartin made his re-mark about the old feud, than a joyous bark was heard from the manor end of the woods. It was Bran. A minute later the delighted wolfhound ran from the trees and leapt excitedly around Theo, who was almost in tears of relief that his pet had been restored.

It was to take almost all day before the bottom of the pool was at last exposed to the air. At first all that the people on the bank could see was mud, stones, and weed. The long-disputed fish had swum out with the draining water, and so had numerous newts. Frogs hopped away into the damp grass and bluebells, and the roots of the coppiced hazel were already beginning to dry as everyone gazed around for something, anything, that might be the lost treasure.

Fittingly, it was Theo who found it. He perceived something oddly symmetrical, rectangular actually, lying only six feet from the bank. "There!" he cried, and jumped down into the mud, which sucked and squelched around his Hessian boots as he struggled to reach the thing he'd seen. Conan jumped down as well, and both men took hold of the object.

"It's a chest!" Conan cried.

Mr. Elcester was as amused as he was excited. "A treasure chest? Pirates could not have done better!"

Lord Carmartin chuckled, and nodded at the two men in the mud. "Well, heave ho, my hearties, let's see what's what."

Conan and Theo struggled mightily to drag the chest out of the mud. It came away with a revolting sucking noise, and much of its rotten wood simply disintegrated, but it was lined with metal, which still held firm as the two men hauled it to the edge of the bank. As Mr. Elcester and Lord Carmartin helped to pull it up to the grass, Conan gave another cry. "There's a second chest down here. Help me, Theo!"

Together they strove to lift the second chest, which soon joined the first on the bank. A third chest came to light, then a fourth and last. When all were lined on the shore, and Conan and Theo had clambered out of the mud, everyone gathered around to see the first chest opened.

Eudaf Hen's treasure was indeed magnificent, an incredible hoard of gold, jewelry, weapons, precious stones, and coins that had to be seen to be believed. And as if that were not sufficient, as the sun began to set, and shadows lengthened in the other direction, Conan saw another shape in the mud on the other side of the pool, close to the hollow oak. It appeared to be a sunken Celtic ship!

Over the following days a small army of men dug away at the mud, until a well-preserved vessel, somewhat resembling a Viking longboat, was revealed. How it had gotten there could only be imagined, for it must have required a great many men to carry it overland from the Severn, and its purpose was evidently for a funeral, maybe even that of Eudaf Hen himself. More riches were contained in the burial craft, and soon several rooms at the manor were filled with precious things that showed just how opulent the summer house of Eudaf Hen—and villa of Macsen Wledig—had been. This corner of Roman Britain had known an opulence that must have been held in awe at the time, for it was still held in awe now.

The story of the treasure was soon the talk of England. Newspapers eagerly spread the tale far and wide, and many came to admire the contents of Hazel Pool. Even the Prince of Wales came to see, and his presence ensured that most of the *beau monde* came as well. That summer· saw so many crowds that the villagers feared they were never to have any peace again, but grumbling wasn't very great, for everyone prospered. Anyone who had a bedroom to let could be assured of a paying guest who was eager to see all he could of Eudaf Hen's Treasure, by which formal title the discovery was now known. The path to the pool was soon very well trodden indeed, and the Green Man so well frequented that it was the most famous inn in England. Elcester was no longer a quiet Cotswold backwater, but a place where it was *the* thing to go! Taynton and Vera did so well that Conan's prediction soon came true, for they purchased a fine inn in Bristol, and another on Cheltenham High Street. Bath was next, with a particularly elegant property close to Pulteney Bridge. But the grandest of all was a prestigious hostelry on the Strand in London, where it was not long before many a stagecoach company chose to a site a ticket office, for any inn that was owned by Bellamy Taynton could be guaranteed to be good. His name was made, and so was his fortune; and he and Vera were so happy together that they could not believe they had wasted so much time before.

Daniel Pedlar did handsomely as well, for so many horses required new shoes that at one point he feared he would not be able to manage. But manage he did, and fill his purse he did, for many a fine lady and gentleman saw his work with wrought iron, and soon he had a full order book, even to providing new weathercocks for the Tower of London.

The Reverend Arrowsmith's life had also changed for the better, although not materially, of course. His wife was a new woman, and he liked her far more than before. He wasn't to know, of course, that she was leading a shocking double life, being mistress of the vicarage during the day, and a follower of the Green Man whenever she could at night. There wasn't a ceremony before the yew that she did not attend, and over the following years she was very careful to initiate her twin sons into the old ways as well. Her clergyman husband would eventually go to his grave without realizing what had long been going on beneath his roof. He died a contented man, so it could not have been a bad thing.

Not long after the triple ceremony before the Black Druid, Theo and Eleanor were married a second time, at no less a place of Christian worship than Gloucester cathedral. Crowds turned out to cheer as the bride and groom drove through the city in an open landau, and after a honeymoon in Paris, the new Mr. and Mrs. Glendower made their home at Carmartin Park, which was transformed from its bitter old days. Lord Carmartin himself was transformed as well, and was truly happy with the way things had turned out. At first he had been bent upon punishing Taynton for having abducted Eleanor all those years before, but when Eleanor herself begged him to forgive the innkeeper, what else could any loving father do but grant her wish? The leniency was helped along by Taynton's own conscience, for he apologized time and time again, declaring that he could not now believe he had done such dreadful things. If only to silence this very vocal penitence, everyone soon went out of their way to reassure the reborn Cadfan Meriadoc that he was well and truly forgiven.

Mr. Elcester was happy too. His financial difficulty was a thing of the past, almost a bad dream, and he now had more Roman and Celtic artifacts to pore over than he had hours in the day! He was blissfully contented as he cataloged them all, and a certain lady of an antiquarian turn of mind happened to come to the manor one day. They hit it off so splendidly that soon there was talk of wedding bells for the father as well as the daughter.

But Ursula's wedding bells rang out in far-off Rome, where true to his word, Conan had taken her in order to make certain that history repeated itself to the full. There, on the gloriously warm and sunny evening of Midsummer Day, he took his Lady of Ribbons to wife. That night, as the wedding party celebrated in the Piazza di Spagna outside their hotel, the new Lady Merrydown at last became truly her lord's wife. There were no rules to be broken now. . . .

Later, as she slept in her husband's arms, squirrels scurried in the vine that grew outside their window, and Conan glanced out to see shooting stars lighting the velvet sky, just as he knew they had done fifteen hundred years before.

In the secret glades of Elcester's hidden valley, where bluebells would bloom again in the spring, the Green Man danced as he always had, and always would. And he sang as he danced. "In and out the dusky bluebells, In and out the dusky bluebells, In and out the dusky bluebells, I am your master. Tipper-ipper-apper—on your shoulder, Tipper-ipper-apper—on your shoulder, Tipper-ipper-apper—on your shoulder, *I* am your master. . . ."